Diner Revelations

Regarding Hayworth

Book IV

L. P. Suzanne Atkinson

lpsabooks
http://lpsabooks.wix.com/lpsabooks#

This is a work of fiction. Names, characters, and incidents either are the product of the author's imagination or are used fictitiously.

Cover Design by Adam Murray
Cover Photography by David Weintraub & Emily Roy
Editing by Lesley Carson

ISBN
978-0-9958-6962-2 (Paperback)
978-0-9958-6963-9 (eBook)

1. Fiction, Contemporary Women
2. Fiction, Psychological Suspense

Distributed to the trade by the Ingram Book Company
Printed in the USA

Table of Contents

We seek the truth and will endure the consequences.
—Charles Seymour

When you have eliminated the impossible, whatever remains, however
improbable, must be the truth.
—Arthur Conan Doyle

To the living, we owe respect, but to the dead we owe only the truth.
—Voltaire

Other works by L. P. Suzanne Atkinson

~Creative Non-Fiction~
Emily's Will Be Done

~Fiction~
Ties That Bind
Station Secrets: Regarding Hayworth Book I
Hexagon Dilemma: Regarding Hayworth Book II
Segue House Connection: Regarding Hayworth Book III

For David

Thank you to Pauline, Wyneth, Kat, Marguerite, Barb,
and my editor, Lesley Carson.

Chapter 1

Gaby

Three years, one month, and twenty-eight days have passed since Roz Dover vaporized. She was last seen when she left the Hayworth Community Hospital after she worked her shift as a cleaner. It was eleven o'clock in the evening on August 6, 1981. Her car, a faded green 1975 Ford Pinto was located on an abandoned farm property a number of days later. The keys were in the ignition and her shoulder bag was found on the passenger seat. There were no indications of a struggle.

Gaby Ridgway sits at her over-sized kitchen island, sips French vanilla flavoured coffee from a hand-turned mug purchased at a local craft market, and watches the sun begin to honour her with its presence on this crisp fall morning. It is Monday, October 1, 1984 and she expects the day will be sad indeed. She will accompany Joe to the local veterinary clinic. Blanche is to be put to sleep today.

She admires, as she most often does from this vantage point, the great room of the house she and Joe built and moved into about eighteen months ago. She loves the rich oak wood work, the bright white kitchen, the rock fireplace, and the curved staircase more each day. The view, past the expanse of a new subdivision in the distance and out toward fields melted into a continuous sky, takes her breath away.

Last night's meeting was like the others. Each year, around the anniversary of Roz's disappearance, the RCMP host a community information session in the faint hope new clues might come to light. They communicate what they can provide for public consumption, in the undying belief someone might remember an obscure detail. The session was late this year, because of Ronny Étang's disappearance and the eventual resolution of her abduction. Ronny's ordeal took place the first week of August, so the annual community information session about Roz Dover was postponed for a couple of months. No matter. The RCMP possessed no additional details to share with the group assembled.

Gaby absently checks her wispy hair to ensure it's still held securely in the clip at the nape of her neck. The fastener won't stay, but it will do for now. Martha, Gaby's husky and blue heeler mix, wanders over and plunks down with little grace and less ceremony at Gaby's feet. "You will stay here this morning, old girl. No need to be in the truck, all in a lather and excited to go somewhere. We'll come straight back home and fetch you if we decide to go into the shop or out to a job site." She leans over from her perch on her stool and ruffles the dog's ears. Big but good describes Martha. It's like she understands every word.

Gaby's mind drifts back to last night's meeting. Almost everyone with any connection to Roz, or the circumstances of August 6, was there. Cheryl Nadler, Patrick Hollinger, Amanda Wolski, Ila and Crystal—Roz's former roommates—both Fiona Werbowski and Sean Knox of the RCMP, Rose and Maggie Woodward, Roz's parents who travel to Hayworth each year for this gathering, and a host of other people who are not as familiar to Gaby. Her friend, Fiona, led the group and tried to focus, this year, on anyone who might have been around town on the evening Roz disappeared. She requested attendees check their old calendars and appointment books on the off chance someone was out for another reason and might recall Roz's car or anything suspicious.

Gaby can remember exactly what she was doing through the whole time period because she was a family counsellor at the Hexagon back then, stalked by a client she later thought might have murdered Roz. This client was Charlene Quinn—Roz's third roommate. Without a body, the cops were never able to pin the murder on her, although she was convicted in the murder of a hitchhiker in Nova Scotia.

No one in Hayworth seems to be in possession of information other than details uncovered at the time of the initial investigation. Roz's disappearance eats away at every member of the community. The people who knew about

Ronny's kidnapping were apoplectic until she was found, and the case was determined to have no relation to the Dover situation. Gaby knows the depressed little northern prairie town couldn't have survived another tragedy.

She lifts her head and turns toward the oak stairs as Joe lumbers into view. He cradles Blanche in his big arms. She was a large cat at one time, but her condition has rendered her both emaciated and frail—lots of long white hair to cover a little bag of bones. They have never known for sure how old she is. Joe carried her home from a construction site years ago, well before he and Gaby ever met. He was certain she had been abused and suspected her blindness was the result of a toxic solution thrown in her face. Today is the day. It will not be easy.

"You know, your choice of jeans and a denim shirt might not be the best." Her remarks are spoken in a soft voice and punctuated by a sad expression.

He meets her eyes, nods, and crosses the great room. As he stops to place Blanche, with a gentleness she finds heartbreaking to observe, into her basket, he glances back over toward Gaby. "I know. I know. I couldn't help myself. To be covered in white cat hair today seems appropriate, somehow."

She hands him a cup of steaming black coffee and crosses the kitchen to the toaster on the counter. "Toast?"

"Sure. Whatever you're having. I don't have much appetite. You were smart to book the vet appointment on a day we're closed."

"Yeah. I didn't think either one of us could face Blanche's demise on a work day. Since Monday's our weekend, this seemed to be the best option." She drops a couple of slices of homemade brown bread into the toaster and presses the lever down. She circles the island and wraps her arms around the man who has been her rock, her partner, her confidante, and her lover for almost three years now.

"I have a plan. Let's come back to the house afterward, get Martha, and go for a drive. I want to see the location where those two big houses are being built north of here. The wives—sisters—brought me their blueprints." A spark of interest registers in his eyes. "Neither property is close to ready for final measurements and design, but a drive would help me visualize where they will be."

"Okay. We'll go over to the diner for lunch and then take a run out. We haven't eaten there much since Amanda bought the place."

"We don't eat out like we used to before we built the house."

"Her food will be as good as when Margo Johnson was the owner." He continues to hug her while he waits for his toast, seemingly relieved, for the moment, of the burden of anticipation about their trip to the vet. "Let's change the subject. Do you ever wonder how nobody saw activity of any kind the night Roz Dover disappeared?"

Gaby unwraps herself and returns to the toaster. She pulls out two slices and pops in two more. "Oh, I think someone saw something or knows something, although they still don't know they know."

"Now what the hell is that supposed to mean?" Joe spreads globs of peanut butter and thick red strawberry jam, from the local farmers' market, across his toast. He glances over at Blanche every couple of minutes as he teases Gaby about her observations of human nature.

"Someone was out. Someone saw activity of some sort. Maybe Fiona needs to have an RCMP member in Truro, Nova Scotia have a talk with Charlene Quinn. She was skulking about that night. She wandered around in her truck, hounded me, and searched for Patrick. If she didn't hurt Roz, maybe she saw who did. Instead of being the murderer, she could be the witness." Although she's certain she shouldn't stick her nose where it doesn't belong, a chat with Fiona the next time she stops by for coffee at the shop might be an idea.

Blanche knows their routine is amiss. Gaby can see the questions in the tilt of the old cat's head, but she's too frail to protest as Joe places her with gentle precision into her carrier. The drive to the clinic takes less than ten minutes. They trudge up the steps and into the waiting room without the need to talk. Gaby and Joe are as one when they enter the building and approach the front desk peppered with treats, a jar full of catnip toys, and another for SPCA donations.

The young woman behind the counter is a new employee, at least to Gaby. Martha and Blanche have always been pretty healthy and annual appointments have been the only necessary visits. Staff turnover happens—the nature of life in the north. The young woman, resplendent in black nail polish and shiny red lips, rifles through the file cabinet in search of the folder with Blanche's name.

Gaby's thoughts are propelled back to June of 1981 when she first encountered Charlene Quinn as a client at the Hexagon. In her varied experiences as a family counsellor, her relationship with Charlene was a unique journey. She was extreme, with her black painted nails, bright red lips, orange or platinum dyed hair depending on her mood, plunging necklines, and elevated hemlines. She courted fear, shock, and the manipulation of others. The unavoidable end result of Gaby's experience with this sociopath resulted in her choice to turn away from her profession and go into business with Joe.

Charlene stalked Gaby for months. She confessed to murder. Although Gaby never acted in an unethical manner, she was investigated by her professional association because of a letter Charlene wrote to them. The time was a stressful and a dark chapter in her life. One of her best decisions was to take Joe up on his offer to help him create Dodd's Contracting and Interiors. Their business has done relatively well, if you take the condition of the Alberta economy into consideration. Sale contracts have been steady, so they have pondered the idea of hiring someone to man the shop throughout the summer. Then they could visit job sites together more often, and the help would free up their evenings. She hopes the summer will be fun.

"Dr. Chisholm will be with you in a couple of minutes. Blanche, right? Please keep her in her crate." The black nails and red lips have spoken.

Joe shrugs and Gaby gives him a tiny nudge in the ribs—a mind your manners nudge, but she remains quiet.

"She's fine. No problem." He peers down at Gaby and squints. She understands. They perch together on leatherette benches. Furry dust bunnies float around their feet. Maintenance must be a constant challenge.

Dr. Chisholm is young. He avoids direct eye contact with Gaby or Joe. He mumbles and the pale skin on his forehead has a sheen of perspiration. He wants to know if they plan to stay while he administers the injection. Gaby hears Joe's breath catch in his throat. She rests her hand on his arm before she speaks. "We will stay with Blanche and then take her body home. We don't want her to be alone." She senses the muscles in Joe's arm relax.

The young doctor presents a white lab coat that hangs over hunched shoulders as he turns his back on them to prepare the medication. "You may take the cat out of the carrier and place it on the table, please." He communicates directly to the beige laminate cupboards in front of him.

Joe, without a word, reaches into the crate for his beloved Blanche, and Gaby pulls the pink blanket out as well. She spreads it on the stainless steel table. Joe settles the old girl, as he calms her down with steady and gentle pats. Gaby puts the crate on the floor and returns her hand to Joe's arm. He doesn't turn, but leans into her touch. The movement is barely detectable.

Dr. Chisholm turns around and, without another word, shaves Blanche's paw and injects the solution into the front of her leg. The process is over in a few moments. "Okay, we're done here," is all the young man says before he opens the back door of the exam room and slithers into the recesses of the clinic.

Joe, stoic to a fault, continues to rub Blanche's now lifeless side. Gaby is patient. She hopes the black nails won't come in and ask them to leave, but Joe surprises her. In one motion he scoops up Blanche, wrapped in her pink blanket, and bends down to put her into her crate.

"Let's get the hell out of here. We'll go home and bury her, Gaby. Okay with you?" His eyes are misty.

No words are required. Her throat is raw and her heart aches for him. He trudges out and down the steps to the truck. Gaby returns to the desk to pay the bill.

Once home, Joe grabs a shovel and makes his way through the back yard to a small grove of trees. He digs the hole with a fury Gaby has never seen. She gathers Blanche, still wrapped in her pink blanket, from out of the carrier, and makes the two hundred foot trip down to the trees. Martha remains on the step, responding to a hand signal from Gaby for her to stay.

✳✳✳✳

They park Joe's big blue monster of a truck in front of the Hayworth Diner near noon. There are only two other vehicles in the lot, but one might expect Mondays to be their slow day. "You stay put, Martha." Gaby gives the standard command, but where the hell can a dog go, as she sits in the front seat of a pickup with the windows rolled down three inches? Her natural response is to give a command, anyway.

Inside, they find themselves drawn to one of the booths located by the long row of windows. They have shared many meals in this exact spot, from the time Joe first renovated her kitchen at 15 Poplar Street, through the bathroom renovation, her troubled year as the counsellor of a sociopath, and then all through their somewhat reluctant, although terribly intense, courtship. Like oftentimes in the past when life proved stressful, they return to the diner yet again.

Amanda Wolski approaches them with menus and water. "Hi, you two. Long time no see. Decided to try the place out again since ownership has changed hands?"

They both nod but Gaby responds first. "Wanted to come down and see the change in management. We close the shop on Sunday and Monday so we can get out and about a bit. How long now, a month since you took over?"

"A little more than a month. Time flies."

"How's business been?"

Amanda, bright red and curly hair piled in a mass on the top of her head, leans against the back of the booth near Joe, as she gazes over at Gaby. "Not bad. I'm pretty sure I made the right decision. Mason has started school...."

Gaby interrupts. "The little guy is in school already, Amanda? I am amazed!"

"The bus lets him off here and he stays with me until Chester is finished work at five. Then they both have supper, go out to the farm to pick up the baby, and then go home. Chester's mother minds Melanie. The staff—Patrick, Danny, and Nancy—do most of the real work. They take care of me. Business is fine." She brushes a wisp of curl off her forehead.

"What about the manager work at The Station?" Gaby knows Joe often wonders how the two of them did repair work at the old apartment building once he moved out. Chester was after him to help with odd jobs every time he turned around.

"Oh, the place pretty much runs itself. I still collect rents and Chester does the odd repair, but the owners told me to hire any help we need—not a problem. Once we get up on our feet, I hope we'll be able to build a house out near the Wolski property. Maybe sooner than later." She winks at Gaby. "I'll be back in a minute to take your order. The lunch special is a turkey and bacon club, with or without fries." She turns on her heel in response to Danny's big paw when it smothers the service bell located on the pass-through counter.

"I'm not surprised Enterprise Investments told her she could hire whatever help they need, Gaby. Chester wasn't any good at the handyman stuff. He would stare at a dripping tap like it had fallen from space. He would say he would fix whatever was broken and then never get back to the tenant. Rose called me, instead, a couple of times when she had a problem." Joe shakes his head. "Want a special? We can share the fries."

"Sure. Sounds good." Gaby's thoughts drift back to when Roz Dover's car was finally located on an abandoned property—the next farm over from the Wolski spread. They might get that land for a song, now. No one knows how Amanda and Chester afforded the diner. Word on the street was Amanda inherited money, but details were sparse. Gaby has always understood Amanda's parents died when she was a child and she was brought up in foster care. One wouldn't think there would be any money. Who knows? Maybe her parents set up a trust fund and lawyers needed to track her down. Maybe she had to reach a certain age.

Amanda approaches the table a second time. "Two specials, Amanda. One with fries and one without. I'll have tea. Joe, what about you?"

"A cup of coffee, Amanda. Thanks."

After Amanda returns to the kitchen, Joe addresses the elephant in the room. "How big of an asshole was Dr. Chisholm this morning? Is it me, or is he a heartless son of a bitch?"

Gaby graces him with a barely discernible smirk. Her Joe has returned. "Your assessment is right on the money. I have been contemplating whether or not I should call the owner of the clinic and report Dr. Chisholm's behaviour."

"Don't bother, but the next time you make an appointment for Martha, ask for anybody but that cold fish." He reaches across and takes Gaby's hand in his big mitt. "Thanks for coming with me today, love. I don't think I could have taken the old girl in without you."

"I know." She pats his hand just as Amanda returns with their lunch.

****

The drive north to the location of the two new homes being constructed outside Hayworth takes about fifteen minutes. Right now, all they can see are footings recently poured, and the start of two wooden basements under construction. The crews are there today. Gaby and Joe stay out of the way. Gaby wants to get a feel for the space. It's much easier to design a kitchen when you know where the sun will come in and what the view will be out the kitchen window.

They wander around for about half an hour. Gaby keeps Martha on a leash since the work site is active. "I'll be able to give the two sisters estimates based on the blueprint measurements and their preliminary decisions on product. Doesn't appear we'll be in a great rush. What do you think? Three months to finishings?"

"At least." Joe stands beside her and wraps a denim-clad arm around her shoulder. "They'll be anxious to get both buildings closed in as soon as possible. I hate to see people try to build while winter rushes at us. I don't expect they'll be in by Christmas."

"No thought of any pressure there. They had to wait until after harvest in order to start. Both hope for late February, beginning of March right now. We will plan on then for a tentative schedule." She makes a quick note on a scrap of paper retrieved from her pocket; kept there for such occasions. "We'll have fun when we measure for kitchens in unfinished and unheated houses in northern Alberta in January." Her sarcasm is unmistakeable. She giggles as she leans into his arm and they trudge through the stubble back to the truck. Construction work in the north is never without challenges.

Chapter 2

Amanda

The afternoon has flown by. Amanda arrived at the Hayworth Diner about thirty minutes after most of the lunch crowd had dispersed. Danny, her short-order cook, and Patrick Hollinger, her old friend from The Station and her right hand man since she purchased the restaurant, were busy with clean-up. They will also do the prep for supper so she and Nancy, her waitress, can manage the evening service. She moves warm glasses from a tray to the shelf behind the counter, and thinks about the changes in her life since she received her windfall back in July.

Murdock Blackney is always the same. Amanda thinks of him as round and brown. His office has brown paneling. He wears brown suits with waistcoats, in an obvious attempt to camouflage his rotund figure. She has difficulty, for some reason unknown to her, in calling him by his first name although he repeatedly insisted she do so, all the time he worked for her in the past.

"Hi, Amanda? Murdock here. Can you pop down to the office anytime soon?"

Amanda hesitated. Her divorce from her first husband became final years ago. She and Chester remarried to make their union legal. What could have gone wrong now? "Do we have a problem, Mr. Blackney?"

"Call me Murdock. No problem, in the strictest sense. I believe I may have good news for you but I don't want to discuss the issue over the telephone."

"I'll come down right away, but I will have Mason and Melanie in tow, if you don't mind."

"Bring the children. How old are they, now?"

"Mason is five and Melanie is two. No kindergarten in the summer. You will be subjected to the company of them both." She chortled. "Are you prepared for kids?"

Her lawyer didn't mind. The news couldn't be bad, if he was anticipating a visit with her children. "I'll be there around two o'clock, if the time works for you."

"See you then, Amanda." The line was dead before she had an opportunity to say good bye.

The meeting with Murdock Blackney didn't take long. She was shocked, and absorption of the news required a measure of time. She recalls their conversation. She must have sounded like an idiot. "Jeremy's dead? What? He's still young, like me. What happened?"

Murdock was careful with his explanation. "Jeremy Bradway, your former husband, died suddenly. The cause appears to have been an undetected heart condition although the exact cause has not been shared with me. He fell to the ground during a basketball game with friends and subsequently died in hospital. He never regained consciousness. I have been contacted by his solicitor—the same fellow with whom I communicated regarding the divorce we discovered you had, but not until after you married Chester—and according to him, you are the sole beneficiary of his estate. Jeremy did not attend to his affairs after the divorce, and you are still the one person named in the will. You are about to inherit a significant sum of money, Amanda—almost three-quarters of a million dollars."

Amanda sat and bounced Melanie on her lap while she watched Mason drive his cars around on the molasses brown wood floor in the tiny law office. She imagined she was peeking through the window at herself sitting in a paneled box.

Murdock continued. "There is no expectation Jeremy's parents will contest the will. The law firm told me you could anticipate a cheque once probate has been completed in the very near future. The resolution of his affairs is not complicated, apparently, and they estimate approximately thirty days. I have a document for you to sign and I will need to tell them where to forward the money."

The one sentence able to exit Amanda's brain at the time was, "I don't know what to say." She held Melanie between her knees as the little girl stood still and clasped Amanda's thighs. Mason stared at her with a quizzical expression, like he was worried his mother might be upset. Amanda's only thought was how the money meant she and Chester could move forward, and this would be one more step on the path toward no more troubles.

The month following her meeting with Murdock Blackney disappeared in a blur of plans, discussions, offers to purchase, negotiations, and more discussions. Amanda wanted to buy the Hayworth Diner and Margo Johnson, the local accountant and part-time entrepreneur, wanted to sell. It was a match made in heaven. Granted, there would be issues about how The Station could be managed, but they always planned for a house of their own in the future. Now, with the money, they could realize their dreams much sooner.

Chester exhibited initial reluctance. Her handsome, fun-loving husband has changed over the past few years, as she has. Secrets pressure a couple. Amanda worries constantly. Every day, as Chester sets off for the Ford dealership and his work as a mechanic, she has these horrible thoughts about how he will never come home, like the universe will pay them back. Her parents were both killed in a car accident and she grew up in foster care. She has always felt undeserving and worthless. Chester once gave her value, but not anymore. Melanie's birth did not help to remove the pall hanging like a dirty fog over their relationship. Now, her first husband has dropped dead, and her anxieties are multiplied. She is bound and determined to make this inheritance from Jeremy a new beginning for them both.

Since their purchase of the diner in mid-August, along with the start of the school year, they have made a valiant attempt to settle into the semblance of a routine. Early each morning, Amanda takes her little girl out to the Wolski ranch to spend the day with her mother-in-law. Then she takes Mason to kindergarten before she returns to The Station to complete her daily chores. By noon, she starts her shift at the diner. Mason gets dropped off by the school bus and spends the latter part of the afternoon with her, until Chester picks him up at five. Then they go out to the farm to get his sister and go back to The Station where Chester does their supper if they haven't already eaten at the diner. Amanda arrives back to their apartment as soon as she can get away. The days are long and not ideal, but she likes to keep busy and she won't be as stressed once they get used to the changes.

****

Patrick lounges in the staff booth at the back with Mason. They are intent as they colour a placemat designed to occupy the minds and fingers of young ones as they wait for their meal. Mason loves to colour. Patrick seems to enjoy the activity as well. As a ploy to keep the little guy out of the kitchen, he oftentimes stays after his shift, to keep an eye on him.

"Saw you at the meeting last night but I didn't see Chester. Home babysitting?" Patrick's approach is easy going, as usual. The diner is quiet and he chatters away to the little boy while he includes Amanda with his question.

"Yes. Chester isn't interested. He says the police don't have a clue, literally, and he won't waste time there when we're busy with work and kids."

"Didn't he get a call that night?"

"Yeah. He went out to give a couple a boost. He never saw Roz or anybody else."

"Charlene must have murdered her, Amanda. Everybody knows she was around then. She went and bothered Gaby Ridgway and then parked in front of The Station for what seemed like hours. The cops should go talk to her again. When Chester left The Station, he must have seen her."

Amanda remembers the old red Land Cruiser ensconced in front of the apartment building. Charlene spent a lot of time there. "He says he didn't. Told the cops he didn't see a thing." She provides her standard response. "The answering service handled his call. He gave some people a boost and then came home. The people were from down south and he was never given their name."

She's happy when the opening of the glass entry door tinkles the bell mounted on the wall above the frame, and a group of teenagers from the high school tumble in. They pile into a booth and wave at Amanda. Soda fountain cokes all around. She knows the drill.

While Patrick continues to mind Mason, Amanda checks out Danny's progress in the kitchen. The air smells heavenly as he takes two large, deep dish apple pies out of the big wall oven. She made them when she first arrived. Danny, the middle aged and gruff short-order cook has become accustomed to Amanda's preferences over the last while. She has decided to buy as few pre-made desserts as possible. They will be homemade, like every dinner they serve. Pork has been roasting this afternoon, so her weekly pork special—a carry-over from when Margo owned the diner—continues in the tradition expected by the public. Each night has its own feature dinner. Customers appreciate familiarity.

Danny, apron betraying evidence of his busy day, nods. "Almost done, Amanda. Nancy coming in soon? The prep is ready for the two of you tonight. I wish the new dishwasher fella' had worked out, but maybe Patrick will want extra hours. He doesn't have much of a life. Never has."

"Hush now." Amanda admonishes her cook. "He's right out in the restaurant with Mason. I'll ask if he'll stay, but I think he's met someone." She acknowledges Danny's wide eyes and raised brows from across the kitchen.

"What? Did he meet another loony tunes in therapy? I don't believe you!"

Amanda considers his disparaging remark to be a term of endearment. She knows Danny's discovered a new respect for Patrick despite the gruff tone.

"I'm pretty sure. Now, don't mention a word. Don't ask him. We'll find out in due time. Hold on. I'll see if he wants to help out tonight." She approaches the window which separates the kitchen from the customers. "Hey, Patrick!"

He reverts his attention from what seems like an intense conversation with Mason.

"Want to stay and bus for us tonight; handle old Bertha while Nancy does orders and I work the back?"

"Sure, Amanda. Happy to help out. Pork roast night is always busy. I can stay. Will you feed me?"

He grins from ear to ear. Amanda hopes her suspicions are correct and he's started to date.

"Of course. I'll even pay you, Patrick!" She guffaws as she turns back toward Danny and supper preparations. The high school kids have settled their bill and left. Chester should be here within the hour.

****

The place is busier than expected and Chester manages to be late, too. Nancy serves dinners, Amanda works the back. Patrick busses. Everybody keeps an eye on Mason. He can be a handful if he sets his mind to "helping" in the kitchen. Eventually, Chester rolls in the door.

He fills the room in the way you might imagine a charismatic politician or a popular movie star would. Every eye in the diner—young, old, male, female—turns to gawk at him saunter down the aisle created by the window booths and the counter, until he reaches the staff booth in the back. He seems to only have eyes for his little boy.

Dressed in blue jeans and a grey plaid shirt, open at the neck, with his dark wavy hair hanging down over one eye, and his perfect teeth shining out of his tanned and chiselled face, it isn't any wonder everyone stares. Chester Wolski is a walking work of art—and he's well aware.

The silence of awe is broken by Mason. "Daddy, Daddy!" He wiggles his pudgy frame out of the bench seat, and upsets a jar of crayons in the process. They crash across the diner floor, as he throws himself, with unceremonious clumsiness, at his handsome father. Amanda peeks through the pass-through and thinks, for a second, perhaps her patrons might actually clap. She wipes her hands and heads out through the saloon doors.

As Chester, Mason in his arms, leans down to give her a peck on the cheek, she asks, "Do you want to stay for the pork dinner? I'll call your mom and tell her you'll be another hour and ask her to make Melanie some supper."

"Sure. What time will you be home?"

Her eyes dart around the diner. Patrick has started to bus tables. The place is almost full. "I could be later than eight, Chester. You can manage if you don't have to do supper, can't you?"

"Sure, but tomorrow night I'm on call. You'll have to find another way." He doesn't meet her eyes as he talks; his gaze is focused on Mason instead.

Amanda sighs. She tries to hide her frustration. The purchase of the diner was to help them, but right now, with two little ones, the business is more of a challenge than a help. Chester never tries to reorganize his schedule to accommodate her. Oftentimes, there's a scramble at the last minute. "I'll call Danny when the diner quiets down and ask him to work supper instead of lunch. I think I'll be okay." She pats Mason's chunky little leg as she turns and makes her way back behind the saloon doors and into the kitchen.

"Problem, Amanda?"

Patrick steps into the space. The saloon doors flap behind him.

"I'm good, just busy. Sometimes I'm disappointed when all anybody wants is the special and meal preps are monotonous, but tonight I don't mind." She attempts to be gracious toward this young man who she knows would do pretty much whatever she asked. "Here. Put down your tray and take these plates out to Chester and Mason, please." She hands him a pork dinner special and a mini hamburger and fries for her little boy. She manages to toss a few carrot sticks on the side although she's doubtful Mason will even touch them.

Nancy places four more orders on the pass-through counter. Nancy is a brick. She is a local, born and raised right here in Hayworth. She started to work full-time at the diner the minute she graduated from high school. Amanda suspects she's near forty, but would never ask. She's slim and trim; walks everywhere—dashes, if the truth be known. She's devoted to her nieces and nephews; never misses a game of one sort or another; has never missed a recital or a graduation, either. She's the kind of aunt every kid needs. Amanda likes her a lot.

Patrick carries the dinners out to the staff booth. She can overhear him as he chats with Chester.

"You know, Amanda and I talked earlier about the night Roz Dover disappeared. She said you were out on a call. I can't believe you didn't see psycho Charlene in her red Land Cruiser parked in front of The Station. You took a call that night, right? Somebody needed a boost over at the hotel?"

Chester acknowledges the question but focuses his attention on Mason, as he helps him slather ketchup on his fries. "Never saw her or anybody else, bud. Did my job and headed back home. The night was pretty quiet. I've told the cops a couple of times."

Patrick presses. "Are you sure, Chester?" Amanda knows Patrick has been obsessed with Roz's disappearance because of his involvement with Charlene Quinn, the young woman who was one of Roz's roommates and who the police suspected was pivotal in her disappearance. Most often, when he becomes obsessed, she can find a way to refocus the conversation and assign him a task.

"Yeah, man, I'm sure. Can't help. Never could."

Amanda addresses Patrick through the window. "You want to grab your tray and clean up the front booth, Patrick?"

As she gets his attention, he turns toward her and nods. "Sorry, Chester. The doc says I fixate. I guess I'd better get back to work."

****

The restaurant is quiet by seven-thirty. Amanda takes time to get the kitchen and front counter organized for the morning. Usually Danny's here well before opening, but she asked him to start work later in the day and he agreed. Patrick fills the dishwasher one last time and takes a bottle of cleaner along with a fresh cloth to wipe down the tables. The diner closes at eight. She doesn't expect anybody else tonight.

"You can take off, if you want to, Patrick. I'll watch the dishwasher until the light goes out and handle anyone who comes in."

"Not a chance, Amanda. We've never let you or Nancy work alone in here. Danny and I never let Margo work alone when she owned the place, either." He scrubs the table with extra enthusiasm. "Not right in this day and age. I think everybody still has the jitters after Ronny's disappearance. Have you heard her? She calls her escape the 'great crapper caper'." He leans against the pass-through and watches Amanda wipe down the stainless counters. "Do you need me to help?"

"No. I think we're good. And yes, everybody was pretty upset about Ronny's ex grabbing her. Of course, I didn't know until the crisis was over. You, on the other hand, knew every detail and never said a word. You know how to keep a secret, mister."

Patrick's self-satisfied expression is slow and easy. His arms are crossed. Like always, his hands are almost white and blotched with bursts of red from tending the dishwasher. He hates rubber gloves. He may have changed a lot over the years—he's improved his hygiene habits and has more clothes than one pair of jeans, a jean jacket, and a filthy T-shirt—but certain peculiarities remain. He leaves his apartment lights on all night, he won't wear rubber gloves when he works, and he obsesses about particular issues to the point where you wish he would shut the hell up.

"I have a couple more secrets, too." He raises one hand like a mock stop sign. "Don't ask. I'll tell you when I'm good and ready—when and if I end up with any news to tell."

"You're not gonna quit and leave me high and dry, are you, Patrick? I don't know what I'd do without you, you know." Her voice softens as she reaches for a towel to dry her hands. "When I bought the place, I told Margo I expected the deal to include you!" She teases him.

"You found a good deal, what with me, Danny, and Nancy. We're a team and you fit right in, so...no, I'm not gonna quit. Happy as a clam!" He waves his arms around the room. "Seems like Bertha's done for the night. I'll put the cups out on the front shelf and then we can get outta here."

Patrick's right. They are a team. Their circumstances will work out, as long as Chester comes to realize he needs to contribute more, both now and down the road. On her way out, she grabs the book of house plans she has stashed under the counter.

Chapter 3

Audrey

Today is move-in day for Audrey Baranski as she takes up residence at The Station. It's a cold and sleet-filled Saturday, November 10. Two days off in a row from her job in the cafeteria at the Hayworth Community Hospital has afforded her the time she needs to get settled.

Her parents, Ivan and Iona, are as reluctant about her move as they have been with every detail of her life since her diagnosis back at Christmas almost six years ago. They didn't want her to take the medication. Her father said she acted like a zombie, and he was right for a while. Gaby Ridgway, her counsellor, supported and encouraged her parents to accept the need for her endless prescriptions. Gaby convinced them to allow her take the job at the hospital. Gaby isn't her counsellor anymore and hasn't been for three years.

Audrey has improved to the point where her parents came to understand she needed a spot of her own. As she continued to live out in the country, she was forced to depend on them for drives to and from the hospital. She works shifts and the situation has been more than inconvenient for everybody. This apartment has been vacant for a long time, but Patrick Hollinger, who lives upstairs in Number Six, told her he thought Enterprise Investments were able to rent the place again. The previous tenant kept the lease for ages.

Audrey met Patrick at the hospital. He sees Dr. Wilkerson, the psychiatrist. He would often come down to the cafeteria for tea before his appointment. He says he doesn't like to sit in the chairs area because the reception room is full of sick people. He's right, of course, but it still sounds funny.

"Come help me with your bed." The boom of his question explodes out of her burly father as he sets down a platform rocker in the middle of the main room of the apartment. Number Four is a plain, two bedroom unit with a kitchen along one wall, a wide open space, and bedrooms connected by an adjoining bath. "Your mother can't help with the bed!"

Her father's voice sounds impatient and gruff, but Audrey knows his tone disguises other emotions. He is afraid for her. He doesn't want to be, but he is. "I'll help, Dad. Tell Mom she can unpack these dishes I just brought in." A couple of weeks ago, when she was first told the apartment would be available for November, she and her mother shopped for all the necessities—they went to Carter River and outfitted her kitchen. They bought linens she would need, as well. They decided she would use her mattress from home, along with the stenciled pine headboard and dresser. Iona donated the extra couch from their den, and the platform rocker. Now her mother has a good excuse to buy more updated versions.

By lunch time, most of her possessions are put into their proper places except for her clothes. She treats her parents to lunch at the diner before they set out for home. She describes the residents at The Station one more time, and takes the opportunity to introduce her parents to Amanda Wolski.

Over homemade chicken soup and biscuits, she sings the praises of the current tenants. "Beginning with the Wolskis, Amanda is married to Chester. They have two little ones and live in the basement suite."

"How can she manage a restaurant and take care of her children?" Iona is old school and Audrey knows she doesn't approve.

"His mom helps." Audrey smiles and tilts her head. Her long brown hair, tied in a tight ponytail away from her face, swishes against her squall jacket. The light from the window reflects her perfect skin, unadorned with make-up of any kind. Audrey has to have her hair tied and won't use any cleanser but the most basic Ivory soap on her skin.

She continues. "Rose Woodward lives below me in Number Two and her sister Maggie lives across the hall from her in Number Three. You know Rose. She works for Dr. Gunton. Maggie works at Segue House. Cheryl Nadler, a social worker at the Hexagon, lives across the hall from me. She's been there almost as long as Patrick Hollinger, who lives up in Number Six. He told me about the apartment and he works here!" She opens her arms and displays her hands palms up, like she has finished a performance.

Her mother is attentive as she nods. Her father acts disinterested, but Audrey is positive he never missed a word. She expects he already found out who lived in each unit before he ever let her sign the lease.

Audrey is not prepared to tell her parents how she once ate supper here at the diner with Patrick, one day when her shift ended early. He said he would pop in to say hi after he gets home later tonight. They are both night owls and have talked about their fears of the dark and a return of their voices.

Patrick busses tables and nods on his way past—very professional and nonchalant. She's warm inside, like they have a secret. Audrey knows she isn't very good at reading people, but she thinks Patrick might like her.

****

After her parents drop her off and she listens, without interrupting, to their instructions, Audrey busies herself. She hangs up clothes and makes her bed. This will be her first supper in her own apartment as a free and independent woman. She takes a moment to gaze around. One hand covers her mouth. She is overwhelmed with the gravity of her change in circumstances.

She hears a very gentle knock on the door. She runs to answer without a thought as to who might be on the other side. She flings open the door and finds herself face to face with the single most handsome man in the town of Hayworth. Chester Wolski stands on her threshold.

She's surprised. He starts to talk before she can straighten out her thoughts. "Hi. I'm Chester Wolski. My wife and I manage the place and, since she's at the diner, I thought I'd pop up and see if you might need a hand with your move-in."

Audrey is overwhelmed. She feels hypnotized or drugged somehow. Although at a loss for words, she opens the door wide, an act which enables him to saunter into her new oasis and personal space. *Why have I let him in? I don't need help.*

Chester wanders around her living area as though he's never seen an apartment at The Station before. He peeks out the window, runs a long-fingered and manicured hand across the back of the rocker, and turns to grace her with what appears to be a leer. His thick and dark hair hangs down over one eye and his smirk-like expression reveals perfect teeth. "You need a carpet and a table and chairs, Audrey."

He says her name in a way that sounds like syrup feels. He draws out the syllables. No one has ever said her name like this before. Her insides flutter. "I know." She sputters her words. "My mom said we could go back to Carter River after pay day and I can shop in a couple of the second-hand stores. Dad said we could take his truck."

"You could go in my truck. I would love to take you." His lecherous expression seems to seep into the pores of her skin.

"Oh, I couldn't ask you to drive me! You have little kids and a wife who runs a business. I don't think you need to chauffeur me to Carter River to hunt for furniture." She surprises herself at how assertive her words sound to her own ears. She knows she's more mousy than assertive, but she wants to be friends with Amanda, and all of a sudden, she thinks Chester might be flirting with her and she is profoundly uncomfortable.

He shrugs his broad shoulders, as if he could care less one way or the other. "Suit yourself. I know a couple of great places, though." He raises his eyebrows for emphasis. "I guess you have to get back to your unpacking. Don't forget, if you need any help, let me or Amanda know. You take care now." His hand is on the doorknob as his last sentence leaves his lips, and then he's gone.

After his departure, she continues with her chores, but obsessive thoughts start to take control. *Why would he come up here? Does he flirt with everyone or is it me? Does Amanda know he acts like this? Should I not let him into my apartment? Does Patrick know what he's like? He must be ten years older than me. Does he have a problem? Am I making too much of this?*

She forces herself out of what she is afraid might be the road to an abyss of negativity and random ideas fabricated by her imagination. She knows this is what gets her into trouble. She's been through enough therapy and taken enough medication to understand her weaknesses.

Men intimidate her. When she first went to university, in Edmonton in 1978, she lived with roommates. She convinced herself she had been gang-raped by the boyfriends of the other women. The situation was a hallucination; all in her mind. Only one of the girls went out with a boy, and he never stayed over. She was such a mess, certain this horrible incident happened to her. Even now, while she dutifully takes her meds and understands the physiology of the paranoid and psychotic state she experienced, she can still convince herself it happened. The voices and the sensations seemed so real.

She tried to explain the delusions and hallucinations to her parents, but the words scared them. They didn't know what to say or how to treat her. Thank God she has now built up enough tolerance to the anti-psychotics that she's stopped acting like a zombie. Gaby helped. Once she landed the job at the hospital, it forced her to interact with people. She works every day to overcome her fears. Patrick is supportive because he suffers from schizophrenia, too. She rearranges the dishware her mother stored in her cupboards. It takes one to know one; kind of like AA, according to Patrick.

She starts to prepare her supper. She has the leftover casserole her mother made yesterday. She will heat it in the oven and toast a piece of the bread Iona included. It seems ironic. She still isn't as independent as she would wish to be.

As she starts to get organized, there's another knock on the door. This time, she remembers to ask first. "Who's there?"

"Hi! Rose and Maggie Woodward from downstairs."

Audrey rushes to unlock and open the door. Rose is the first to speak. "I'm Rose Woodward. We've met at Dr. Gunton's office, Audrey. Welcome to The Station." She thrusts a red, chapped hand toward Audrey, who avoids the act of handshaking at all costs, but compromises her preferences on this occasion and takes Rose's hand in hers. "This is my sister, Maggie. She works at Segue House, the women's shelter. I don't think you two have met before."

Audrey turns to greet Maggie, an ethereal, childlike creature who beams through a curtain of chestnut hair on both sides of her face. "Hi, Maggie— and Rose. Would you like to come in? How nice of you to stop by and say hello."

"Oh, we hope to do more!" Maggie gushes and turns to her sister for confirmation. "We want you to come for supper at Rose's tonight. She's made tomato and macaroni casserole. I've made a salad and we have Amanda's buns from the diner. We have leftover lemon pie. Will you come?"

Audrey catches her breath. She is overwhelmed and searches for an escape, but her attempts prove fruitless. "I guess I could come down. This is very nice of you."

"We are like a family here, Audrey. We want you to become part of our little neighbourhood." Rose sounds pragmatic. "Now grab your keys and come along with us. The casserole should be ready anytime, now."

****

Back in her apartment later in the evening, Audrey reviews her visit, and realizes the time spent wasn't as bad as she had anticipated. She learned a great deal about the two sisters, as well as the other residents in the building. Her concerns, related to Chester, were assuaged, as both women swooned over how handsome he is, but neither said an untoward word about him. They expressed their admiration for Amanda, but thought the time had come for the Wolskis to give up management of the building. Rose felt Amanda should spend more time with her children. They hinted about how Amanda came into money recently, and the couple wanted to build a house our near Chester's family farm.

They talked about Joe Dodd a lot. He lived in Number Four for many years before he built a house with Gaby Ridgway. Audrey never let on how she knew Gaby, or how she had met Cheryl Nadler on previous occasions, either. She made sure not to mention her friendship with Patrick. She said she knew him from the diner and thought he was a pretty nice fellow.

Rose and Maggie chattered away about their jobs and their lives in Hayworth. Maggie is enamoured with a policeman named Sean. She gushed about him and giggled, but didn't reveal much in the way of details. Audrey expects Maggie is challenged to keep her private life a secret from Rose.

She checks her watch. Patrick isn't off shift until after ten o'clock on the weekend. Still an hour to wait. He said he would stop in, on his way up to Number Six, to see how her move went. She thinks he seemed excited. She curls up on the familiar sofa and waits with a patience she has learned throughout her illness. She balances a book in her lap but doesn't read.

An hour goes by, and then she hears the soft tap on the door. In deference to Cheryl, across the hall, she whispers, "Who's there?"

He whispers back. She can tell his face must be mere inches from her door. "Me, Patrick."

She opens the door and he steps in, like a spy in a mystery novel.

"Hi! I'm all settled and ate supper with Rose and Maggie Woodward. Do you want to come in and sit down?"

She's relieved when he says, "Sure!" He surveys her space. "The place is coming along. Joe never owned much stuff and the apartment looks like when he was here—no clutter but all the essentials." He plunks himself down in the platform rocker.

Audrey becomes decidedly formal all of a sudden. "Can I get you a drink? I have juice and can make tea."

His expression is gentle. "Let's have tea, Audrey, to celebrate your move. How did your folks handle the whole process?"

Audrey hesitates. Patrick is the one person who understands her fears; her challenges. "Dad was gruff, as usual. Mom was helpful. She said she'd take me to Carter River in the truck. I need to find a second-hand table and chairs, plus a carpet. Those pieces will fill the place up a little." Patrick looks relaxed in the old rocker. "But, there's an echo, still."

"Mine has one, too. When my dad was here, he wanted to roar off to Carter River and get me lots of new stuff, but I told him most of my furniture bits are old friends, now. I don't want new, but a carpet might be nice, now that I think about it."

She hands him a white pottery mug of black Red Rose tea, and takes a seat on the sofa. She cradles her own warm mug in both hands. "Patrick, I have a question and I don't want you to think I'm paranoid, okay?"

"Sure, Audrey. I won't think any such thing. Fire away." His eyes have questions, but his expression remains open and relaxed.

Audrey is encouraged. "Is Chester an okay guy?"

"I guess. He's pretty full of himself, but he's a good mechanic. They sing his praises down at the Ford dealership. Why do you ask?"

"He came up here this afternoon, before supper. Came in the apartment and wandered around. Said if I needed help, to ask him. Offered to take me to Carter River in his truck, but I told him my mom wanted to drive me."

"He's the manager—or, he and Amanda are the managers. Askin' if you need help seems fair."

Audrey shakes her head and senses her pony tail brush her back. "He seemed funny—like flirty. I can't explain with words, except I kind of wanted to take a bath after he left. It felt creepy, Patrick. Is he the same with other people?"

"I don't think so. Maggie has never said he bothered her. Neither has Ronny, when she lived here, or even Cheryl, for that matter. Of course, they would never say much to me. You could ask one of them sometime. I'm not the person who would know. Guys like Chester—they flirt for fun. They like to get women all flustered. I think it's a power-trip."

He chuckles as he takes a sip of his tea. "Now, you're gonna say I've spent too much time talkin' to Dr. Wilkerson. She told me once how I needed to learn the ways of the world. She thought I was so busy listening to the voices, I didn't pay attention to the real folks who were around me."

"I still do that sometimes."

"She was right," he continues. "I don't think you have to worry about Chester. He loves Amanda, and he's devoted to those two little mites of theirs. You should see him when he comes into the diner to pick up Mason."

Chapter 4

Patrick

Clare Hollinger, an unmanaged schizophrenic, killed herself in the basement of the family home. Patrick found his mother hanging from an orange extension cord. She dangled there, right in front of his television, dressed in her flannelette nightie with the lace cuffs. He was fourteen and the voices already tormented him on a regular basis.

By the time he turned sixteen, he was withdrawn from most of the world around him. Raymond, his father, was much more concerned about his two younger daughters, Natalie and Sarah. It was obvious he didn't want them to turn out like their mother; to inherit her affliction. Patrick never revealed how he was the child swallowed by a relentless deluge of voices and paranoia. He left home back then, afraid his sisters might one day find him the way he found their mother. He ended up in Hayworth in 1977.

A lot has happened since his arrival in the northern prairie town. Ben Tullis, the elderly antique dealer who used to live in Number Three, was good to him. He has always been fond of old toys and she found many to add to his collection. She treated him like a person, with a respect he often believed was undeserved. She reminded him to wash, to change his clothes, and to make eye contact when he talked to people. As she was dying of pancreatic cancer, he contributed, along with his neighbours, to her care so she could stay at home. The other residents at The Station began to appreciate him as a good person.

She left him a couple of furniture pieces in her will, along with enough money to get his missing front tooth replaced. Cheryl Nadler helped him obtain an appointment to see Rachel Wilkerson, the psychiatrist who travels to Hayworth every couple of weeks and uses an office at the hospital. Margo, who owned the diner before Amanda bought the business, started to let him work a few shifts out front rather than just wash dishes. He gained enough confidence to even call his father, who came out to Alberta to visit.

Ben's death opened up a whole new world for him. He remains unresolved about his friendship with her. Would his life have changed if she had not become sick and died? The question often haunts him. She offered to buy him a tooth but he said no. She wanted him to see a shrink but he said no. She suggested he call his dad but he said no. He resisted any options for intervention, but her death changed his mind. She made amends with her family when she conquered her fears and contacted her grandson. He tried to follow her example. Circumstances have worked out. He loves his life in Hayworth. His job at the diner satisfies him. He is content. The people who live at The Station are like family. He sees his father and sisters at least once a year. He is his own man. And now, he's met Audrey.

As he follows his routine to prepare for the day shift, he imagines what their date will be like tonight. He has planned a real date which will involve escorting her, in his car, to the hotel dining room. Patrick appreciates how his father managed to buy him a little Pontiac Acadian in Edmonton on his way up to Hayworth from Alystair, Ontario. It was the first time they saw one another in years. He doesn't drive much. He prefers to lope down the streets of Hayworth at all hours of the day or night depending on his shift, regardless of the weather. But this is a special occasion and he intends to employ every tool at his disposal to impress Audrey Baranski.

He leans over, squints, and peers at his complexion reflected back at him from the scarred bathroom mirror. Alex Gunton might be a miserable SOB doctor when it comes to bedside manner, but he was able to prescribe a kind of paste the pharmacist concocts, and the pock marks and zits on his face have all but disappeared. He studies his reflection. There was a time when he never glanced in the mirror from one week to the next. Rose Woodward— she's worked for Dr. Gunton for ages—told him the doc could have the drug store make up this miracle cream. He didn't believe cream could solve his complexion issues, but he learned from his experience with Ben, to never reject someone's suggestion out of hand.

Before Patrick turns toward the apartment door, he surveys his space with an expression of satisfaction. Ben's leather sofa has pride of place. His antique toys are displayed with care and attention on the bookshelf. He has a real bed, now, instead of a mattress in the corner, and a wooden table with two chairs. Joe Dodd found the set at a job site, abandoned. He brought them to Patrick. They are sort of reddish brown wood. They work. He glances at the kitchen. He has more dishes, too, and actual groceries in the cupboards and fridge. Dr. Wilkerson told him he needed to eat better. She said good food could help his mental health as well as his complexion. Dr. Gunton doesn't get the total credit. No more French fries and gravy for dinner at the diner. He eats real meals.

They won't have their supper at the diner tonight. Instead, they will go to the hotel dining room. Patrick knows the food is posh and not like a turkey dinner they might get at his workplace, but he wants the atmosphere to be special. He won't have to worry someone will ask him to replace a control on the fryer, or fix a rattle in the dishwasher, and ruin the mood.

Dressed in his signature jean jacket, even though the temperature is cool, he trots down the two flights of stairs and out into the crisp November air. Although daylight has arrived, the sky is dull and appears to be on the edge of dusk. Patrick sniffs the breeze and winces. There could be snow before evening.

His shift is scheduled until three o'clock this afternoon. Then he has an appointment with Dr. Wilkerson at the hospital, after which he will take Audrey to supper. His thoughts drift for a moment to Raymond Hollinger. His father would be thrilled to think his son has gathered up his courage and asked a girl out. Patrick shrugs. Well, at the ripe old age of twenty-nine, the time has come for him to go out on a date or two.

****

The diner is busy for a Thursday morning in the middle of November. All hands are on deck, except for Amanda who will arrive closer to noon. Danny, the cook, flies around the kitchen. With a balanced combination of haste and precision, he creates omelets and scrambles eggs like a mad man. Nancy, Amanda's long-time waitress, corrals Patrick when he strolls in the back door. "Grab an apron. We need you out front. I called that Colin-character to come in and manage the dishwasher."

"I'm not late, am I? My shift starts at eight-thirty and the clock says eight-fifteen!"

"No, we're busy. There's a big trial at the courthouse. There must be a dozen RCMP members in town to testify. We didn't know."

"I can bus and do the dishwasher, Nancy. You didn't have to call in reinforcements." Patrick thinks maybe Nancy figures he can't hold up his end.

"Not my point. I need you to wait tables. I'll be here until mid-morning and then I have to go out for an hour." Patrick knows his eyes ask the question. "I have a doctor's appointment, kinda' last minute. Not serious—I hope," she adds as an afterthought.

"Hey, Danny, how's it goin'?" Patrick and Danny maintain a respectful work relationship now. For years, Danny baited him and fed his paranoia. Not anymore. The two work together like a finely oiled machine.

Danny turns to Patrick and raises a finger to the white kitchen cap he wears when he's at work. The hat is more like the version a surgeon would tie on before performing an operation. His face is flushed, but he can manage the grill like a master. Patrick has a lot of respect for him.

"If I can help, Danny, let me know."

"You can run a load of plates and glasses before Colin gets here. He'll take a half hour to get organized."

"Consider it done. I'll tell Nancy and I'll be right back."

The whole morning was like this. Everybody helped in any way they could. By the time Amanda arrived for lunch service, Nancy was back from her appointment, the kitchen was prepped for lunch, and the focus turned to a not-very-happy Nancy.

"The doctor says I might have a problem," was what she said, telling them she would have to talk to Amanda, first. Everyone was nervous. The lunch crowd started to pile through the plate glass doors. Patrick thought about how many guns were in the diner, as he counted the RCMP who had turned up again for lunch. He bussed tables, took orders, helped Colin with the finicky old dishwasher, and worked the till when Amanda was in the back office with Nancy. The diner bounced.

By two o'clock, the place was empty. Mason was expected to arrive from school. Nancy went home without a word to any of them. Danny was still in the kitchen doing supper prep for Amanda. "Can you stay and help me with supper tonight, Patrick? Nancy was supposed to work, but she's no longer an option."

Patrick didn't know what to say. He felt flushed and shaky. He didn't think he'd ever refused extra work. He responded to Amanda with sad eyes and winced. "I have a date tonight, Amanda. Can Danny stay? Sorry, but I don't want to cancel." He hoped he didn't sound whiny.

"My God, Patrick, if you have date, then by all means go! Danny said he would call his wife if you couldn't stay. I prefer you, so I can cook, but Danny can stay." She patted his hand. "Who's the lucky girl?"

****

As he sits in Rachel Wilkerson's office and gazes across the desk at who he still considers is the most beautiful woman he has ever known, Patrick shares his obsessive concerns about Roz Dover's disappearance. In the past, Rachel has advised him to leave the detective work to the police, but every time there's a community meeting, he's propelled back to the night she disappeared.

"I can't believe nobody saw anyone. I think the RCMP should go down east and talk to Charlene Quinn. She was out. If she didn't kill Roz, then she must have seen other vehicles around. She could be their witness."

He refocuses his attention from his hands, and interprets the familiar expression on his psychiatrist's face. "Now, don't think I'm paranoid. Yes, I obsess a bit, but lots of people obsess when they work through a problem. Right?" He needs her understanding today. He knows his mental illness is not in play here. He's sure a clue has been missed in the investigation; a behaviour, an observation, a witness, or a detail.

Dr. Wilkerson gets up from behind her desk and moves to the chair across from Patrick. She is wearing a wrap-around dress with a long necklace which hangs down almost to her waist. Her thick brown hair is tied back with a clip. Patrick finds this off-putting. She most often wears her hair down so it tumbles on to her shoulders.

"Your self-observations are absolutely correct, Patrick. You are obsessing about a circumstance well out of your control. This is not your problem to solve." Her frown is thoughtful. "Is there a function you can perform that you think might move the problem along?"

"Suggest the RCMP talk to Charlene? I imagine other people have thought about the same idea. Maybe they've talked to her already and she doesn't know any more than the rest of us." He meets Dr. Wilkerson's eyes. "I don't know. I guess there's not much I can do right now."

"Your assessment is accurate, Patrick. If you are not a witness, then you do not have a role in this."

He decides to change the subject. "Can I tell you about my date tonight?"

Rachel leans forward. "You sound excited, Patrick. Tell me about your date."

****

At five forty-five, as they previously decided, Patrick pulls his little Acadian around to the front parking lot at The Station, unlocks the outside door of the building, and races up the first flight of stairs to Number Four. She opens the door before he can knock. Of course, she has heard him come down the stairs and run out back to get his car. She is so pretty.

Their reservations are for six. He steals a quick glance at her as they drive the quarter mile to the hotel. Her long straight hair is tied back like always, but she has a blue ribbon wrapped around the elastic holding the pony tail. It's sweet. She never wears jewellery and tonight is no exception. She stares straight ahead, out the Acadian's cracked windshield. He starts to tremble, becoming even more nervous than he was earlier.

"Have you been over to the hotel to eat before, Audrey?" He tries to socialize. He's developed an easy way of interacting with customers at the diner, but this is different. He's tongue-tied; red and hot behind his face.

She turns toward him. "Once—for my mother's birthday. I wasn't well and didn't enjoy the experience." She must have noticed the expression of concern on Patrick's face because she quickly adds how she's sure tonight will be different. Patrick hopes she means it.

The restaurant in the Travel Rest Hotel is called The Grill. It's off to the right of the entry doors. The space is dark and quiet. Reservations were not needed, but Patrick made them anyway. Reservations seemed appropriate, given the circumstances. They are shown to their table by an older fellow. He has salt and pepper hair and a handlebar moustache. He's very attentive and pulls Audrey's chair out with a flourish.

The menus for the restaurant are huge. When Patrick holds his up to read, Audrey disappears behind the red and white laminated list of offerings. He decides on what he wants as fast as he can, folds the menu up, and places it back down on the table. "Do you know what you would like to eat, Audrey? I'm so used to diner food, I think I'll try something different and have the steak Diane. What about you?" He hopes she can hear him through the barrier.

Audrey peeks around her menu. She looks lovely in the glow of a little candle stuck inside a pink glass dish that looks like a rose bowl. "Is it good? I don't know. Do they cook it well? Maybe I'll have the same." She lays the enormous bill of fare down with careful precision on top of Patrick's. The waiter appears out of nowhere. "You tell him," she whispers.

"Two orders of the steak Diane, please, medium-well. And what to drink?" He defers to Audrey.

"Oh, do you have ice tea?" She glances up at the moustache.

"Of course."

"Two ice teas, then," Patrick adds. He's happy they've chosen the same dish. Neither of them should drink alcohol because of their medications. They exchange a glance that shares their silent conspiracy.

He starts the conversation and attempts to be calm, although his stomach is not excited about the introduction of food, no matter how fancy. "I didn't see you at the hospital today. I had an appointment with Dr. Wilkerson, but there was no time to come down to the cafeteria to say hello."

Audrey frowns. "I wasn't there, anyway. We were short-staffed and I was on the run all over the hospital to pick up trays. The girl who's supposed to do pick-ups called in sick at the last minute. I don't mind, but at the same time, I like my routine."

Patrick understands. His routines are his lifeline. Whenever he has to perform a task outside the boundaries, like when he travels down east to visit his family, or even going out on this date with Audrey, he is anxious and constantly tries to talk himself out of making an excuse to avoid a change. This day has been full of breaks in his routine. "I felt the same way about tonight—for sure not a regular day." He flashes precious confidence through his unbroken grin and almost clear complexion.

"Oh, I'm really glad you understand. Nobody ever understands, Patrick."

Still compelled, somehow, to drive the conversation, he decides to tell her about Benjamine Tullis and how she was an influence in his life. Rachel Wilkerson has said he needs to open up to people. "Ben Tullis was the first person in town who was nice to me. We became friends. Did you know she died down in Number Three? Everybody took care of her. We all had jobs. She had cancer."

Audrey's expression is hard for him to read. "Are you bothered because she died at The Station?" He continues. "I like it. Maggie Woodward likes it, too. We sometimes think we can sense her there with us."

"Her death in the building doesn't bother me, Patrick. I wish I had known her, too. Maybe I would be able to feel her presence. Do you think people like you and I are more sensitive? Sometimes I feel like I have special powers; that I can see and hear more than other people."

Patrick tries very hard not to let his diagnosis drive how he thinks about the world around him. Therapy has helped with this. "No, Audrey. Certain people are more in tune or more aware, that's all."

They enjoy their dinner and share a piece of cherry cheese-cake for dessert. Conversation doesn't lag, although Patrick senses the need for more time together before Audrey will be comfortable. He leaves her at the door to Number Four. She reaches up and kisses him on the cheek before she slips into her apartment. He can feel the spot on his skin tingle as he takes the stairs two at a time.

Chapter 5

Gaby

"Are you ready? I don't want to be late, Joe." Gaby shouts up the stairs before she hears him start to descend.

"The special is turkey dinner at the diner, Gaby. What's the rush?" There's a teasing quality to the low rumble of his voice as it tumbles down the steps in front of him.

She gazes up as he emerges into her line of sight. Dressed in dark khakis and a pale green striped long-sleeve shirt, her heart flips a bit when he catches her eye. "You clean up pretty nice there, mister. Can't take you out with me to a Christmas dinner if you dress like any old Joe the carpenter."

She turns to Martha, plunked like the guard she is, beside her foot. "You get to stay here tonight, old girl. The weather's not fit for us, let alone for you. One more quick pee and then you can curl up on your mat until we get back." Gaby communicates with her dog like she would with another person. Always has.

"Joe, will you let her outside for a minute while I finish up?" He nods and grabs his coat as she runs upstairs one last time. Earrings. She needs earrings. For tonight, she's chosen comfort and warmth. The diner can be drafty, especially when a north wind blizzard threatens. She's chosen wide-legged and high-waisted pants. They appear to be wool, but aren't, thank God. Coupled with a short white angora sweater, her self-assessment reveals she will come across as more Christmassy with a pair of crystal chandelier earrings and a matching clip for her hair. The clip will no doubt fall out before the evening is over, but at least she can start off with a coordinated outfit. She examines her reflection in the bedroom mirror. Passable for an old girl pushing forty-four. She clatters back down the stairs, and soon realizes she will have to put her shoes in a bag since there's no possible way she can avoid cumbersome winter boots tonight.

The diner sports twinkle lights for Christmas. Amanda was clear about how this would be a celebration of the Wolskis' purchase of the diner, but since the date happens to be December 15, the theme has become a combination of the two occasions. Joe pushes open the plate glass door supporting a sign which states in bold black letters: Closed for a Private Event. Gaby notes how the wind is howling already. She hopes they won't have to shovel one another out.

Chester is already there, of course. He greets them with a wave as he pushes through the saloon doors used to separate the main dining area from the kitchen. "Hello, you two!" Amanda peeks out through the pass-through.

"Are we the first ones here?" Gaby can hear Joe thinking there was no need for the rush. She grins up at him.

"Not by a long shot." Chester reappears. Doors flap behind him as he wrestles a case of beer to the front counter. "Patrick and the beautiful Audrey are helping in the back."

Introductions are promptly made. Gaby acknowledges Audrey, but reveals no clue to indicate they already know one another. Joe shakes Audrey's hand and exchanges pleasantries with Patrick.

"So, this is the new tenant in Number Four. Very nice to meet you, Audrey. I hope you will enjoy living at The Station as much as I did."

"We couldn't get over how long you held on to the place, Joe. Thought you would never let go!" Patrick snorts and turns a bit red as he jokes with Joe about the empty apartment.

"I had a three year lease. We..." he turns to catch Gaby's eye. "We thought holding on to the lease was a good way to see if circumstances would work out for us. She kept her house, too, Patrick, until a couple of months ago when she sold out to Ronny."

"Gee, Joe. You think it's serious between you two?" Patrick teases his former neighbour. Joe elbows him in the arm.

"Maybe," is his response, as the door seems to blow open. Maggie Woodward and Sean Knox tumble in, preceded by Maggie's sister, Rose. Before the door is fully secure, Ronny Étang and Fiona Werbowski squeeze into the space behind them. The snow has started to fall with a vengeance.

"Hey, Ronny! You look none the worse for wear. Great to see you. Likin' your new digs?"

Chester, with little or no finesse, in Gaby's opinion, references Ronny's ordeal last August as well as her subsequent purchase of Gaby's house.

Ronny is a good sport. "I'm good, Chester. And I adore my new place. Not that I didn't like The Station back when I lived there."

She catches Gaby's eye and they exchange a glance. Chester can come across like an oaf sometimes, regardless of his handsome good looks.

The person with the most challenging entrance is Cheryl Nadler. She appears like a mirage before the plate glass entry in knee-high, heeled patent leather boots. She clutches a bowl of pasta salad, covered in what looks like a shower cap, in gloved hands. Joe jumps to hold the door for her.

Gaby studies the assembled group while coats are hung and seats are selected. Station residents, former Station residents, and close friends of those residents, including both Sean and Fiona, as well as herself, are in attendance tonight. They are an intimate group, for sure.

Maggie and Constable Sean Knox have dated ever since the horrible episode in the summer involving Ronny. Sean because of his work, often turns up at Segue House, the women's shelter. Ava Burrway is the manager of the women's shelter and Maggie has served as her right hand for years. The general consensus is she will be Ronny's right hand in the New Year. Their mutual admiration was a foregone conclusion.

Ronny's kidnapping in August brought this group closer, somehow. At the time, Ronny rented Gaby's little house at 15 Poplar Street, although she lived in Number Three at The Station when she first moved to Hayworth. She and Fiona, Sean Knox's RCMP partner, have become the closest of friends, more so since the abduction. Gaby can appreciate why. Fiona is a wonderful officer. She was kind and supportive to Gaby throughout the time she was stalked by Charlene Quinn and subsequently under investigation by the Canadian Counselling Association. Those incidents seem like a lifetime ago, now.

Amanda has set up the booths across the front of the diner. Ronny and Fiona will sit across from Gaby and Joe. Maggie and Sean will sit with Patrick and Audrey. Cheryl and Rose will sit with Chester and Amanda. The place sparkles and smells wonderful. Periodically, a wind gust causes the old building to shudder. Snow swirls around the vehicles parked out front.

Gaby isn't worried. Joe's big old four wheel drive truck will get them home no matter what.

While Amanda and Chester assemble a buffet-style turkey dinner on the front counter, Gaby takes the opportunity to circulate a bit. "I see you brought your famous pasta salad, Cheryl."

The petite and perfectly turned out social worker admits with self-amusement to Gaby, "Old habits never change. I've actually eaten here since Amanda took over...well, once I ordered a sandwich. Anyway, I prefer to contribute, even if I'm told not to."

Cheryl is a clean freak and more than a wee bit obsessive-compulsive. She was much worse in the time before Ben Tullis died, according to Joe. She still never has a hair out of place and only eats food prepared in her own kitchen, but to those who know her well, she has changed a great deal. Gaby and Cheryl worked together at the Hexagon for years—Gaby as a member of the Family Counselling Division and Cheryl as one of the Adoption Services social workers. Cheryl continues with this job, but also serves as a mentor to new workers.

"I, for one, expect to have lots of your pasta salad my friend. Merry Christmas, Cheryl. Will you be around for the holidays?"

"Yes, as a matter of fact. I like to work between Christmas and the New Year so staff with kids can take the time. It's no big deal. I expect Rose and Maggie—and maybe Sean, now—will invite me in on Christmas Day. They usually do. What about you?"

"Oh, Joe and I like to curl up by the fire, call family, and eat too much. We close the shop for almost a week to give the crews time with families. We give each other a book every year—our tradition."

"Sounds wonderful."

Gaby notices a wisp of sadness settle in her eyes. "Maybe Amy will come out for Christmas one of these years."

"You never know, although I can go down and see her if I want to; stay in a hotel and celebrate with her for part of the time. Haven't been able to scrape up enough courage to manage this option yet. Our relationship is still new." Amanda taps her glass. "We'd better sit down."

"Everyone. Dinner is served. Please come up to the counter and help yourselves. Cheryl has brought her pasta salad. This dinner is to thank you— our Station friends both past and present—for your support as Chester and

I try to balance the work of apartment managers, restaurateur, and Ford mechanic. Two kids are a minor complication."

She giggles as she raises a glass of wine poured from the box beside the platter of turkey. "We both want to let you know, although the news isn't public yet, we hope to hand over the reins of The Station in about six months. There are still a few negotiations." She puts her hand beside her lips like she has shared a secret with them. "Not public knowledge yet, but we may build a house! Gaby, stay tuned." To the collective oohs and ahhs, she encourages them to enjoy their dinner. "There's pecan pie for dessert. Leave room!"

Then, she takes her glass and moves over to the table where Cheryl and Rose have situated themselves.

So, Amanda and Chester want to build a house for sure, and somebody else will be hired to manage The Station. This is great news. There's no smell compared to a brand new blueprint unfurled across her desk, to get the creative juices flowing.

Although Gaby knows everyone thought she was certifiably crazy when she quit her job at the Hexagon and went into business with Joe, the experience has proven to be more rewarding than she could have imagined. Of course, there are pressures. They regularly employ two independent contracting crews of four men each. They are installers and need to be kept busy. She needs to sell kitchens, hardwood floors, and tile bathrooms. As long as she can sell, everybody can work and get paid. There have been sleepless nights along the way. She'll admit to this, but the work has its advantages. Of course, she misses the clients from her Hexagon days, but she doesn't miss the government interference and mind-changing, the blaming, and the paperwork. No matter how organized any one person can be, government mandated paperwork is always tedious.

Fearing she has tuned out the party and become lost in the weeds of her own thoughts, Gaby listens as Joe regales Ronny and Fiona with a foolish story about Martha and a customer. He tells them about someone who came in the shop from Carter River. He wanted twenty-five kitchens built in two months for an apartment building he was constructing.

"Now, Martha is a pretty good judge of character, and she took a dislike to this guy. Remember, Gaby, she would lie down at the opposite end of the office when he was there, and growl under her breath." Joe takes a sip of his beer.

Gaby nods confirmation to the others. He loves this story.

"Anyway, the guy wanted one kitchen ordered and installed first, instead of filling the twenty-five unit order all at once. His request seemed weird. Contractors for buildings can't waste time ordering a sample kitchen. Then, he wouldn't leave a deposit. We didn't know him from a load of hay, so a deposit is part of the routine. In the end, we took Martha's behaviour seriously and called the lumberyard in Carter River. I know a guy there. He told me this fellow tries to get a kitchen for free and then cancels the remainder of the order. Good old Martha. She knew the guy was crooked the whole time!" He throws his head back and his roar of laughter booms off the ceiling as everyone wiggles back out of the booth and makes their way to the counter.

The meal is fabulous. Everyone visits with everyone. Over pecan pie and herbal tea, Gaby works up the courage to ask Fiona the question she has been anxious to ask all night.

"Fiona, I know we all thought Charlene Quinn was implicated in Roz Dover's disappearance."

Fiona peers over at Gaby with dark and quizzical eyes. "We could never prove she was involved."

"I know. But she was out and about in town. She was at my place and then, according to Patrick, she sat out in front of The Station until late. Did anyone ask her if she saw other people around? Maybe she's a witness."

Fiona glances at Ronny. Gaby notices. "Charlene was questioned extensively, Gaby. She said she didn't see Roz. It's why I continue to plead with the community to rack their brains and try to remember details about the night. For all intents and purposes, everyone in Hayworth was in bed by eleven except Charlene, Roz, and whoever was involved in her disappearance."

"Chester was out." Patrick has materialized from the kitchen, and starts to bus tables in order to help Amanda.

"I know, Patrick." Gaby can tell Fiona is trying hard to be patient. She relates to the frustration her friend must carry because the police have not been able to assemble the pieces and put this puzzle together. Gaby is sure the situation eats at Fiona no differently than the rest of them; like what happened when Ronny was grabbed by her ex-husband in August. People were frantic in no time. The community was afraid whatever happened to Roz had also happened to Ronny. Resolving her situation and putting Duncan Taylor back in jail was a great relief to everyone, but the episode served to emphasize the lack of resolution in the Dover case. "Chester has told us he saw no one that night except the couple at the hotel who needed a boost."

"I think somebody should go down to Nova Scotia and talk to Charlene in jail. I bet she knows more than what she first said. And what about the people who needed the help? They could be witnesses, too."

"Patrick, you and I think alike. I wanted to ask Fiona about Charlene tonight, too." Gaby catches Fiona's eye. Her cheeks are flushed. She is no doubt annoyed with them both.

"We don't know who Chester helped at the hotel. No names were exchanged."

"The answering service would have a record, Fiona. Didn't anyone contact them?" Gaby doesn't want her voice to sound too judgmental, but she can't believe they didn't check with the service. It would stand to reason Chester didn't have a name, but the service should know who called. If the people qualified for a roadside emergency, they would have to make a claim.

"They were contacted, but all we seem to have now are dead ends. Sorry, guys."

Patrick picks up the scraped-clean dessert plates and stacks them in his open left hand. "I still think you guys need to talk to weird Charlene. What's she got to lose? If she didn't kill Roz, why not put the screws to somebody else? She would enjoy herself."

As he trots off to the kitchen, Fiona admonishes Gaby. "You know we shouldn't even talk about this out in public, despite the fact you were involved to a certain extent. I will ask a couple of questions and then come down to the shop for coffee. No promises. I hope Chester didn't overhear us."

"But, you know Patrick might be on to something, right?"

"Ronny, let's go thank Amanda and be on our way. I for one, have to work tomorrow." She cannot avoid a hint of exasperation in her tone as she talks.

"Before you go, Fi, can we talk about the fundraiser ball for a second? The date's been set for February and the tickets are ordered. I'm a little worried we might sell less tickets since we juggled the annual weekend from October to February. I guess whether or not we made a mistake remains to be seen. Can we set a date for right after the holidays so the three of us can go over final details?"

The women compare dates and make a decision. While this is goes on, Joe leans across the back of the booth and talks with Sean and Maggie.

The evening was a blazing success. Gaby can see Patrick in the kitchen, as he loads the dishwasher and helps Amanda clean up. Audrey picks up stray plates and utensils. She seems to be managing her illness better than Gaby ever thought she would. Full-time work at the hospital and the move into town have both helped her have a focus. Patrick could well be a good influence.

****

Gaby is alone in the shop, focused as she reviews the kitchen designs for the two big houses outside town. Martha crawls out from under her desk to make her way to the door about ten seconds before the chimes have a chance to tinkle in the showroom. Gaby has a mirror above her doorway and knows Fiona is there before the constable has an opportunity to shout, "Hello."

"Come on in. I'm at my desk."

Fiona lumbers in and plunks herself down in the chair by Gaby's desk. She skips any chit-chat and gets directly to the point. "I know Patrick is a bit paranoid, but what's your excuse? Think we haven't done our job down at the detachment?"

Gaby can't tell by her expression if the constable is kidding or not. "I guess I've been obsessing. The business with Ronny's disappearance brought the whole ordeal back, Fiona. I know her case was resolved, but then the community met again, and still no headway."

"Don't you think we all feel the same way? In any event, I talked to one of the detectives assigned at the time—every idea helps. He told me a couple of officers interviewed the answering service employees and they found no record of a call, so no name. Chester says the service called him and he went out. Somebody doesn't keep good documentation."

Gaby starts to get up.

"Wait. I'm not finished, Gaby. I imagine you will be pleased to know we have contacted an investigator in Truro who will travel to the women's institution—they frown on referring to the place as a prison—to talk to Charlene. Who knows? A conversation with her can't hurt. This is strictly confidential, Gaby."

She waits for Gaby's nod before she continues. "I have no intention of repeating the information to Patrick. I know he's better, but I don't want to feed into any of his issues. Can you keep this to yourself?"

"Can I tell Joe?"

Fiona's response is reluctant, but she agrees. "Talk to Joe, but no one else, okay?"

Chapter 6

Amanda

Cold still grips early March. Amanda, Chester, and the children are off to his parents' for a special Sunday dinner. Amanda has reassigned her diner duties for the day to Danny, Patrick, and Nancy. She stands in front of her full-length mirror hung on the wall between their two dressers. She has put on another few pounds to add to her frumpy physique which never relinquished itself from the baby weight of her second pregnancy. Hard to believe her baby is more than two years old now.

She tucks in her long-sleeved T-shirt, covers her protruding belly with a baggy sweater, and turns to check out her profile. A baggy sweater hides a thousand sins. Her crimson red curls, gathered into a bunch and secured with elastics and a blue ribbon, shake as she admonishes herself. There are significantly more than a thousand sins to hide.

Amanda isn't sure, but she suspects her father-in-law is about to tell them he has managed to secure the land next door to the family farm. Chester won't be happy, but she wants to use the rest of the money she inherited to build a new house out by the Wolski's. She needs to be close to Chester's parents. She wants to be away from The Station and its responsibilities. Life has become too complicated.

"Are you coming?" Chester's impatient voice interrupts her self-conversation. "I have the kids ready to go out to the car. Mom will wonder where the hell we are."

Amanda trots out of the bedroom, in a hustle as she inspects her children and soothes her husband. "We're ready. Let me get the pecan pie I have for her. Mama would be disappointed if I didn't bring a pie from the diner." She projects an impish grin toward Chester. He doesn't appear to appreciate her tease.

They muddle out to her 1980 red Toyota Tercel hatchback. The kids, complete with a knapsack full of colouring books and toys, crawl into the back. Although the car is Amanda's and purchased second-hand from the Ford dealer when she bought the diner, Chester gets behind the wheel. She could have bought new, but she wanted to save as much of her inheritance as possible in order to build her dream home.

Mason and Melanie are excited. A visit with Grandma and Grandpa is always fun, even though they are at the farm almost every day, in Melanie's case, and often for Mason as well. "What's for dinner, Mommy?"

"I don't know, Mason. Grandma is cooking a surprise dinner."

"I hope she makes Christmas dinner and we have presents and turkey!"

Amanda attempts to clarify her son's expectations as she glances over toward Chester. His eyes remain glued to the road which has started to become slippery in spots as daylight turns into darkness, and the air temperature drops all of a sudden. "No, not Christmas. You get one of those a year. And before you say any more, not your birthday, either. Supper will be good, no matter what Grandma makes."

Melanie gurgles words not quite comprehensible but they resemble "good supper." Amanda isn't sure.

By the time Chester turns the Tercel in to the long gravel lane, the children are peering out the windows and drawing with pudgy fingers in the vapour they've created. "What do you think this is about, Amanda?" Chester sounds annoyed. He doesn't like surprises. "Mom and Dad don't invite us out for Sunday supper very often. We spend enough time here during the week."

"I hope it's news about the property next door." Amanda remembers stories of the two estranged bachelor brothers who shared the property for many years, but never got along. After they both died, the estates were in such disarray, it seemed their distant relatives finally gave up trying to settle anything. "The family of those old guys fought and argued forever, but maybe, in the three and a half years since Roz's car was found, they decided to play ball with your father and sell."

Chester's expression is one of pure horror. "We can't let Dad buy that land, Amanda! Who in God's name would want that land?" His voice has an element of panic Amanda has heard with regularity over the last few years. The first time she was introduced to this particular tone was the day Mason was born. Chester likes to be in control and when he isn't, he panics.

"To own the land next door would be wonderful, Chester." She maintains an eerie calm in her voice. "I don't care about Roz's car. It was a long time ago. No one cares anymore." She knows she sounds cold-hearted but she's determined to have a brand new house near her in-laws, where she will be safe.

Borys and Tesia Wolski wait at the back door of the old farm house. The light from the porch bathes them in a soft yellow glow. Borys is a big man with mature good looks and an abundance of shocking white hair. One powerful hand rests on the shoulder of Tesia, also tall and attractive. Her hair, threaded with new silver and faded gold, reflects both her present and her past. It falls to her shoulders and is held back from her face with a pair of tortoiseshell clips.

"Come in. Come in. Get the little people out of the wind!" She bends to greet the children while she wraps her blue crocheted shawl tighter around her significant shoulders. Tesia notices, when Chester scans the yard for other vehicles. "Your brothers and their families are not invited tonight. Only you."

Amanda, ever alert to the least little change in behaviour of those around her, wonders if her hopes might be realized and the evening has to do with the property next door. Chester has two older brothers, Alex and Paul. Both help with the grain farm. Both have built homes on the Wolski property. Chester has always known the farm would never be able to support a third son, hence his education as a mechanic and his job at the local Ford dealership. He loves his work. He's never once wished he could stay on the farm full-time, although he often goes to lend a hand when needed.

Once inside, Amanda's eyes absorb the familiar space. The Wolski house is a traditional peaked roof farmhouse built in the 1940s. The main floor supports a formal living and dining room on the front, with a kitchen and gathering area at the back. When you enter from the porch located on the side and near the driveway, you go through the woodshed to access the kitchen parlour. A set of stairs runs from the front door up to two bedrooms and a bath. Both bedrooms are under the eaves. All three brothers used one of those rooms. Lately, the Wolskis have said they might add on a bedroom and bath downstairs. Amanda knows they would be reluctant to move into town when Alex and Paul become the sole operators of the family business.

The room is drowning in the aroma of cabbage rolls, perogies, and roast pork. No matter how popular her pork roast dinner is at the diner, Amanda's senses revel in the smell of Tesia's version. Amanda knows she will never, ever, meet the Wolski standard for a hearty meal. "I brought a pecan pie, Mama. I'll set it on the counter over here by the tea things." Amanda loves how she can call Chester's parents mama and papa. Since she was nine years old, she has yearned to be part of a real family, and will do whatever might be necessary to maintain her current status.

They eat well, by any measure. The children behave themselves, at least to a degree accepted by grandparents, if not by Amanda and Chester themselves. Over pie and tea, Borys plunks his big elbows on the table, gives Tesia a glare which undoubtedly states she is not to admonish him for his bad manners, and clears his throat.

"This is an evening of celebration. Today, I signed the papers to buy the farm next door." His voice has a hint of flourish mixed with emotion. Amanda, not surprised but terribly pleased, keeps an eye on her husband.

Chester doesn't react for almost a full minute. When he responds, Amanda is shocked at how calm he is, like he has given up the battle to stay in town and away from the property with the long, convoluted history and recent negative reputation. "Will the boys lease the land, Dad? You know I don't want to give up my job. I won't be a farmer. We can't afford the land if the boys don't lease it back."

Borys sighs a gust of relief. "Son, we have the details arranged. You do not have to pay for the land any more than your brothers did. In exchange for the property, you let them farm the acreage and we are square." His eyes are rimmed in dampness now.

Amanda holds her breath, as she waits for her proud and troubled husband to find fault with the arrangement. "This means Amanda can build her house and the boys can farm? Just like that?" There is no emotion in his voice. His eyes stare directly at his father.

Borys nods as he emits a rumbling chortle which always sounds like thunder in the distance. He allows his eyes to meet Amanda's. "By God, my girl, I think we have ourselves a plan! Mother, brandy for our tea. We need to celebrate, now."

Mason and Melanie are both curled up on the kitchen sofa, sleeping, by the time the conversations about planning start to wind down. Alex and

Paul knew about the deal for a few weeks but were sworn to secrecy, in the event the offer to purchase didn't work out. The negotiation with an estate of unreliable and cranky beneficiaries who barely know one another was not without its challenges. However, the bad press garnered when a missing girl's car was located on the property served to encourage them to cooperate with one another and eventually divest themselves of the asset. Borys reveled in telling the story of his meeting with them in Edmonton; how he stuck to his guns regarding the price he offered; how he told them no one but him would ever take an interest in the old place. They relented. He was the victor. He told them the story three different ways.

The ride home is stressful. The roads are icy. Tesia even suggested they should spend the night, but Amanda was adamant in her refusal. She was anxious to get Chester alone so they could talk about their future home and move.

Chester, much to Amanda's annoyance, has very little to say. "I guess we are going to build a house and live out there. I was steamrollered and ended up with no say." He's pissed, although he never revealed this to his parents. "I don't know how you expect to supervise workmen on a job site while you run the diner, Amanda." He glances over at her. In the glow of the lights from the dashboard, his eyes are steely calm. "And you know you will have to be there."

Amanda practically bounces on the passenger seat. "Our life will be great now. Maybe we'll be able to leave The Station and move out to your folks while we build. Apartment management would be one less responsibility for us, then. I think I might even know somebody who would be interested in a move over to The Station." Her plan falls into place with more precision than she expected.

Chester's sigh fills the car.

"Don't be disagreeable, honey. We can live out near your parents in a brand new house that's paid for. I can work at the diner and you at Ford. Once Melanie is in school, both kids will be able to get the bus to and from, and your mom will keep them after school. Our life will be perfect again. No one cares about Roz anymore. We can pretend she never happened."

****

The next morning, before she leaves for the diner, Amanda calls her bookkeeper. Greta Seeley has kept her books ever since she purchased the diner. She works at the local service station, and does their paperwork, along with the books of other clients, on the side.

"Greta, it's Amanda. How are you this morning?"

"Hi, Amanda. I didn't expect to hear from you. Is there paperwork you need completed for the accountant? Margo never mentioned an issue." Greta has been referred to many clients by Margo Johnson, a local accountant and the former owner of the diner. Margo always tells businesses about how a good bookkeeper can save you lots of money when year-end arrives. Greta has been kept busy as a result.

"No, Greta. I want to talk to you about another matter and I hoped you could stop by the diner sometime today; maybe this afternoon when the lunch crowd is gone?"

"No problem. You're not about to fire me, are you?"

Amanda snorts. "Not a chance! You won't get rid of me and my poor penmanship so fast. See you later today, okay?"

She gets her apartment building chores accomplished in no time. They don't amount to much besides a sweep of the inside stairs and the foyer. The tenants would never leave any garbage around, so there isn't a lot to do. Enterprise Investments, the owner in Edmonton, has approved outside painting this spring. She already has a contractor in mind. There will be no disruptions with the painting, even if Greta takes over the building. Chester dropped Mason at school. Melanie plays in her stroller at the foot of the stairs, and doesn't make a fuss, as Amanda clomps to the top and sweeps her way back down. Both of her children have been easy. She has never experienced any problems completing her Station tasks with them in tow.

As the Tercel rolls down the Wolski's drive, Melanie starts to clap and sing a song. It seems to relate to her grandma, but Amanda can't understand her. As usual, Tesia waits at the back door. "Hello, you two. Today is chilly for little girls." She gazes down with unabashed fondness at her granddaughter who makes a gargantuan attempt to navigate the back stairs with her mother's help.

"Good morning, Mama. I hoped to ask a question of you and Papa before I go to work."

"Come in. Come in." Borys is sitting at the big kitchen table drinking tea while he reads a quarterly journal published for wheat farmers. "Borys, Amanda needs a word."

Borys removes his frameless reading glasses. He leans over to pick up Melanie who has positioned herself with one hand on her grandfather's knee. "What can we do for you this morning? Did you think you might play hooky and stay with us and your daughter for the day?"

"Not exactly, Papa. I want to know if we could move in here in a few months, while we build our house." She forgets about the preamble she had composed in her mind—how she would need to be out here; how work at The Station might be too much.

Her in-laws communicate in silence, as couples married more than thirty years can do. Tesia is the first to speak. "We would be happy to have you and the children here, Amanda—for as long as you want. You and Chester work hard. We can help, can't we Borys?"

His handsome face seems to light up the old kitchen. "To have my grandchildren on my property is a dream." His voice is a rumbling purr. "When will you move? What does Chester say?"

Although Amanda feigns confidence, a shred of nervousness still filters through. "Chester will be fine. I need to find someone to take our place at The Station. I have a woman in mind, though. I will talk to her this afternoon."

Her mother-in-law nods.

"Then, Chester and I will make a plan and I will talk to the owners. A move after school closes will be best. Now, I have to run. You be a good girl, Melanie." She jumps up and leans over to kiss her little girl. She inhales the sweet baby smell of her wispy hair and softly touches Borys' shoulder.

Tesia walks her to the door and envelopes Amanda with both arms. "We are very happy. We will be a little cramped, but it won't be for a long while. We are very happy," she repeats.

Amanda surveys the yard on her way back to her car. She will have more control out here. She needs to guard her investment in their future.

*****

Back at the diner, breakfast and coffee service are in full swing as Amanda trundles in the back door, waves at Danny, and shouts "I'm here," to Nancy, busy as she busses tables in the front.

The time goes fast and before she has a chance to give the next facet of her plan any real thought, Greta Seeley comes through the door and plunks herself down on a stool at the counter. By now, Patrick has begun his shift and he pours her a cup of tea.

Greta Seeley is a short, chubby woman in her mid-twenties. She has two young children. Everyone seems to know her story. She turned up at Segue House when her drunken husband ran out on her and left her holding the bag of rent and food with no money. She decided to volunteer the surrender of her children to Child Protection Services until she could get herself qualified as a bookkeeper. Her children are back with her and she seems to be in a good place with her life.

Amanda hears Greta's voice and pushes through the saloon doors from the kitchen. "Hi, Greta! Glad you could make time for me. Come sit in the staff booth and we can have a chat. We still have a few more minutes before Mason gets off the bus."

"Mason comes here after school? Mine go to day care—expensive. My salary from the service station goes to child care. Stupid, eh?"

"Well...I have a proposition, Greta. Tell me what you think. Chester and I plan to move out to his parents' farm once we start to build our house out there. I need to give up the management of The Station and I thought, before I turn in my notice to Enterprise Investments, perhaps I could interest you in the position."

Greta's posture changes from relaxed to alert. Amanda is afraid she's going to refuse out of hand, judging by the shocked expression on her face.

"Before you say no, hear me out. The apartment would be free. You have to clean units when they are vacated, which is practically never, and sweep the stairs and foyer every day. There is a list of repair people to call if a shower leaks or a stove goes on the blink. There is a guy who plows and shovels in the winter and he will also mow in the summer, if you don't want to do yard work. You could stay at home with your kids, do people's books, and get your apartment for free!" Amanda expels a gust of air, satisfied she has hit the high points to effectively make her argument.

Greta's round face seems even more round in its surprise. Her lips are pursed into a pink bow. "Are you serious? Do you think they would want me when you leave?"

Amanda nods. "Listen. They are in Edmonton. I am here and can make a recommendation. Decisions are much easier for them when they go along with my suggestions."

Greta visibly relaxes.

"I'm sure there will be no problem. Do you think you can move in after school closes? We can be out by then. All I have to do is talk to Chester." She leans over and winks at Greta. "So...do we have a deal?"

Chapter 7

Gaby

"Hard to believe two months have already passed since the Segue House Ball, Amanda." Gaby makes conversation from her spot in a booth at the front of the diner. Joe should be back from a job site any minute.

"I know. This is your second dinner on me, right?" Amanda is gracious.

Gaby thinks she looks tired, despite her elevated mood. Her skin has a sallow tone in a hue akin to the yellow ribbon in her hair, while the muscles in her face seem to droop in a way more common in women of an older vintage. Her appearance is no surprise, when one considers the events in her life of late. She has purchased the diner. She runs her business as well as manages The Station, and at the same time she has two little kids to raise. Gaby doesn't know how she stays afloat.

"Yes. Dinner Number Two. A dinner a month for a whole year was a big donation to the auction for Segue House, Amanda. Margo Johnson, when she owned the place, used to donate a couple of dinners for two—not twelve!"

"I know. Chester said I was crazy and the staff added their two cents worth, but the fundraiser netted a lot of money. What did Joe pay again?" Her eyes twinkle.

Gaby pretends to take a serious interest in her fork. "Five hundred?"

"So...by my calculations, it would be almost forty-two dollars for your two dinners. And what does the special cost these days?" Amanda's tone mocks. Gaby is quite capable of doing the math.

"Okay. Okay. You've made your point. Joe over-paid big time for the twelve dinners. He wanted to contribute. You know Joe."

Right on cue, the glass door swings open and in lumbers the love of her life. Gaby takes a second to study her barrel-chested, particular, animal-loving, contractor beau. Despite aging less than gracefully as the years of hard work take their toll, he still doesn't come across as too bad for a guy now nibbling away at fifty.

After her first husband died and she moved to Hayworth in 1977, she never even entertained the idea of another relationship. Grant Pendleton died when he was young; when they were young. She fought hard to put the tragedy behind her. She moved away from her home in Ontario so she didn't have to be the guidance counsellor who was widowed at forty years old.

Joe managed to snuggle into her life as both a friend and a support system. Their relationship grew. Love crept up on them both. Sometimes the best events in life are the least expected. "I haven't ordered yet. I knew you would get here in good time. Thought you might be stuck in the mud out at the job site, considering all the rain this April."

She lifts her cheek and gets a kiss before he turns toward the men's room to get washed up. "Back in a flash. This is our 'specials' night, right?" His back is already retreating down the hallway to the washrooms.

"I'll order. Take your time." Gaby and Amanda exchange looks of mutual sympathy and indulgence for husbands who are never where they're expected to be.

"By the way, since spring is supposedly here, can I show my draft blueprints to you and Joe?"

Gaby is a little surprised. "Blueprints? Do you and Chester expect to build this year?"

Amanda's face lights up. "Yes! His dad bought the property next door. The beneficiaries of the two old guys' estate decided the money was better than their quarrels and a tax bill every year. I am really excited!"

"What about The Station?"

"Taken care of. Greta Seeley will move in after school closes. We will move out to the ranch to better supervise the building. I know where I want the house and have put sticks and tape in the ground as best I can. I want you and Joe to do as much as you are able. Joe could be the general contractor, couldn't he?"

"By all means, Amanda...if you're certain it's what you want."

"What does Amanda want, Gaby?" His voice teases them both. "She better not want me to pay! I paid through the nose at the charity auction." He taps Amanda's shoulder before he slides into the booth seat across from Gaby. "Just kidding. What's up?"

"You go ahead and tell him, Gaby, while I go get your waters and let Danny know we need two more specials."

"She and Chester are building their dream house next door to the Wolski's farm, where they found Roz's car, Joe." She leans across the booth and lowers her voice. "Remember—the family fought with one another about who owned what after the brothers who lived there died. My understanding is none of them have spoken to one another in years. I can't believe Amanda wants to build a house out there. I imagine Borys Wolski bought the property for a song. Anyway, Greta Seeley—she's a bookkeeper and does private clients and also works at the service station—will manage The Station after July 1st." Gaby leans back into the vinyl booth and sighs.

"Man, I was gone to the can for five minutes. You can pry information out of people better than anyone I know." He smirks as Amanda returns with their waters.

"Will you do it, Joe?"

"Do what?" He looks first at Gaby and then back up at Amanda.

"Didn't you ask him yet?"

"Nope. You ask. It's your house."

Amanda's cinched red curls vibrate. "I want you to be the general contractor and build my new house for me. There are no money worries. I inherited money, as you might already know. I used part of it to buy the diner. Payment will be cash. Chester won't be very involved. He's busy and not interested. What do you say?" The information comes out in a rehearsed rush, almost as if she expects people to think she can't afford to do the job.

Joe is all business. She recognizes his cue. They are together on this. "How about you set a time to come into the store and sit down with both of us? We can review your plans and explain how we work. Then you can decide if you want to stick with Dodd's and sign a contract."

Amanda appears a bit crestfallen. "I thought I could have you handle the details and I'll pay the bills." She pouts a bit.

"No way, my dear. Gaby and I like to make a contract and deal with those details up front. There are enough surprises when you're building a house.

We don't need to ask for trouble."

"Can I come down tomorrow, in the morning?"

"Of course you can, Amanda. Joe and I are there by eight-thirty, if the time works for you."

"I'll stop here and get everyone coffee and cinnamon buns."

Before they can argue, Danny slams the bell and two specials magically appear at the pass-through.

****

A cold spring wind whistles around the shop and catches Gaby full in the face as she climbs out of her little black Mazda pickup and faces the double locks on the back door of Dodd's Contracting and Interiors. She expects to see Amanda soon. Joe will be along in due time. He drove over to another job site to check and make sure the drywall installation suits his standards. He's still hands-on even though they have site foremen to carry the load. Martha wags her tail in metronome fashion. She waits patiently as Gaby fumbles with keys while she balances both a purse and a bag full of paperwork.

She discusses her plans with her dog. "I have to get to the bank today. Will you help me remember? Time to earn your keep, old girl. Enough of this sitting around and charming the customers." At seven-thirty, they flounder into the hall and Gaby reaches up with a gloved hand to hit the master switch.

The back entry and office are flooded with illumination. She rounds the corner, flicks on the track lights, and the long, narrow showroom springs to life. The space consists of a series of kitchen and bathroom vignettes. She and Joe created displays of cabinetry, plumbing fixtures, and countertops in the best way they could manage in order to provide their customers with a visual of available choices. Each small section contains various sample brands, brochures, and accessories. The shop is quite long from front to back. They managed to install displays along each wall while the centre area showcases individual options, like bathroom vanities and ceramic tile selections. The transformation has been an incredible amount of work and, every time you think the place is finished, a product is discontinued by the manufacturer and they have to redesign a complete display.

She walks to the plate glass front door, turns the sign to open, and flips the deadbolt after she drops her armload of belongings into her chair in the office. Martha continues to trot along beside her. "I think I'll make coffee, even though Amanda said she would bring coffees from the diner. Who knows? She might be late. This way we will have our caffeine one way or the other. What do you think?"

She looks down as she continues her dialogue with her dog. "Fresh water for the old girl?" Martha wags her big tail as they trundle off to the kitchenette alcove tucked into the back hall.

Gaby likes the quiet. There are no messages on the answering machine. The phone isn't jangling off the hook. She has a bank deposit to prepare and those two blueprints to review again as she starts to assemble presentations for the sister houses located next door to one another north of town. The contractors are inside now, as they complete the rough-in electrical and plumbing. Time to make plans for the finishes. Amanda should be around in a little more than thirty minutes.

When the front door opens at about eight-fifteen, Gaby pops out of the office and is surprised to see Amanda poised in the entry. "Hi, you. You're here at the crack of dawn. Joe isn't back from his morning check on a job site, but he'll be here anytime. Come down to the office."

Amanda is laden with coffees, a bag already stained with what appears to be butter leaked through the sides, a shoulder bag almost as big as herself, and a stack of draft drawings under her arm. She follows Gaby down the length of the shop. Gaby can't help but notice how her attention jumps from one display to the next—the true sign of a customer both excited and overwhelmed.

"Thanks for the goodies. Cinnamon buns, right? Joe will be ecstatic. I'll put his coffee and a bun over on his desk."

She returns to her seat and focuses on the issue at hand. "Let's talk for a minute about what you'd like, Amanda. Have you explored lots of options? Do you have particular preferences?" Gaby finds better success with customers if she listens to their wants and needs first. Sometimes those don't correspond with their budget, but the job has proved much easier when she elicits information from the very beginning. No need to work on a kitchen design all day and then discover the customer wants a wall oven and counter cooktop, rather than a traditional stove.

Amanda has removed her down-filled puffy pink coat, which clashes mercilessly with her fire engine red curls, and plunks herself down in the seat beside Gaby's desk. Her sigh is audible. "Before I take a big bite out of a cinnamon bun, I have to tell you I have no idea what I want. I've thumbed through magazines and stuff, but I've never lived in a nice house so I don't know."

She stares into her coffee, as if deciding how to explain. "My previous mother-in-law's kitchen was unreal. The cabinets were white and shiny. There were gold-coloured hinges on the cupboard doors, a black sink and countertop, and gold taps. The walls were tiled in what seemed to be marble; probably was, with the kind of money they could spend." She begins to munch on her cinnamon bun.

Gaby considers her family counsellor experience to be of great use on many occasions. She allows Amanda the pleasure of a simple chat for a few minutes before she tries to tackle the situation. "Do you want a kitchen like your mother-in-law has?"

"I said 'previous'. Mama—Mrs. Wolski—has farmer cupboards. They're old plywood slammed together. My first in-laws were filthy rich. I'll have to tell you about them one day."

Gaby senses her evasiveness, so moves the conversation along. "Shall I have a peek at your preliminary blueprints and then we can do a wee tour of the showroom? You can get an understanding for what you find attractive."

"As long as the finishes are expensive...and classy, Gaby. My new house has to be classy. No tacky trims."

Gaby practises patience brought on by years of experience with all sorts of people. "Now Amanda, do you think I would consider it acceptable for you to live and work in a tacky kitchen?"

On cue, Martha scrambles out from under Gaby's desk and prances toward the back door as Joe makes his entrance accompanied by a gust of cold spring wind. "Good morning, ladies. Do I smell cinnamon buns and fresh coffee? A guy might want to work here steady with this kind of service."

Everyone chuckles as he flops down into the chair at his desk and rustles in the bag.

"I was about to give Amanda a tour of the displays to collect ideas."

Amanda is quick to add, "Joe, please review the plans for the house. Chester and I want you to build our new home, if you think you are able, schedule-wise. I don't care about the cost. I want the very best. You understand."

Gaby and Joe communicate silently. He gets up and moves the drawings out to the big work table in the showroom. A change has happened to Amanda. She has become a "take charge" sort, as compared to the quiet, mouse-like creature who used to manage The Station.

By the end of their visit, Amanda has chosen very expensive oak cabinetry, solid surface countertops newly available to the area, and crystal knobs for the hardware on each cupboard door and drawer. A decision is made. Gaby and Joe will do a full proposal after Joe clarifies he will not be available to start until late in July. They settle on a time to meet again once the blueprints are finalized, based on lot elevations.

"This seems to be the new Amanda, Joe. Price is no object. She made it clear she has some sort of inheritance, although I'm not sure from where. She mentioned how her previous mother-in-law was filthy rich. I think we'll have our work cut out for us."

"This does not seem to be the Amanda I knew when Ben Tullis was dying. Amanda did so much for the old lady; always right in there to lend a hand."

"Do you think she's changed a lot, Joe?"

"Ever since she bought the diner, or maybe even before then, she seems to have turned into boss-lady extraordinaire!"

Gaby guffaws, enough to get a rise out of Martha. "What do I hear? Is this your French for today? Is the air thin up there on your high horse?" She continues to titter as she packs up her bank deposit and turns toward the back door.

****

When the bells above the door tinkle at around three in the afternoon, Gaby is expecting no one in particular. She is pleased and surprised when Fiona Werbowski, in street clothes, pops into the shop.

"Hi there! Haven't seen you in a dog's age. No offence, Martha." She pats her dog who, as usual accompanies her to the front of the store. You're not on shift. Can I interest you in a new kitchen or a countertop?" Gaby teases. She knows Fiona lives alone in an apartment.

"Nope. Not here to shop. I wanted to take advantage since I'm off the clock, so I decided to come in and talk to you about the Roz Dover case."

Gaby knows she looks surprised.

"I suppose you thought I forgot to get back to you. We did manage to make a request for a member in Truro to go and question Charlene Quinn, but investigations take time."

"Fiona, I know you would never forget. There's no pressure. My distinct impression, the last time we talked about the case, was that I had stuck my nose into issues decidedly none of my business." She hopes Fiona sees she can be contrite and apologetic.

"Come on in and sit down. Joe's gone to a job site and I need a break from these house plans. Tea? Coffee?"

"No thanks. I'm off to Segue House for supper a little later. I'll have tea over there."

She sits, nonetheless. "I'll get to the point. Charlene Quinn continues to repeat how she saw Ford's tow truck leave The Station the night Roz disappeared. She said she might have fallen asleep at one point. Anybody could have come out of the back lot or driven by on the street and she wouldn't know. The other observation she claims she knows for sure is that she saw Chester's old pickup leave the parking lot, too. She went home after both trucks left. Her roommates were asleep and, of course, Roz wasn't there so we are no further ahead."

"Didn't Chester have the service truck at The Station because he was on call? Could someone else have been on call that night? Why would Charlene see Chester's pickup? Would he have taken his own vehicle on the call?"

"Too many assumptions, Gaby. We figure Charlene's confused. We think she saw the service truck for sure, but her memory has recalled the old pickup, too. There's no other explanation."

"Fiona, I developed a clear understanding of Charlene Quinn when I was her counsellor. I struggle to believe she would get a critical detail mixed up. It isn't her nature. If she says she saw both trucks, then it happened."

"All I can tell you is we are following the evidence and not suspicions, Gaby."

"You said the investigation never found records of his job that night. Could Chester have been working off the books and therefore took his own truck?"

"I might ask him about it to clear up the questions, but the fact remains— Chester went out on a call. Charlene saw him. Period. I wish there was more. And by the way, they said Charlene was cooperative and polite. She said to say hi to Gaby Ridgway."

"It's beyond creepy to know she thinks about me, Fiona. One minute I consider her a possible reliable witness, and the next I'm back to a place where I know she can lie like a cheap carpet and I could be convinced she might have killed the girl herself."

Chapter 8

Patrick

"The diner's been busier than I thought, Chester. I couldn't get away. Mason's doing his best to behave himself, but please come and get him at five. I want him to go home with you. I called your mom. She knows we won't be there. What?" A giant sigh escapes despite her obvious attempt at control. "No, I can't, Chester." Her voice starts to shake. Patrick can sense her anxiety while he sits in the back booth with Mason and helps him colour. Nancy skirts by with an armload of dirty dishes.

"Do you need help? Mason's a big boy now. He can sit by himself for a few minutes." The child beams up at Patrick and offers him a red crayon.

"No, sit with the kid while there's a lull." She directs her eyes toward Amanda, as she continues to talk on the phone mounted on the wall beside the swinging doors. "I'd rather be back in the kitchen cleaning up. Another couple of runs and there'll be enough for the dishwasher. Do you plan to manage old Bertha tonight?"

"Yeah. I'll bus and wash." He admires his long-time friend. Nancy experienced a health scare a while back. He was petrified she might get sick and die, like his friend, Ben. The problem turned out to be minor. She was off work for a week, but then returned fit as a fiddle. He was relieved. Concern about your friends is a new responsibility. It has materialized with the changes he's made in his life these past few years. "I hope Amanda's okay. The situation seems pretty rough between her and Chester. Do you know what the problem is?"

Nancy casts her dark eyes, laden with mascara, downward toward Mason. "I'll talk to you later." She hustles into the kitchen. The saloon doors flap behind her.

Amanda barks into the receiver. "Come and pick up your child, Chester. Besides, I won't be home until after eight and I have to confirm the contract with Joe and Gaby. Come in and we can talk. I have to go." She hangs up the telephone with what Patrick estimates is unnecessary force, spins on her heel, and tromps into the kitchen. Patrick hopes most people order the meat loaf special tonight. He doesn't think Amanda is in any mood to take the time necessary to create particular items on the menu.

After a few minutes, he gets up from the staff booth and leans toward the pass-through into the kitchen. If Nancy is finished her tables, he will load the dishwasher, but he's reluctant to leave Mason by himself even though the diner is empty of patrons. You never know what the little tyke can get up to in five minutes.

"He doesn't want to build a house out on the property his folks bought for us! He makes me crazy. We have been given a piece of property free and clear. The house won't have a mortgage because I have the cash, and he's up in arms about the costs. Nothing satisfies him. He's pissed off at the world all the time. He told me the other day he was in a fight at work. That's never happened before."

"Maybe he's stressed out, Amanda. What with two kids and the diner...and now the house."

Patrick takes the opportunity of a short lull in the conversation between the two women to ask Nancy if she wants to man the front so he can come in the back. He explains to his boss. "Don't want to leave the little duffer out here by himself."

"Nice to hear someone's responsible," Amanda grunts.

Nancy blasts through the double doors and before they flap, Patrick makes his way into the kitchen and over to the dishwasher. He listens to Amanda as she bangs pots and mumbles for about five minutes before he interjects. "Amanda, if there's anything I can do to help you, you know you can ask, right? You've been good to me. I hate to see ya unhappy."

"I'm not unhappy, Patrick. You're wrong." She turns and leans a round hip into the stainless steel counter while she rubs a stray red curl off her forehead. "I have wonderful parents-in-law, two great kids, and a gorgeous husband who has a steady job. I inherited enough money to buy this place and build a new house. There is no reason on God's green earth why I shouldn't be the happiest woman in Hayworth, and I want to be. Chester will have to get used to the idea of us building our dream house on the property next door to his parents. I don't care about how Roz's car was found there. If the history of the property bothers him, he'll have to learn to cope." She pants a little when she's done her speech.

Patrick isn't sure he should respond, so he chooses to mumble, "Oh, Chester will come around. You'll see."

No sooner are the words out of his mouth than the front door chimes sound and in he comes. Amanda is first to peek through the opening to check, but they both hear Mason squeal with delight at the sight of his father.

"Daddy, Daddy." His chubby legs are like propellers as he tries to wiggle his way out of the booth.

"Okay, Mason. Don't fall." He picks up the boy and nods to Nancy who glances toward the kitchen. Suddenly, every table in the place appears to require another wipe before the supper crowd.

Patrick decides to find a task to do at the counter and starts to leave the kitchen as Chester enters. "Mason, you go on out with Patrick. I need to speak to your mama."

Mason starts to complain but after he sees the glare in Chester's eyes, the little boy pushes out through the doors and throws himself into the staff booth. Patrick sidles in beside him as the child prepares to run the red crayon he's grabbed, across the top of the table.

"Service was busy at lunch. There was no time to get the prep done for supper. Danny's off today and I didn't have the heart to call him in. Sorry I couldn't get out to the farm after school with Mason." Her frustration is punctuated with a heavy sigh. "Changing the subject, we have a quote from Joe and Gaby. They will contract the house and take care of the details. We pick out what we want. I have it in writing."

Chester's voice has a pitch Patrick has never heard before. "Are you telling me this house will cost us a hundred and twenty thousand bucks? Even more if you decide on pricier stuff inside? You're kidding, right? Shouldn't we try to save our money for our kids? For college?"

Amanda keeps her voice subdued, like she's talking to an old person and she wants him to focus his attention exclusively on her. "This is my money

L. P. Suzanne Atkinson

and I will spend every dime as I see fit. I do not care if you want me to sweep stairs at The Station for the rest of my life while you gallivant around. Those days are over. Joe and Gaby will build us a new house. They will start in the summer, and this discussion is over. Here." She hands him an envelope. "This is the basic quote. Review the figures. If you have any questions, we can go and see them together once the blueprints are finalized. If you don't, I said I would call them by the end of the week. We need to be put on their schedule. You owe me, Chester."

The diner becomes quiet. Patrick can hear the rumble of old Bertha and the scratch of a red crayon dragged back and forth across a paper placemat.

The saloon doors flap as Chester pushes out, picks up his son, and leaves the restaurant without another word, envelope in hand.

****

The day felt like it would never end. You could cut the air in the diner with a knife. As Patrick unlocks the door of Number Six and enters his sanctuary at a little after nine, he still can't keep his mind from fixating on Chester and how he seems to have changed. He tried to talk to Nancy about him when they were out front and he was bussing tables. Nancy pursed her lips, glanced at the pass-through, and kept moving.

Patrick's apartment is on the top floor of The Station. The layout is different than the other units because of the gable windows. There is one big room and the bathroom. He loves this place. Before Ben Tullis died, back near Christmas in 1980, he still heard the voices and did not take proper care of himself. Now, at the ripe old age of almost thirty, Patrick considers he is his own man. There are both positives and negatives in this regard. The positives are obvious. He has a good job. He is close to the people at The Station and has other friends from the community like Gaby Ridgway and Ronny Étang. His bills are paid and he admits, albeit with an element of caution, how he has developed a crush on Audrey Baranski.

The negatives involve his ability to become obsessed with an idea or an issue; like a dog with a bone. He knows he can have a one track mind and when it happens, he loses focus on what's important.

He's thought about Audrey a lot in the last days. He doesn't want their relationship to be based on the fact they have both heard voices. He wants them to have more in common than mental illness.

When he hears the soft knock on his door, he knows it's Audrey. He was thinking about her and conjured her up in his mind. He doesn't even take a moment to verify his suspicions through the peep hole. He opens the door wide and there she is, like he knew she would be. Her skin shines with a pale pink rosiness he can't explain. Patrick always notices the skin of others. She's wearing black jeans and a black hooded sweatshirt. She has flip-flops on her feet—in April. Her hands are in her pockets and she stands perfectly still.

"I heard you come home and thought you might like company. I hope you don't mind." She glances down at her bare toes and her skin gets a bit more rosy.

"Come in. Come in. Do you want tea? I can make tea. My friend, Ben, used to always make tea. I have two kinds. One's regular and one's herbal." He blathers. She scuttles in on her flip-flops and perches on one of the chairs at his little table.

"Tea would be good. The herbal one. What kind do you have?"

Patrick digs the box out of an upper cupboard near the sink. "This one is black currant—a gift from Rose." He doesn't have a kettle but fills his one saucepan with enough water for two cups and sets the pot on the stove burner. "It won't take long." He settles into the other chair at the table.

She twists her fingers.

"What's new, Audrey?"

"Did you hear we might get a new building manager?"

"Yeah, sure, but not until late in June or the first of July. Greta's okay. Her two kids are cute. She does Amanda's books for the diner." He studies Audrey's face for a clue as to her concerns. "I met her ages ago. Is there a problem?"

"Probably not. I wonder about people I don't know. Chester Wolski was over here with her this afternoon. I thought it was weird."

"He might have given her a few tips about how to run the place."

"Still kind of soon for training, don't you think?" Audrey's suspicions are obvious.

"Greta Seeley seems like good people, Audrey. I don't think you have to worry."

"No, I know, but Chester bothers me. For him to be here in the middle of the afternoon...."

"He came down to the diner near five o'clock to pick up Mason. Chester didn't seem very happy. Neither one of them did." He pours the hot water into mugs with care, and places both on the table. He returns to the single walled kitchen to get a couple of spoons and a saucer for the tea bags.

Audrey jumps up and turns toward the door. "I'll be right back."

Patrick doesn't know what to think as she darts through the door and he hears her gallop down the stairs. He hopes Cheryl Nadler, who lives across the hall from Audrey, hasn't gone to bed already.

She returns with two huge ginger cookies on a plate. "They made these in the cafeteria today and I thought you might like one." She blushes.

He can have a cookie at the diner almost anytime he wants, but one Audrey has brought him tastes extra good. The couple munch quietly for a minute. Patrick tries not to get crumbs on his face. He provides paper towel to substitute for napkins. "These are great, Audrey! I could eat these every day of the week."

"There's one cook at the hospital who makes them, so we have them once a week. I love ginger." She pops the last bite into her mouth.

Patrick watches her lips move. The act of eating with someone seems personal somehow. There's lots about relationships he doesn't understand. He'll talk to Dr. Wilkerson in a few days.

****

Dr. Wilkerson proves to be her usual wonderful self when Patrick appears for his scheduled appointment at the Hayworth Community Hospital later in the week. She's dressed in a yellow silk blouse and a tweed skirt. A brown suede jacket hangs over the back of her chair. Her ears and neck are trimmed with heavy gold accessories.

Rachel Wilkerson rarely sits behind her desk when Patrick is there. He appreciates how she sits in the second chair in front of her desk and treats him like they are together for a conversation; not like she's a psychiatrist at all.

"What's on your mind today, Patrick?" She crosses her long legs and leans back into the typical fabric stacking chair issued for institutional use. It seems as if the one task she wants to accomplish in life is to listen to his deepest and darkest thoughts.

"Can we talk about my friend, Audrey? I like Audrey Baranski a lot but

I want to make sure my interest is not because we're both schizophrenics trying to stay sane." He smirks. "Like a pair of alcoholics trying not to drink."

She responds without any change in her expression. "Mental illness is what brought you together, right?"

"No. She moved into my building."

"Therefore you have more than one circumstance in common."

"I guess."

"What else do you have in common? What sorts of topics do you talk about?"

"One of the main issues is Chester Wolski. Audrey thinks he tried to put the moves on her. She isn't sure because she reads details into conversations when they're sometimes not there. She imagined she was gang-raped and then the doctors figured out she had lost it. But I think she was right this time."

He seeks permission to continue. Rachel nods in response to his questioning eyes.

"Chester is very handsome. He flirts with girls all the time. She saw him the other day over at The Station with Greta Seeley, the new manager who will move to the basement apartment in a couple of months—once Amanda and Chester move out to the farm. Audrey thinks he might have put the moves on her, too, but I don't know."

"Has Audrey suggested Chester has flirted with her lately?"

"Not in so many words, but maybe. He creeped her out when he came for a visit right after she moved in. We've also talked about the night Roz disappeared. I still think Chester must know what happened. I think maybe the RCMP went to talk to Charlene Quinn in prison, but they would never tell me what she said. I can't believe she didn't see him out that night. Maybe the RCMP could have screwed up the whole situation."

"Have you fixated on this, Patrick?"

"I know what you're about to say: 'Let the cops do their job. Not my concern. I can't help them. Don't let myself get obsessed', right?"

Rachel's expression is indulgent. "Maybe we need to switch chairs."

"I know I should let go but I still want to tell you what I think, Dr. W., and I promise I won't say this to anyone else, not even Audrey. Roz told Charlene Quinn she had a crush on a hunky mechanic at the Ford dealership. She used to take her Pinto there. Chester is a big flirt. He's one of those guys who's so good looking he thinks every woman will throw themselves at him. You should see people's reactions when he walks into the diner." Patrick frowns. "I think Chester and Roz were gettin' it on. Maybe Chester didn't even have a service call the night she went missing. Maybe he used it as an excuse to Amanda so he could get out of the house. I suggested the RCMP talk to the people he was supposed to have helped at the hotel, but there isn't a record. That's weird, too."

"Patrick, you realize you have now suggested Chester is implicated in Roz Dover's disappearance."

"Yup. And I think he's getting away with whatever happened." Patrick leans back in his chair and meets his psychiatrist's eyes. "These are my own thoughts, Dr. W. I'm not obsessing. My hands are tied, but man, has Chester ever changed in the last few months. He wasn't happy when Amanda bought the diner and he's even more unhappy because they're building a house on the land his father bought for them; land where Roz's car was found. He and Amanda don't seem to get along at all right now. It's like workin' on one of those big puzzles, but there's just enough pieces missing you can't tell what the picture will turn out to be in the end." He sighs in frustration.

"I think you will have to get used to the missing pieces, Patrick. We may never know what happened to Roz Dover. Let's review your medication before we finish up. We want to ensure you are, in fact, not obsessed with this, but rather observing the workings of the world like anyone else."

"What do you think about Audrey, Dr. W.?"

"I think people meet under different kinds of circumstances. What you make of the relationship afterward is what becomes important. You will know if she's the right girl." She moves around to the back of her desk to get her appointment book.

Chapter 9

Audrey

"I know, Dad. I'll be fine." Audrey sighs and tries, without much success, to avoid sounding exasperated as her father lists off a litany of cautions and instructions.

"Don't get into a car with strangers." "Keep track of your money." "Pay your bills on time." "Make sure your door is locked." It's a Saturday evening in early June. She often spends Saturday or Sunday with her parents. The schedule depends on her days off.

Ivan Baranski's voice continues to rumble after she's out of the International grain truck he has utilized to drive her back into town. The big vehicle, like a dump truck but specifically designed to transport grains, is his pride and joy. Audrey knows he is proud to drive the truck to town just in case somebody sees him. The vehicle is five years old, but Ivan considers it new. "Almost new," he says. "Paid for in cash."

"Good night, Dad. I'm fine. You worry too much."

Audrey lets herself in to The Station and remembers to lock the door behind her. After she trudges up the now familiar flight of stairs, she unlocks her door to Number Four and walks over to the front window in the kitchen to watch as her father navigates the International down the street. She is alert to the silence; appreciates the absence of interference. She likes the quiet. Before her medications began to work, she hated emptiness because the voices took over right away to fill the void. She has learned to float in the peace of silence now, and not struggle like a drowning swimmer.

Audrey begins her routine to settle herself for the night, but is distracted by the unexpected sounds of a commotion emanating from the front parking lot.

"Honest to God, Amy! You didn't have to carry every stitch of clothing you own. You're here for three months, not three years."

Without any concern she might be seen, Audrey stands at the window and observes the two women who resemble one another like twins. Audrey has always admired Cheryl Nadler, the social worker who lives across the hall from her. She is unapologetically rigid in her routines and in the way she presents herself. She takes full advantage of her short stature and perfect figure, which Audrey compares to her own stick-like and angular physique. Cheryl is committed. She jogs every day. Her hair is always precise in its sameness, like she manages to have a trim before she's in need of one. She's crisp and fresh—morning, noon, or night. Audrey envies her neighbour's personal discipline. Also, Cheryl is the only tenant who has a washer and dryer in the apartment. She does a lot of laundry because Audrey can hear the machines as they hum away on certain days.

"I didn't know what to pack, Cheryl. Do they wear regular clothes to the store, or do they dress up a bit? I wanted to be safe...and I didn't think you would want to buy me a new wardrobe." Her teasing expression reveals white teeth. They gleam and mirror those of the older woman beside her.

Although the girl called Amy addresses Cheryl by her given name, Audrey is almost certain this must be Cheryl's daughter who has flown in from down east to work for Dodd's Contracting and Interiors for the summer. Patrick has told her about Amy already; how Cheryl went to Nova Scotia and found the child she gave up for adoption when she was a teenager. Amy started to visit Hayworth when she was sixteen. Audrey calculates she must be almost nineteen now.

The two women begin to haul bags across the lot and up to the door. Without any thought as to why, Audrey opens her own door and runs down the steps. "Can I help you? Hi Cheryl." She gives the younger girl a shy smile. "You must be Amy. I'm Audrey and I live across the hall in Number Four."

Amy shrieks. "Help! I, especially, need all the help I can get. Can you grab the other end of this suitcase and we can carry the damned brute up to Cheryl's?"

Audrey wastes no time, and picks up the other end of the almost exploding luggage and off they go. Cheryl is left to manhandle the big heavy front door, purses, and an overnight bag Amy probably carried with her on the plane.

Once they reach the top of the stairs, they wait for Cheryl to catch up and open the door.

Audrey doesn't want to admit to being nosy, but she is very curious about Cheryl's apartment and whether the space reflects her preconceived notion of the woman herself. The apartment doesn't disappoint. Number Five resembles a picture in a magazine. The dining room table and chairs are glass and chrome. The living room furniture is leather or suede or a combination. There is no pattern. Each piece is beige. There are no rugs on the floors. The counters are bare.

"Where do you want me to put this? Do I have to sleep on a camp cot again?"

"No, Amy. You'll find a real single bed for you, set up in the corner of my room. There isn't enough space in my laundry room."

Amy lifts her perfect eyebrows as she explains to Audrey. "Cheryl thinks a laundry room is more important than a room for her soon-to-be nineteen-year-old daughter who expects to work Tuesday through Saturday all summer. Do you have roommates?"

Audrey's voice is quiet. "No. I live alone." She glances over at Cheryl for approval. "But you can come and visit anytime you like."

"Where do you work?"

Audrey isn't used to multiple direct questions and feels compelled to overcompensate. "At the hospital; in the cafeteria. I work days, but different shifts." She becomes anxious and stares at the floor. "Do you need any more help?"

"No, I think we can manage, Audrey, but thanks again for rescuing us. Are you off tomorrow? Perhaps you can stop in for tea." Cheryl is very formal all of a sudden, like they've never met before.

"I work until three, but I'll come by afterward." Audrey, overcoming her reluctance, holds out her hand to Amy. "Nice to meet you, Amy. I expect you'll enjoy working for Joe and Gaby. They are nice people."

Amy puts her hands on her hips in mock horror. "Now how do you know I've been hired by them?"

Audrey is on the spot and doesn't want to reveal how she acquired her information. She sputters a quick response. "Hayworth's a small town. Word gets around." She's out through the open door and over to her apartment before more words can be exchanged.

****

When Audrey gets obsessed with an idea, the thoughts anchor themselves, stubborn and unmoving, inside her brain. Whether a bad idea or a good thought, once the obsession takes hold, there is little she can do to dispel whatever the topic happens to be. In this particular case, the topic is Amy.

Audrey rises at the crack of dawn on Sunday morning. Her shift starts at seven, but she gets up at five to give herself more than enough time to cook the peanut butter cookies she mixed and stored in the refrigerator last night. She has never been anxious to be friends with anyone before, except for perhaps Patrick. The sensation is odd, like nervousness before a performance on stage, or taking a big test.

Once the cookies are baked and tucked into a tin, she trots down the stairs and off to Hayworth Community Hospital. The clear and fresh morning air makes the thirty minute walk worthwhile. All she can think about is knocking on Cheryl Nadler's door after work with peanut butter cookies; of sitting with these two normal women and having tea. She shakes her head a tiny bit as she washes lettuce in preparation for salads. Patrick is a great guy, but facts are facts. They are both chemically managed schizophrenics. Cheryl and Amy are normal people. This might be an opportunity for her to hang out with normal people away from the hospital cafeteria.

The day drags. There isn't much pressure involved with her job. She washes vegetables, chops food, and sets up the trays to go upstairs to the patients. Oftentimes, she will serve dessert into bowls. Sometimes there's a new admission, or a person in the outpatient department who needs a meal. She will get volunteered to make the trek upstairs to deliver. Most of her colleagues try to avoid any unnecessary running around.

Twice during her shift, she asks Babs, the supervisor and cook, if there are more chores for her to do. She unloads the dishwasher a couple of times and mops the floor by the prep area. Babs wants to know why she's so hyper and if she's okay. Audrey guesses Babs is afraid she might be drifting into an episode. "I'm a little antsy, Babs. Meeting a couple of people after work for tea. I made peanut butter cookies—your recipe!"

"Well, your meeting must be a special occasion, then." Babs, heavy-chested and supported by swollen ankles at the end of edematous legs, wipes her hands on the front of her now-soiled apron and glances up at the extra-large round clock perched on the opposite wall. "Why don't you go home, Audrey? You've put in a hard day. Nobody needs to know you left at two-thirty. Hey, wait! I'm the boss! I say 'go' and share those cookies." She gives Audrey a wee nudge. "Tell me all about your tea party tomorrow." Her breasts rock back and forth and her hairnet, holding the greying strands of permed curls in place, shudders as she snorts at her own joke.

Audrey doesn't have to be offered a kindness more than once. She rushes to the staff room to peel off her uniform and hairnet. Both go into a string bag along with her shoes. She jumps back into the jeans and sweatshirt she wore to work this morning, ties up her sneakers, pulls her pony tail elastic tight to the nape of her neck, and races for the door.

She's home by three, which feels almost as good as a day off. She heard muffled noises through the door of Number Five, and noticed Cheryl's Toyota Celica still parked out front when she came in. Audrey's stomach flutters. She decides to change into pale pink cotton pants and a white blouse with frills down the front. Her mother gave her the outfit and she's never worn it before. She starts to undo her ponytail but can't force herself to let her hair hang down. Certain situations still threaten to make her crazy. She knows her limits. Instead, she grabs a black clip, wraps her hair into a knot, and secures the resulting bun to the back of her neck. She examines herself in the mirror, a behaviour she usually avoids, and decides she appears better than one would expect after running around in a steamy institutional kitchen all day.

As she gets to her door, she stops. *Keys and cookies. Don't forget your keys and the cookies.* She retraces her steps back into the kitchen and grabs the plate; the special one with the provincial flowers on the rim. Her mother received the dish as a wedding gift and gave it to her when she moved. She locks her door and takes the necessary three steps across to Cheryl's apartment. Her knock is soft.

"On my way! Hi, Audrey. We heard you come home." Amy's voice breaks through from the other side the moment the door swings open.

Audrey catches her breath. Amy is dressed in very tight blue jeans which are worn at the knees. She has on an over-sized sweatshirt. It slides off one pale shoulder. Her feet are bare. She has a big wad of bubble gum in her mouth and huge black reading glasses perched on the end of her perfect nose. All Audrey can think is she could be Cheryl if the social worker ever managed to relax. Amy comes across as Cheryl gone off the rails.

"I brought cookies, Amy. I hope you like peanut butter." Audrey takes a tentative step into the apartment as Cheryl comes around the corner from the second bedroom outfitted as her laundry room.

"Hi, Audrey. We have both been anxiously anticipating your visit today. I'm in the midst of laundry chores but will take a break for tea. Amy, will you put the kettle on, please? Remember to set it on the trivet and not directly on the counter."

Amy makes a face. "Cheryl has been in her laundry room most of the afternoon, ironing her panties."

Cheryl responds with a little, less than genuine, laugh. "I don't iron panties, Amy." She acknowledges Audrey. "At least not anymore."

"Well, you iron the sheets, for God's sake! Ironing sheets is just as bad."

"No need for us to air out 'clean' laundry in front of company, Amy." She glances at Audrey and winks. "Everybody has their own way of doing chores. Come on in and sit down at the table. I bet your cookies are delicious. You girls enjoy." She turns on her heel and hustles back to the laundry room. "Call when the tea's ready."

After Cheryl is out of ear shot, Amy rushes over and whispers to Audrey. "Cheryl is obsessed with perfection. After one day, I'm the one who will soon be crazy. You have to help me."

"How can I help?" Audrey finds herself whispering, too.

"Want to have a walk this evening? I'll come over and get you. Cheryl always goes for a run before supper. She wants me to go, but we can take a walk later, okay?"

Audrey is confused. "Of course. No problem, but I don't know what I can do to help."

"Kettle's boiled!" Amy yells her message and Cheryl appears again. She sets heavy placemats at three spots on her glass table top and a fourth in the centre. She puts a spoon and napkin at each place and moves the plate of Audrey's cookies from the spot beside her, to the extra mat. "Pour the tea, Amy. Did you warm the pot, first?"

"Of course. Like you taught me. I'll carry the cups to the table while the tea steeps. You sit down."

Although her behaviour seems out of character to Audrey, Cheryl does as she's told and sits at the table. She eyes the cookies. "Those smell divine, Audrey. Did you make them yourself?"

"Yes. They are Babs' recipe." Cheryl's face is blank. "Babs is the cook at the hospital."

"Well, I expect you and Amy will enjoy them."

"Will you have one, Cheryl?" Audrey tries not to feel slighted.

"No. I never eat between meals and I prefer not to eat other people's food— one of my little rules. I may eat out if I'm away, which is rare. A few years ago, when I drove down east to see Amy, I booked a hotel room with a kitchen and made my own food. It's a rule I have," she repeats.

Amy transports the teapot to the table and, with exaggerated care, makes use of another trivet Cheryl has placed strategically for the purpose. "Cheryl has lots of rules, Audrey."

"I try not to impose them on other people, though. You know I work hard at not imposing my standards, Amy! Consider what you have chosen to wear today. I rest my case."

Audrey takes a sip of very bitter black tea and nibbles on a cookie. Amy takes two cookies off the plate and devours each one in a couple of bites. "Man, these are tasty. You're a good baker. Cheryl, we need to have food besides chicken and pasta salad."

Cheryl responds with an expression of impatience, but appears to want to keep conversation light in the presence of company. "Did you have a good day at work, Audrey?"

"Yes, Cheryl. The actual job isn't great. It's just a job, I suppose, but they understand me. The staff are nice and there are never any issues we can't work out. I don't like stress. The job is good for me."

"Audrey, maybe we can go for supper at the diner one night. Patrick, upstairs, works there, right? And does Chester Wolski hang around since his wife owns the place?" Amy reaches for another cookie.

"Don't spoil your supper, Amy."

"I like to go to the diner when I can, Amy. I don't make a lot of money, so I don't eat out often, but we can go." She isn't sure why, but she's hesitant to reveal her close friendship with Patrick. She wonders if Amy is the kind of girl who would try to muscle in because she's pretty and she can. It happens.

Cheryl glances down at her wrist watch. "I must get ready to go for my run. I assume you will accompany me, Amy?"

Amy shrugs. "Sure, Cheryl. I'll clean up the table."

Cheryl has already filled the sink with steaming hot and soapy water. The cups, saucers, and side plates are in to soak. With a raise of her perfectly plucked eyebrows, Amy scoops up the last cookies and hands Audrey her plate. "Thanks for the cookies. I'll talk to you later," she whispers into Audrey's ear. Audrey can feel the words carried on Amy's peanut butter scented breath.

****

The two young women take their planned walk through town on Sunday evening, and go together again on Monday afternoon, before Amy starts her job at Dodd's Contracting and Interiors the next day. A plan is hatched whereby Amy will try to inconvenience the very particular Cheryl to the point where she will permit her to move across the hall and rent a room from Audrey.

Audrey isn't totally on board. Amy will be gone in the fall but she will still have to get along with her neighbour, Cheryl Nadler, in Number Five. Nevertheless, Audrey is swept along by the conspiratorial and outgoing Amy.

Before Monday is over, Amy has convinced Cheryl to agree to an arrangement with Audrey, so she can have her own room as the best option for them both. Her argument concludes Cheryl needs her space, she needs her own room, and the two younger women have a more aligned lifestyle. It seems to sway the social worker. She will still be able to keep an eye on Amy without the two of them tripping over each other. Amy makes her thoughts clear to Audrey. Crowded conditions are not the issue. Cheryl does not cope well with tasks and circumstances which might interfere with her rituals, her schedules, or her routines.

Audrey suspects her parents will be thrilled their daughter has a friend, a roommate, and someone to contribute rent money. Ivan Baranski might stop asking Audrey if she wants to move back home. Perhaps this decision will be her best option.

Chapter 10

Gaby

The early June sunshine blasts through the front window of Dodd's Contracting and Interiors, and welcomes Gaby as she emerges from the back of the shop. She flicks the track lights into action. They shed soft spotlights on cabinet displays and ceramic samples, as she manhandles her large purse and briefcase around the corner and into the office she shares with Joe when he's not on a job site. Martha trots behind her, ever alert as she eyes the door. Satisfied the shop is safe, she follows her mistress and flops down on her over-sized pillow under Gaby's desk.

"I'll make coffee before I open up, Martha. I told Amy eight-thirty. We still have a half hour."

Dressed in soft navy linen trousers and a fluttery navy silk blouse with white polka dots, Gaby reaches for comfort rather than style when she chooses her attire. She is tall, thin, and considers her wispy curls to be her cross to bear. Absently, she touches the clip attached, none to securely, at the back of her neck. The Bakelite accessory will hold there for a couple of hours but she knows the fastener will be in her bag before noon.

The shop offers a mixture of contractor and designer products. The atmosphere is designed for casual comfort. Customers can come in and relax, discuss their needs, review their options, and explore possibilities. The business is one of the first of its kind in the small town. Before Gaby and Joe opened, customers purchased interior items they needed for their homes through the lumberyard, or they trekked to Edmonton in order to make their choices there. Joe owns the building and rents the other half to a lighting store. Dodd's Contracting and Interiors opened a few months after Alberta Lighting. They both provide a balance for clients seeking more upscale products than the usual fare one can purchase at a lumberyard.

As Gaby finishes making coffee, the front door rattles. She peeks around the corner and sure enough, there's Amy. She's shifting impatiently from one foot to the other. Gaby wipes her hands on a tea towel hung from a cabinet door in the little staff kitchen, and hustles out to let Cheryl Nadler's daughter in. Martha is already on the mat, and wags her tail as she gazes up at the young girl on the other side of the glass. They have met. Martha likes Amy a lot.

"I'm here!" Gaby twists the deadbolt on the metal and glass door. At the same time, she flips the sign from closed to open and lets the girl come in. "You are here bright and early! Ready to get busy?"

Amy is the image of her mother. She's petite, with dark hair tired in a knot at the base of her neck. Cheryl always wears her hair short, but Amy's style serves to accentuate how much the two resemble one another. Their voices are the same. If you were to close your eyes, or hear one on the phone, you would be hard pressed to tell which woman was speaking. Their tones are soft but clear and firm; low but confident and forthright. Gaby was pleased for Cheryl when she managed to find the child she gave up for adoption when she was a teenager. They have spent a number of summers together, and it is safe to assume their relationship has blossomed over the ensuing years.

Gaby wanted help for the summer and Amy seems to fit the bill. She will mind the shop if Gaby needs a day off or if she requires a job site measurement during business hours. Amy's presence won't free up her days as much as her evenings, which is important this summer as she and Joe have serious plans to make.

"Good morning, Gaby. Cheryl told me you like punctuality—perhaps not as much as she does—so I thought I would be smart and show up a bit early." She giggles at the reference to her mother's obsessive nature. "Thanks again for offering me the job. University gets more expensive every year."

"What do you want to study?"

"Cheryl wants me to specialize, but General Arts is all I can manage right now."

"Well, an arts degree is a good start, Amy. Come on down to the office and we'll get organized. We can have coffee and I'll show you the ropes." Gaby is pleased Amy has chosen to dress in simple white slacks and a T-shirt without any advertisement across the front. She has a small wallet sized purse with a shoulder strap. "By the way, Amy, I like the way you have dressed, today— perfect for the shop. I don't mind blue jeans, if they're tidy and clean, but I don't want you to wear revealing clothes or items torn or worn." She steals a peek at the girl as they make their way to the back of the shop. *This might work out.*

****

Amy and Gaby share sandwiches and chocolate chip cookies Gaby has brought from home. The bell over the door chimes just as they finish. Chester and Amanda enter the shop.

"Hi, Gaby! I brought revised blueprints!" Amanda bounces from one foot to the other. Her eyes sparkle as they dart around the shop. It looks like she's reassessing her options. Gaby has seen that look on the faces of customers before. It oftentimes results in revisions; lots of revisions.

Gaby knew Amanda would be around sometime today when she could break away from the diner, but she didn't expect Chester to be with her. "Hi, you two. Welcome." She turns toward Amy. "I know you folks have met many times, but I would like to introduce you to my new assistant for the summer, Amy MacDonald." Gaby places a hand on Amy's shoulder, including her in the conversation.

"Assistant? What a great idea! Congrats to both of you!"

Chester scans the young woman up and down, appearing amused somehow.

"Come on in." Gaby points to the blueprint Amanda cradles like a newborn in her arms. "May I have a peek? Let's roll this out on the work table and see the final picture, shall we?"

Amanda, with a certain hesitation, hands over her precious cargo to Gaby as they make their way to the centre of the shop. Chester straddles a stool, but Amanda begins to wander through the space. She fingers tile samples, touches countertops, and opens various cabinet doors in the displays.

"Coffee?" Gaby wants to ensure the couple is comfortable before they get down to business.

"I drink too much coffee at the diner, Gaby, but thanks."

Chester nods. Amy scoots into the back to get him a cup. She returns in a flash and puts the pottery mug down in front of him.

"You need to ask how he drinks his coffee, Amy. Not everyone chooses black." Amy has to learn the rituals of how to make customers comfortable.

"Oh, I know he drinks his coffee black. I've made him coffee at the apartment."

Chester observes Amanda and Gaby with an expression stuck somewhere between smugness and a sneer. "Amy and I are old friends. We've met lots of times, right kid?"

Amy makes her way to a stool behind and to the side of Gaby. "Yes, Chester often stops in to see if Cheryl and I need any help."

"Generous of him." Gaby does not mistake the sarcasm audible beneath Amanda's tone.

"Okay, folks. The revisions will result in minor price adjustments. I will review and update the original quote, but as long as you still want us to do the work, there shouldn't be much difference."

Amanda, with her loose-fitting cotton A-line dress draped over the stool on which she has perched, plunks her elbows on the work table. "Gaby, I want you to handle the details. Tell me the final figure if you want, but the job is yours."

"Now, you both agree Joe and I will re-price the complete package for you. We will manage construction, hire sub-trades, and work with you on decisions as we go. Our initial bid has provided you a contractor price with basic finishes. You can upgrade where you want and with products you can afford."

Amanda is all ears. She leans forward a little farther. "Give me a couple of examples, Gaby."

"Okay. The basic package included a kitchen in the layout as indicated on the plan. We would normally price a flat-panel oak cabinet with basic hardware and rolled laminate countertops. You have already upgraded to a more expensive cabinet, solid surface counters, and fancier hardware." She nods at each of them in turn. "Upgrades add to the overall price. Your kitchen is the first example. When people are building, they get a basic price for the house, finished and ready to move in. Then they decide what upgrades they can afford, what they have to have, and what they can do without. Make sense?"

"Yes, but there are certain products I absolutely want, Gaby. I want a marble fireplace hearth and I want ceramic tile in the three bathrooms."

"We can provide those products, Amanda, but you may find the basic finishes are a better fit for your budget. You have exactly what you want in your kitchen. There's room to compromise in the baths."

Amanda ignores her. "How long will you need to get the bid done once I choose the extras, Gaby?" Amanda is impatient. "I want to be in the house by Christmas. I want to have the family for the holidays."

"Christmas could be a push. Four months to build is standard. We would need to break ground no later than August first. Give me a week. To be honest, the site preparation will take a couple of weeks. Hold on a second." She hastily does some rough mental calculations. "We will start in mid to late July, if we can. After Joe and I complete the budget process, we will detail your choices. Those decisions will not prevent permit applications, and then septic work can begin. Is there power to the lot yet?"

Chester, who has cast lazy eyes on Amy at intervals throughout the meeting, perks up at this. "We need one pole and they are supposed to put it up within the next two weeks."

"Good to know. Lots of work yet to do." Just then, the phone rings. "Amy, will you run and get the phone? Remember the way we discussed how to answer calls. Take a message and I will call them back."

Amy darts into the office. Gaby can't help but notice how Chester watches her retreat, again with a funny snide expression. Gaby's skin crawls a tiny bit.

****

Joe and Gaby are curled up on the sofa in front of their stone fireplace after a long day at work. Martha convinced them to go for a walk when it was well after nine. They discussed their two major projects for the summer and are now relaxed as they review future events. "I'm sure happy Amy will be with me in the shop, Joe. I shouldn't have to work after supper this summer. I can get out to job sites during the day, and we'll both be free to get this damned wedding planned."

"Damned wedding?" Joe leans over far enough to nudge her shoulder. He fakes a sheepish expression. "I assumed you wanted to marry me. Second thoughts?"

She knows he loves to tease her. There is nothing in the world she wants more than to marry Joe Dodd. The last few years have been beyond wonderful. Before her first husband died, she thought she and Grant had a fabulous marriage. She missed him for many, many years. She and Joe have a different relationship. They have experience. They have maturity. They think alike and have similar goals. They are a team. Their marriage is a formality to what has been a perfect match.

People were curious when she first started to date Joe back in the fall of 1981. They asked questions when she quit her job as a family counsellor at the Hexagon and went into business with him. Former co-workers challenged the wisdom of building a house with him. No one could understand why she didn't want to be a counsellor anymore. She knows everyone assumes they were secretly married at some point. Well, August will be an enlightening time for many.

"No second thoughts whatsoever, but if we plan on an August 25 wedding, we need more than a date and my dress for a Sunday afternoon party." She throws her head back and roars. The dress is upstairs, hung under a sheet in the hall cupboard—a simple, empire-waist, cap-sleeved lace affair; not over the top or unique but it suits her slim figure and angular lines to a T.

"Let's invite our friends here to the house like we do at Christmas, get some grub brought in, an afternoon garden party of sorts, and then tell them they're at a wedding. It might be fun? Right?"

Gaby is inspired and delighted by Joe's idea. "I'm in. Who will we invite? The usual suspects? What about family? Your sisters? My sister?"

"Of course, we'll invite the sisters to come." He frowns. "We would have to tell them about the surprise wedding, but they could let on they're here for a regular visit if they happen to run into anybody ahead of time. We can put them up at the hotel."

"Okay. They can be our decoys. 'Come to our party and meet the sisters!'" Gaby laughs again.

Joe pushes on, despite the distraction. "Other than family who are able to attend, invitations can go to Patrick, Rose, Maggie, Ronny, Fiona, Ava, Amanda, Chester and the kids, Cheryl and Amy if she's still here, and what about your old friends from work?"

"I would have to invite Mimi plus Rachel Wilkerson. We could add Pearl, but if we do, then Edith and Frank and Elliot have to be included, not to mention Clark Alden—God give me patience."

Gaby knows, in her heart, she can't leave these people out, even though she hasn't worked with them in more than three years. Dr. Alden is the supervisor of the six social services divisions at the Hexagon. He must be nearly ready to retire. Pearl Markowski was Gaby's boss when she worked for the Family Counselling Division. Edith, Frank, and Elliot were her colleagues. They weren't the most supportive bunch throughout her ordeal. If she were to describe their overall concern at the time of the horrible investigation she went through, she would say they were more curious than worried, but it's water under the bridge now. Mimi, their secretary, was her rock, and Dr. Rachel Wilkerson, in the end, found a way to help her extricate herself from the glue of the investigation by the Canadian Counselling Alliance.

"We also need to invite the crews. If everybody is accompanied by someone, how many do we have? I know there's a helluva lot more than Christmas."

Gaby counts off with her fingers. "I think there will be at least thirty-six people depending on who might invite a plus one. We will have to wait and see if any of the brothers-in-law can get away. Rose will be alone, as will Rachel and no doubt Clark. We can tell the caterer forty-five and make the best of whatever happens." She giggles. "Times have changed. I think Patrick might be involved with someone and I know Maggie is often out with Sean Knox, the RCMP. You know who I mean?"

Joe nods. "What do you think if I ask Murdock Blackney to marry us? He moonlights as a JP. Did you know?"

"How can he do JP work when he's a lawyer?"

"I guess he works as a justice of the peace part-time. He doesn't do criminal or family law anymore. Since he focuses on issues like wills and stuff, he's able to act as a JP. Want me to call him?"

"Works for me. He did a great job on our wills. I like him. I hope he can overcome the urge to wear a muddy brown suit. Everything in his office from the floors to the walls, to his clothes, looks like dirt." She guffaws. "I think I'll call Nina tomorrow. You get hold of Anita and Chrissie. I'll make time to call everyone else. People might suspect, but the day will be fun regardless." She snuggles further into the sofa, satisfied with their discussion, but her mind flips back to work. "I'm exhausted and we have to do up the revised Wolski contract tomorrow. Then they can come in for signatures. She never told me her budget. I hope we aren't way over the top."

****

Amanda and Chester arrive late in the afternoon two days later to review their plans and get their quote. Gaby called Amanda earlier to present the final figure. With Amanda's acceptance, she has completed the contract and provided an inventory of samples. The couple can review their choices and make adjustments as they see fit.

Amanda is excited. Her red hair flies like a halo around her face. She is dressed in jeans and a T-shirt since she has been the chef at the diner all day. Chester carries his movie star good looks with a sullen moodiness. Gaby is silently pleased this is a contract review and not a marriage counselling session, as she plunges in.

"Hard day, Chester? You don't look very happy. I hope you'll like the choices we have for your new house."

He gazes, with lazy boredom, around the shop as he plunks himself down at the design table. "Doesn't matter much to me. Whatever Amanda wants, she'll no doubt get. The money is hers."

Amanda blushes a deep pink. "Well," she addresses Gaby with apologetic haste, "I did inherit the money, but since we're building our house, the whole family benefits." Her voice contains a hint of exasperation. "Show me what we have, Gaby."

Gaby is conflicted and uncomfortable, but she has ample experience to deal with a couple who aren't seeing eye to eye. She starts with certain areas of the building process where she thinks Chester might become more engaged—subjects like water flow and drainage, roof lines and windows, and the garage. He lifts his hooded eyes, but watches Amy as she sorts tile samples, more than he examines shingles and siding.

Amanda, of course, is much more enthusiastic. "I still want those cabinets over there, Gaby." She points to a raised panel oak display topped with Corian counters.

"That's the kitchen we priced from the start, but with your other choices, you've increased the square footage price of the house considerably, you know."

"No need to worry, my friend." Amanda leans over and pats Gaby on the hand. "I appreciate your attempt to help me be frugal, but I can afford to have what I want. Did you put the same cabinets and tops in the bathrooms, like I asked?"

"Of course. Each product is as you requested."

Chester stands up, ready to go. "Time to give my mom a break and pick up the kids, Amanda. When I dropped Mason off after school, Melanie caused a big ruckus. Let's get you back to the diner so I can go." Remembering his manners, he turns to Gaby. "Thanks for this."

Amanda fumbles to write a deposit cheque while Gaby takes her time to fold the customer copy of the contract and stuff it into a big white Dodd's Contracting and Interiors envelope. "Go over this when you can. We have time before the start date to make more changes—you may still decide you need to cut back in a couple of areas," she adds, as she tries her best to ensure Amanda understands she has choices.

Then, with a flirty tone Gaby finds unsettling, Chester catches Amy's eye. "Bye, Amy. See ya later."

Amy lifts her hand in a fluttery wave and returns to the tile display boards, appearing a bit embarrassed. Amanda can't disguise her frown, as she and Chester make their way out to the truck.

There's a tension in the air. Amy hasn't made eye contact with Gaby since the Wolskis left. "Amy, Chester's a flirt. You know how he is, right? He's the same with everyone." For whatever the reason, and she can't determine why, she feels a need to emphasize to Amy why Chester is not an option.

"He's nice to me. He's given me a drive back to The Station a couple of times. He sure is handsome." She blushes a little when she says this.

"All you can do is admire, Amy. Everybody likes to look at Chester, but he's married."

Gaby barely hears her when she replies, "Not happily."

Chapter 11

Amanda

Danny and Nancy will open the diner without her. Chester has shepherded Melanie out to his parents' place and Mason has already caught the bus. She sits on the sofa, crazy red curls wrapped in a yellow bandanna and her green patterned dressing gown cinched at her waist. She is surrounded by magazines and brochures. Gaby told her to make some choices. The final contract price for the house will depend on the quality of the finishes. *Do I want a stainless steel sink from the lumberyard; one Joe can pick up anytime; one the same as everybody else's? Do I want a unique sink with a deep side and a built-in cutting board? A special order will cost three times the money and take six weeks to get here. Or do I want a cast iron sink by Kohler, in persimmon or maybe black?*

Her thoughts spin. The kitchen sink is the least of her problems. There's flooring and ceramic tile, interior doors and lights. "My God! I have three bathrooms!" She sputters aloud to the pale blue walls of the basement suite they will vacate the end of the month. She realizes she has forgotten the details of the particular decisions she's already made. *Maybe I can change a few choices. Gaby said I could.*

Although they talked weeks earlier, the conversation with Chester about the decision to move was not pretty. She still becomes both angry and frustrated if she permits ruminations on the subject. Thank God the kids were already at his parents' place for the afternoon. It was Saturday. He was supposed to do the spring yard work at The Station, but he turned up at the diner for coffee early in the afternoon. The place was quiet. She poured herself a cup and sat down with him in the staff booth at the back.

"My mother says you two have talked about us moving out there until the house is built. Did you think you might talk to me first?" His dark eyes flashed with anger. He made an effort to keep his voice down, which was helpful. Patrick was on duty in the restaurant. Amanda would take on the chef role today. Nancy and Danny were off.

"We talked about the idea of us living out there for the next few of months until Joe gets the house done, Chester." She kept her voice level and measured, in the hopes he would agree and it would be the end of the story, but no such luck.

"I don't want to move out there and you know why. I don't want to build the house but you intend to have your own way, right?" His thick dark hair fell across his eye. She admired how handsome he was on that day. She worried, for a second. She used to get distracted by his looks, although such a circumstance hadn't occurred in a long time.

"We need to get out of town. If you weren't such a flirt, I might find life a bit easier, Chester." She bent forward and hissed this last part. He leaned away from her, like he wanted to force himself right through the back of the booth. "You might as well get used to the idea of moving. I gave our notice to Enterprise Investments and told them we would be gone the end of this month. Greta Seeley was approved to move in with her two girls. The position is a perfect fit for her. Now she won't have to go the service station each day to do their invoices and pump gas when they're short-handed." She could feel all the details come out of her in a puff.

"I guess you've got our life figured out." He snarled his whispered response. "Greta does, too. I've talked to her a couple of times already." Then his snarl sounded more like a sneer.

"You've talked with Greta? Why? I've made the arrangements." She sighed.

"Well, you wouldn't tell me what was going on."

All of a sudden, he was huffy. Typical, so she tried another tactic.

As he stood up to leave, she let her hand rest on the sleeve of his plaid shirt. "We need to be out near your parents, Chester. The kids will thrive. They won't have to be carted back and forth every day, once school's out. We can keep track of the build and have more time at home." She tried to appeal to the part of him who still wants to be a father and a family man.

"Okay. Okay." He relented. "But Joe Dodd better get his ass in gear and build the place sooner than later. I do not want to be under my parents' roof for more than a couple of months. You talk to Gaby. Make sure they're on time."

Amanda examines the samples laid out around her. *I guess I can't make too many more changes or we could be past Christmas when we try to get construction finished.*

After a quick shower, she tidies up, jumps into her Toyota, and flies down the main drag in Hayworth toward the diner. Perhaps, after lunch service is done, she can sneak away and have a quick discussion with Gaby. Chester was right. She needs to push for work to start sooner than later. As much as she loves Borys and Tesia Wolski, and as convenient as she expects residence with them will be, she wants to move into her new house more than she can explain.

****

Most of the day has been a blur. Danny has been busy at the grill and Patrick has taken care of the dishwasher. She wanted to get a new unit but Patrick became almost apoplectic, like she was about to scrap his best friend. He found an appliance guy and the two of them gave old Bertha an overhaul. Patrick says she's as good as new. As long as she washes the dishes well enough to keep the health inspector satisfied, Amanda has more pressing issues with which to occupy her time.

The phone rings three times before she can answer. "Hayworth Diner. Amanda speaking."

"Hi, Amanda. Will you and Chester be home tonight? I'd like to pop in and review a few questions regarding the Roz Dover case." Amanda knows the voice on the other end belongs to Constable Fiona Werbowski. She has been involved in the investigation since Roz first disappeared. The woman is like a terrier with a bone.

"Yes, we'll be home, Fiona, but I don't arrive until handy eight. Will I be too late?" She knows her sigh is audible when it reverberates down the phone line.

"Not at all." Fiona is the personification of patience. "I called Chester at work and they thought he was there with you on a coffee break. Is he there?"

"No." Amanda feels a hot flush creep across her cheeks. "I can't imagine where he would be. My father-in-law picked Mason up today. I expected Chester to be here for supper, before he went out to the farm to get the kids."

"No matter. He might be out on an errand for the dealership. I'll come over about eight, okay? You tell Chester I have a few questions to clarify about the investigation."

"No problem, Fiona, but he doesn't have information for you. He went out on a call and then came home. Gave a couple from the hotel a boost. They left their lights on, maybe? I can't remember the details. The whole episode was a long time ago." She imagines her words tumbling out of her face and into the mouthpiece of the phone.

"I know, Amanda, but any little detail could help."

Her fingers shake as she dials the Ford dealership. "Is Chester there? This is his wife, Amanda."

"No, Amanda. He received another telephone call a half hour ago and I told that person to check with you. Can I get him to call when he gets back?"

"Yes, please!" Her voice sounds like she's gasping for air.

"I imagine he'll have work lined up. The boss isn't happy when he goes out to the diner for coffee. He's been off a lot lately."

"Thanks. I'll tell him to stay in for coffee. Give him my message, okay?" When she replaces the receiver, her hand shakes. Chester rarely comes to the diner for coffee—maybe once a month. Another flush creeps across her cheeks. *He better not be up to his old tricks again.*

****

"Chester! What is going on? Where were you today? Fiona Werbowski called. She will be at the apartment at eight o'clock to ask you more questions. God, Chester!" Amanda's voice is barely above a whisper as she sputters into the phone at her husband.

Chester's response is benign. "I've been here most of the day. I ran out to do an errand. Clerical thought I went to the diner. They always seem to think if I'm not here, I'm at the diner. Relax. What did Fiona say she wanted?"

Amanda gulps twice as she tries, with little success, to harness her anxieties into some semblance of control. "She said she wants to review questions, whatever the hell that means. Where were you, anyway?"

"Come on, Amanda. Don't worry." His voice is rolling and soft, his standard attempt to pacify her. The approach works most of the time, but pressure has started to creep under what she has always perceived as her thick skin. She wants to get their house built; to get out on their land; to make this business of Roz Dover disappear.

"Okay. Will you come here for supper or go out to your mom's?"

"I'll go have supper with the kids before I come back into town."

She heaves a sigh of relief.

"Will you call Mom and let her know? I'll get the kids ready for bed. By the time you get home and Fiona arrives, the chores will be done. Don't worry," he repeats.

Amanda sighs. "Okay. There isn't a question she can ask that you haven't already answered. God, Chester, will this ever end?"

"See you at eight. Must run, Amanda." The dial tone sounds in her ear before she has a chance to say good bye. Her eyes settle on the picture of the children, perched on the top shelf above the rows of glasses and cups. They have their backs to the camera. Mason has his arm around Melanie. All this is for them.

****

When Amanda pulls into the lot behind The Station, Fiona Werbowski's patrol car is already parked beside Chester's truck. Since there's no sign of the service vehicle, Amanda is reassured Chester isn't on call. She makes her way to the door of their basement apartment.

The Station is perched on the side of a hill that leads down to a creek which runs through town—in effect, the elevation creates a walk-out suite which serves as the manager's residence. The apartment isn't fancy, but the space has served them well. Nevertheless, she will be happier when the children each have a room of their own, and she and Chester have their own bathroom. Not long now.

Amanda comes through the door to see Fiona at the kitchen table. She's dressed in cotton pants and a T-shirt with a light jacket over top. "Hi! I think I only managed to beat you here by a couple of minutes. Long day?"

"Not bad." Amanda checks Chester's face for a telltale sign, but it's blank. Amanda understands this particular expression has become a habit. He presents his handsome, bored, blank face when he doesn't want anyone to know what's on his mind. Chester has created a mask for himself. "Can I get you a drink, Fiona? Tea? Coffee? Is Sean out in the car? I didn't notice on the way in. Are you off?" *Stop talking!*

"Nothing to drink, thanks. Nice to get out of the uniform every now and then, but my business is sort of official, even though I'm here on my own."

Amanda glances at Chester again, but his expression is more obtuse than ever. "What can we do for you, Fiona?"

"The primary investigators have told me they've learned a little more about the evening Roz Dover vanished." She turns her attention to Chester. "You've told us you received a service call. What vehicle did you take out?"

Chester's answer is immediate. He does not even glance at Amanda before he blurts out, "The service truck. I'm sure I've told you before."

"You have, but a witness has suggested you might have taken your old truck out instead. Do you remember, Amanda?"

"I thought he took the service truck. A witness? Maybe they thought they recognized Chester's old Ford and assumed Chester was the driver."

"You could be right." Fiona pats the bun at the nape of her neck. "You didn't go out, did you Amanda?"

"What? With a toddler? I was three or four months pregnant with Melanie and sick as a dog twenty-four seven. Where would I need to go?" She hears her anxiety. She swallows, hard.

Fiona's expression is noncommittal. "Oh, I don't know. Maybe you took Mason for a drive to put him to sleep? We thought if you were out about the time Roz went missing, you might remember if you saw someone else, or her, for that matter."

"Don't you think, Fiona, if I had seen Roz, I would have told you by now? Come on. You know us. I wouldn't hold back an important detail." She can't help herself. "Who's the witness who seems to think they saw Chester's truck? Anyone we know?" She struggles to keep her voice calm.

"I can't reveal a name, Amanda, but no one has accused you of a crime. We can only hope someone will remember if they saw something."

"Well, Fiona, as much as I would love to help you, there isn't a scrap of information I can contribute." Chester leans toward Fiona just enough for his dark hair to fall over one eye, as he presents the perfect movie star pose.

Although Amanda assumes she isn't much interested in men, the cop blushes anyway. Chester has this effect on women—all women.

"Okay. Well, I've taken up enough of your time. Today has been a long one for everyone, I imagine. I have to say this, though. If you think of anything— even someone who might have an old truck like yours—let me know. We do not intend to stop the search. I think everybody has figured this out after three years."

As she takes a few steps toward the door, Chester reaches out and touches her shoulder. "We're behind you, Fiona. The whole community is behind you." He gazes deep into her eyes. Amanda thinks the cop wants to squirm like a mouse held upside down by the tail, but she maintains her composure and wishes them both a good night.

****

"You were cute." Amanda can't stop the sarcasm as it creeps out. She doesn't try.

"Settle down, Amanda. I have to pour on the charm. It's my secret weapon." He swaggers across the open expanse in the living area and rests a perfect and proportioned square hand on her arm. His hands are always clean. He wears gloves when he works—surgical ones like doctors wear. He prides himself on his clean hands despite his career as a mechanic. "It always works on you."

"Not anymore. Your charm has worn thin, Chester. I want to go check on the kids. Did they go to bed okay? Mason has been cranky the last few days. He wants to stay up later than his sister and he has a point. I'll be glad when they each have their own room." She successfully deflects the conversation, extricates herself from her husband's touch, and pads into the children's room on stocking feet.

She stands in the semi-darkness and watches her children sleep. Mason and Melanie are the best part of her life. She thinks back to her miserable existence in the child welfare system after her parents were killed in a car accident when she was nine. No one, not even her grandparents, wanted her. She learned to expect zero; to take care of herself; to survive despite the challenges. It took her a long time to trust Chester, and even after the trust was built, there have been big obstacles. She married him before she was divorced from her first husband. A mountain of paperwork and the financial support of her old friend and former resident, Ben Tullis, were both required to extricate her from the mess.

The children are pure. They have no ugly history. They are unspoiled by life's inequities and sudden tragedies. Her eyes tear up and her throat burns when she thinks she could lose her children; of them forced to repeat her history. She swallows hard and brushes her eyes with the back of her hand.

"Tea?" Chester has already boiled the kettle. He holds up a box of teabags and pouts in the way he does. Her heart lurches a little.

She nods, unable for the moment to get out a word.

"I suppose we have to get all this crap packed up." Chester's remark is more of a question than a statement.

"I know you don't want to live out of town, but we have to. Your father bought the land. It was cheap because nobody wants the property but us. We have to move ahead, Chester. The details are falling into place."

Chester's face doesn't reveal his thoughts. "I guess, since you have the money, you get the say. Right? And it isn't 'us' that wants the old farm, it's you."

"No! Stop! Your father bought the property. If you have a bone to pick, talk to him. We need to be out there; to be closer to them. The property will protect us in the end."

"I don't know where you get such an idea. Roz Dover's car was found out there. Cops like Fiona will never give up, Amanda. We will have them under foot for the rest of our lives. You know it. I know it."

"Well, we can't turn back now. The contract has been signed and Joe will start the basement soon. I don't want us to change our minds, Chester. I want to be out there where we can protect the property, even if it means we put up with periodic visits from the RCMP. We seem to have managed okay this far."

She sips her tea and gazes over the rim at him. One of her primary functions will be to manage her husband; to keep him on the straight and narrow.

Chapter 12

Patrick

Patrick has been at the diner since the doors opened at eight o'clock. The day has begun to heat up already, which is unusual for late June. The hot weather in the north is most often reserved for August. He opens the windows in a couple of booths. Amanda isn't thrilled when the windows are up. She says the dust from the parking lot creeps in and she's right, but he and Danny need the breeze. The back door has been open since they arrived. He can feel the fresh air brush his skin as it drifts through the pass-through to the kitchen.

"Breeze feels good." Danny places two full breakfasts on the counter for Patrick to deliver to the middle-aged couple seated near the front door. Lyle Smythe and his wife, Dottie, come in every Saturday for a late breakfast. Amanda advertises how they serve breakfast anytime of day and customers like the option.

"Here we go, folks, hot and ready. Anything else I can get you?" Dottie isn't all there. Patrick makes eye contact and graces her with a kind expression. She's wearing a trench coat despite the current weather conditions. Her hair seems mussed, like she didn't comb it when she got out of bed. Her nails are dirty. Lyle is sort of polished for a farmer. His clothes are clean and his hair is combed. Maybe Dottie won't wear clean outfits; won't let Lyle help her. Patrick doesn't know.

Lyle nods his thanks and points to his coffee cup. Dottie plays with her fingers in her lap. "Dottie, do you want more juice? Eat your breakfast. We came here to have our breakfast."

She doesn't respond to his request. Patrick picks up her fork and hands the utensil to her. She beams up at him and takes the fork.

"Thanks, Patrick. For whatever the reason, you have to give her the fork. God knows why." Lyle's voice always seems to hold a hollow and tearful ring these days. Current circumstances must be hard for him.

"Well, I'll be here next Saturday for sure, and I'll let you know then, if there's any Saturday I'm scheduled to be off. Amanda's been pretty busy with her house and the move, and we don't have the shifts yet. I expect she's gonna be gone a lot and we'll have more hours." He starts to turn. "I'll go get the coffee pot."

As he gets back to the Smythe's table, the bell sounds and Chester swaggers into the restaurant. "Hi there, Patrick. Came for a break and a cup. Coffee fresh?"

"The coffee's always fresh, Chester. You know that." Patrick controls an urge to become a little offended. "I'll be right back with the pot. Wanted to warm up Mr. Smythe."

"No rush. I don't have to be anywhere in a hurry."

"I thought this was your weekend to move. Amanda said she wouldn't be around. Danny has to work a double and Nancy will be here by noon." Patrick's anxiety bubbles up. He takes a breath and tries to relax. He moves behind the counter and reaches for a mug off the glass shelf. He keeps his eyes down—a bad habit he has managed to break, for the most part, but Chester makes him uncomfortable. His behaviour becomes worse when he tries not to let his apprehension show.

"Oh, Queen Amanda has every detail organized. I figured I was in the way. Took the kids out to the farm and came back here. She doesn't need me."

"Won't she want your help? Your truck? She can't do the move alone." Ideas flash through Patrick's mind like strobe lights. *How can I help? What can we do? Should we close the diner and go over there?*

"No need to worry, kid. She hired real movers. Most of our stuff has to be stored in one of Dad's barns, and she has a crew to wrap and pack. It's what happens when you have money, I guess."

His tone is somewhere between envy and annoyance. Patrick can imagine how Chester would resent Amanda's money. He's probably happy, though, that she can afford to hire help and he's off the hook.

"Are you here for breakfast?" As the question leaves his mouth, a group of five women tumble in the door. They all giggle and chat at once. Patrick runs to grab a chair tucked into a corner for such an event, and deposits it at the end of one of the booths so the five can sit together. They squeal their delight as he drops menus at each place and tells them he'll be back in a minute to set up and serve coffee. The noise level increases exponentially.

"Hey, Danny! How about an order of bacon and eggs? Give me fries, not hash browns, and Texas toast—not the whole wheat crap. I want white."

Patrick is stunned. Chester has every right to order his own breakfast. He could have walked into the kitchen and been respectful about it. He could have written his request on the pad left on the counter, and asked him to give his order to Danny. *What is wrong with him? When did he turn into such a jerk?* Patrick has always thought Chester was a flirt, but he's become a real jackass since Amanda came into her inheritance and bought the diner.

"I'll write up the order and take it back, Chester. No need to yell out to the kitchen." Patrick's annoyance is obvious.

"My place. I can do what I want. You're my employee. Don't get high and mighty with me."

There was a time when Patrick would have been so upset he would have rushed into the back and pretended the dishwasher needed to be loaded or the stainless steel counters required a scrub. He would have experienced a meltdown, for sure. After years of regular therapy, and a medication to control the voices as well as his nervousness, he is able to almost ignore Chester's remarks and carry on.

"Here's your bill, Mr. Smythe. Always nice to see you and the Mrs." He places the tab on Lyle Smythe's table. He then sets up the booth with the group of women, provides water, and asks about coffee. He returns to the counter, pours three coffees and prepares two teas, organizes the lot on a tray, and returns to deliver the drinks without a glance toward Chester. If Danny didn't hear him when he yelled, well he can wait for his damned breakfast. He turns on his heel, settles up with Lyle Smythe, and then returns to the table to take orders and accept a bit of teasing from the women.

"Hey, Patrick! You're lookin' good. How come we never see you at the tavern?"

"He's shy. Maybe he has a girlfriend."

"He's a man of mystery!"

"How about you sit down for breakfast with a few of your admirers,

Patrick? You know, the reason we eat here is because of you."

The women can have their fun. Patrick plays along. "Love to join you, ladies, but who would wait your table? What can I get you?"

"Maybe I can join you, if Patrick doesn't want to accept such a generous invitation."

The diner goes completely quiet, like the place is empty. Chester has turned around on his counter stool and simpers across at the four women seated in the booth. The fifth remains in the chair at the end, facing the window. Patrick doesn't miss her expression, as her lips form a tight bow and she widens her eyes as she communicates silently with her friends. Chester is losing his charm, as these women do not intend to react. "Too pretty; too conceited." Patrick hears the girl in the chair whisper.

Full of confidence once more, Patrick breaks the tension as he starts the process of taking orders. Ignored, for all intents and purposes, Chester spins back around and bangs his elbows down on the counter. "I guess I'll have to help myself to more coffee."

With the table of five settled to wait while Danny makes their breakfasts, Patrick heads into the kitchen with the orders. "Did you hear Chester when he hollered at you?"

Danny takes the latest order slip from Patrick. "Oh, I heard him. No slip, no order. Tell him you have to write it up before I can cook. It's my rule. God, what an asshole."

Patrick leans a little closer. "Did you hear him offer to keep the table of women company? They whispered they thought he was too pretty and too conceited. He can't ride on his charm and good looks with those ladies."

"No. They like to flirt but on their own terms. You handle them pretty well, though. They like you." Danny is amused as he teases Patrick and drops eggs on the grill.

"Okay, Chester. What did you want, again? Danny says he needs a slip. Since you didn't write one up yourself, you'll have to wait until after table four gets theirs. You don't care, eh? You said you weren't in any hurry." Patrick lets the words float in the air between them. His voice has a challenge embedded around the edges, as if he dares Chester to make a fuss.

"Like I said, bacon and eggs, fries, white Texas toast. Make the eggs scrambled." Patrick can see the cocky expression fade from Chester's pretty face.

Chester's on his fourth cup of coffee by the time the table of five leaves. Lunch preparations are ready to start. Patrick has cleared the tables and loaded old Bertha. "Chester, aren't you going to go help Amanda?" Patrick would like to see the back of Chester's white shirt leave the diner. He's tolerated the guy for long enough this morning.

"Nah. I'll meet her out at the farm around lunch time. Boy, am I gonna miss my views at The Station."

"Your views?" Patrick places heavy white china mugs, hot out of the dishwasher, back up on the shelves behind the counter. "What views do you have out the back of The Station you won't have when you live in a brand new house next door to your parents' place?"

"Audrey and Amy for starters. You're lucky to have a chance to see one or both of those two specimens every time you walk in or out, empty the garbage, or do your laundry." His eyes are sort of glazed over, like he's watching an event far off in the distance.

Patrick feels hot and uneasy again. He and Audrey are good friends. He would like them to be more than friends, but he lacks experience and doesn't want to offend her or risk the relationship they have now. Dr. Wilkerson suggested he tell Audrey what he thinks. He hasn't worked up the courage. Amy is Cheryl Nadler's daughter. In an instant, Patrick realizes his suspicions are true. Chester likes to ogle young girls. He's like a dirty old man, and he's only in his mid-thirties as far as Patrick knows. He's given Audrey the creeps since she moved in, but Patrick thought her feelings might be a function of her illness. He should have trusted her.

Chester continues to talk. "Maggie Woodward isn't too bad either except she's a loony tunes. I guess she's off the market, anyway. I see that cop, Sean Knox, sniffing around a lot. I expect they're an item."

Patrick can't help himself. "Aren't you kind of off the market yourself, Chester? You're a married guy with two kids."

"Oh, I'm what I call 'an observer'. It doesn't cost to have a gander; to daydream. I like to see a girl blush and get all coy, like she's gonna jump out of her jeans right in front of me. Now, there's some fun."

"Like the women who were here for breakfast? Like those women?" Patrick can't help himself. He wants to see how the guy will react when he's cornered.

"Well, they're a little older, and most of them are married." His face starts to turn a pale pink.

"Maybe you're losin' your touch, Chester. They didn't have any trouble turnin' on the charm with me." He continues to wipe the mugs before he places each one on the glass shelf. When he glances up, he catches a glimpse of Danny, standing in the kitchen with his arms crossed, a grin on his big round face as he listens to every word.

****

Patrick finally gets home from the diner, after he stays to help Nancy with dinner service. Audrey pops through the doorway of Number Four when he gets to the landing on his way up to Number Six.

"Hi. I thought you would never get here," she whispers.

"Hi. How are you? I stayed extra to work with Nancy. Amanda moved today."

"Can you come in? I need to ask you a question. I'll make us tea."

Patrick would walk across town to have tea with Audrey. She doesn't have to invite him twice. "Okay." He follows her into her apartment.

The décor isn't a lot different than when she moved in back in November of last year. It is Spartan, like his apartment. Audrey doesn't make a lot of money. Her income goes for rent, for independence, for freedom from the constant supervision of her parents ever since her diagnosis. Patrick understands, as does Maggie, downstairs. When mental illness has dominated your life and you find you need to depend on others for your stability, the biggest challenge is to live alone and take responsibility for your own decisions. There is always the fear you'll make a mistake and end up back where you were, but you have to carry on. You have to prove you can function on your own. Help is okay, but on your own terms, not forced.

"Chester scares me." Her voice is soft and her back is to him at the counter as she pours boiled water into two flowered mugs.

Patrick hears her words but wants to see her face when they talk. He still has trouble judging people by words alone. He needs to see faces. He hates the telephone. "Wait until we are both here in the living room and we can talk, Audrey." He gets up off the chair. "I'll come get my tea."

He's shocked as he approaches her. Tears stream down her pale face. Her hands shake. Her hair is tied back so tight, her eyes appear slanted instead of round. He isn't sure what to do, but he takes a risk she won't be offended or worse yet, scared, and opens his arms.

She collapses into him and starts to cry with a vengeance; big gulps of crying; wet cries that soak through his short-sleeved plaid cotton shirt. He pats her back. She shakes inside her baggy sweatshirt. Despite the warmth in the air, she shivers.

"Come on. Tell me what's happened, Audrey." He leads her to the couch and returns to the kitchen to retrieve the tea, which he places on the coffee table as he sits down beside her. "Talk to me. Are you scared you're getting sick again?"

They settle in, side by side on the sofa for what seems like forever to Patrick. His mug of tea gets cold. She holds his hand and he becomes aware she is more than a friend. He forces himself to focus on the issue at hand. Once she calms down to the point where her sobs are moderately controlled, he asks again. "Are you starting to get sick?"

She frowns. "I don't think so. This is real, Patrick. Chester turned up at my door late this afternoon. The movers left and I thought he and his family were gone. I went to the door. Amy was supposed to be here after work. Dodd's closes at three-thirty today."

"Tell me what happened, Audrey." Patrick's voice is soft but his insides quake. His stomach churns. "Did he hurt you?"

"No, but he scared me. He told me, since Amanda's either out at the farm or at the diner most of the time, he and I would be able to visit whenever we wanted. He said he would be able to come over after work. I don't understand." To Patrick, she's like a lost puppy. "Chester is married to Amanda. They have cute little children. He has a family who loves him. What does he want with me?"

"What happened, Audrey?"

"Amy turned up. She was late, but she turned up. When she opened the door, I yelled to her. Then she knew I was here and Chester said he should get out to the farm. He winked at Amy when he left. See, I know I didn't imagine him. Amy was here. She can tell you he was here. She thinks he's cute, but he frightens me."

"If you want, I will talk to Amanda, Audrey. She needs to know what he's up to. She's been so busy with her house plans and the diner, she likely hasn't noticed."

"Oh, no! Amanda would be really upset. She has more than enough on her mind. They don't live here anymore. Maybe he won't be around much now.

Let's wait and see."

Patrick is reluctant to follow Audrey's wishes. His suspicions about Chester start to rumble around again. *Chester was out the night Roz disappeared. I suspect Charlene saw him. Why don't the RCMP do something?*

He pats Audrey's hand as he gets up. "Let's get some hot tea and change the subject, Audrey. What did you do with your Saturday off? Are you off again tomorrow? Maybe we could go for a walk in the afternoon. I don't have a shift, but we could go to the diner for tea and pie. Whaddya say?"

When he hears her quiet response and knows she is feeling better, a rush of warmth spreads through him. He feels contented from tip to toe.

Chapter 13

Audrey

Her hikes to and from the hospital provide much needed opportunities to think; to mull over occurrences; to calm her mind. Life with Amy as a roommate is like trying to survive a hurricane; always in the path of the storm. Amy is vivacious, funny, very chatty, and an absolute slob. When Audrey is home from work, she spends much of her time cleaning the bathroom and washing dishes. She has requested Amy help out, in a valiant attempt to make their living arrangement work for both of them.

She discussed the situation with her mother again on the phone last night, while Amy was gone on her run with Cheryl. Iona Baranski was no nonsense with her advice. "Be assertive. Be strong. Tell her to do her share or she will have to move back across the hall."

"But the extra money helps a lot, Mom!"

"I know, but come September, she will return home to go to school and you will have to make do without. Besides, if she moves back in with her mother, won't she save more money for school?"

"I don't think rent matters. Cheryl is the one who said she would pay me. Maybe Amy doesn't even have to use her own money."

"What about your friend Patrick? Have you seen much of him since Amy moved in?" Audrey knows her mother is anxious for her to make and keep friends.

"I talk and visit with him when we have days off together and Amy is at work. She's met him. She flirts. I don't think he's interested, but who knows?"

"Invite him out to the farm for supper next weekend when you're both off, Audrey. Does he have a car?"

"Yes, his father gave him a little car a few years ago. He walks most of the time, but he uses his car every once in a while and keeps it parked out back."

"Well, invite him to supper. What about Sunday? If not, we can schedule another day. What do you think?"

"I'll ask him, Mom. What about Dad? Will you talk to him? I don't want him to make a big deal about me and a boyfriend. Dad will want to know if we plan to get married."

"Don't worry. I'll handle your father. You talk to Patrick and let me know, okay?"

Absorbed as she is in her thoughts, she's surprised to see The Station come into sight. She expects Amy to be home anytime now, too. She tries to think of a way she can speak to Patrick so Amy won't discover the topic of conversation is a supper invitation out to the farm. She sighs. As much as she hates to admit the truth, she still does not trust Amy.

There she is. She watches Amy climb out of a white pickup truck. The vehicle is very similar to Chester's. Audrey is puzzled. The Wolskis have already moved out to his parents' place while their house is under construction. Greta Seeley and her kids moved into Number One a few days ago, earlier than expected. She slows down and observes from a distance. She sees Amy lean over close to the driver. Did she kiss him? She couldn't have kissed him. Audrey is certain she has seen behaviour she should not have seen.

Amy jumps down and trots to the front door of The Station. She turns to wave as the vehicle backs out of the front lot. Maybe the truck resembles Chester's but it belongs to someone else. Maybe Chester sold his truck. After she is sure Amy has gone upstairs to the apartment, she increases her pace.

"Hi. You're home early. I thought Dodd's was open until five." Audrey places her purse and keys on the kitchen counter. She leans toward the spare bedroom and the chaos which is Amy, as she elevates her voice to be heard above the raspy strains of Phil Collins as he belts out "One More Night" from Amy's cassette player.

Amy skips out of her room, changed into miniscule jean shorts and a fluffy blouse. Audrey thinks she could be Daisy Mae from the *Li'l Abner* comics.

"Tell Cheryl I can't go on a run with her today. I have a date." She winks at Audrey who has become uncomfortable again.

"Amy. You tell your mother what you're up to. I'm not your messenger." She thinks about her own mother's advice. "Who is your date with anyway?"

"Secret information." Amy winks and puts her index finger across her lips. "If you don't know, you can't tell."

Audrey decides she would not be wise to suggest the mystery man is Chester. It could have been any old truck. What does she know about trucks?

They exchange looks when they both hear Cheryl arrive home and place her key in the lock of Number Five. Audrey firmly shakes her head. "You go see her yourself. I won't do your dirty work." With a determination she discovers and is surprised she possesses, she turns toward the refrigerator and starts to pull out salad ingredients for supper. "Will we eat together, or will you have supper with your mystery man?"

"Oh, I'll eat first. He said he would pick me up down by the Creek Tavern about seven-thirty."

"Okay, I have hamburgers already made. You can toss the salad after you go talk to Cheryl. Why doesn't he come here to get you? I don't understand."

Amy graces her with yet another secretive little wink. "We want our relationship to be private. No need for the whole town of Hayworth to be in our business."

"You mean you don't want your mother to know." Her voice is soft but her point is clear. Audrey feels secure in the knowledge her own mother has encouraged her to invite a boy out to the farm for supper. They might not like Patrick after they meet him, but at least she won't have to sneak around and try to keep a secret from her parents. Then again, she can hardly wait until Amy leaves in order to go upstairs to Patrick's apartment, or call him at the diner, to invite him to dinner next Sunday.

"What's your expression all about?" Amy questions Audrey who is unable to camouflage her own delight right now.

"I can't hide information from my family like you can."

Amy flounces her shoulders. "I'll be back in a minute after I tell Cheryl I don't want to run." She turns around and points the pink manicured nail of her index finger in Audrey's direction. "And you keep quiet. Don't breathe a word, okay?"

"Don't worry, Amy. I don't have details to share." Although she's now almost certain Chester brought Amy home.

****

"Do you have to work on Sunday, Patrick?" After Amy raced to the Creek Tavern, Audrey went upstairs to knock on Patrick's door but there was no answer. She then screwed up enough courage to call the diner.

"Until two in the afternoon, Audrey. What's on your mind?"

"My mom wants to know if you would like to go out to the farm with me for supper this Sunday." *Why do I sound so formal. What is the matter?*

"Out to the farm? For supper? With your parents?"

"Yes. Yes. Yes." Audrey beams. "They come and get me on either Saturday or Sunday every weekend, after I know which day I have to work. I have this Sunday off. Will you come?"

"Sure. We can drive out in my car. My old second-hand Pontiac Acadian still works fine but I don't drive much. I take good care of it, though. Dad managed to teach me a few tricks." He sounds proud and apologetic at the same time.

Audrey tries to reassure him. "Amy is kind of a challenge to live with and Mom thought I might like to spend extra time away from her, and she included you."

"Can I contribute a pie, maybe?"

"Don't even think about pie! She will have the house full of food. Dad will be disappointed he can't come to pick me up in the grain truck, but he'll survive." She giggles.

"Maybe I wouldn't mind a trip in the grain truck."

Audrey hopes he's teasing. "We can talk later about the time, but I'll tell my mom you'll come. You'd better get back to work." She hesitates before she lets him go. "Patrick?"

"Yeah?"

"Does Chester still drive an old Ford truck?"

"An old rattletrap 150, Audrey."

"He's never traded? Still the same old white or beige one he had?"

"That's the one. Why do you want to know?"

"Oh, I wondered if I saw him here at The Station. I wasn't sure. Talk to you later."

****

Audrey responds to a short and crisp series of knocks on her door later in the evening. She already knows Cheryl Nadler is on the other side. She heard her door open and close and the pad of her sheepskin mules as she trotted across the hall.

"Is Amy around?"

"Hi Cheryl. Come in, please. No, Amy isn't here. She went out earlier—right after supper."

"She came over and said she didn't want to go for our run, but she never let on she would be out. Do you know what she's up to? Did she have a date with someone I should know about?"

Audrey examines the social worker, mother, and compulsive woman who has been her neighbour since she moved into The Station. Conflicts spin around in her mind, like leaves in an autumn wind storm. She doesn't want to alienate Cheryl. She wants to be friends with her. She doesn't want Amy to be mad at her. She wants the rent to be half paid until the end of August. "Amy said she made plans to meet someone or a group. I don't know who. I wasn't invited."

"Well, her behaviour was rude, Audrey. Did she say when she'd be back?"

"No. I've been watching TV and was about to call my mother when you knocked. Do you want me to tell her to go over to your apartment when she gets home? I doubt she'll be late."

"How can you be sure if you don't know who she's with or where she went?" Cheryl's tone is abrupt. Audrey, although she tries to remain motionless, takes a small step back from the open door. "I'm sorry, Audrey. This isn't your fault. I was afraid of what would happen if I let her rent your spare room. She's not as mature and responsible as you are. She has been indulged most of her life." Cheryl blushes.

Audrey thinks the older woman has said more than she intended. "Mature and responsible? Me? I depend on my parents a lot, Cheryl."

"You are a good kid and a good friend to both Amy and me. Could you tell Amy to pop over when she gets home? I won't take up any more of your time, Audrey."

"I'll tell her. Talk to you later, Cheryl."

"Have a nice evening, Audrey."

After she closes and locks the door, Audrey makes herself a cup of chamomile tea and calls her mother. "Patrick said he would come on Sunday and we could drive out in his Pontiac Acadian." Audrey knows very little about cars, but she tries to remember a make and model once she hears the description. "What will you cook?"

"I thought I might roast a duck. Do you want to come out before Sunday and help me make perogies? Do you think he likes cheese-cake?"

Audrey giggles. "I think Patrick will be fine with whatever you make. If Dad comes in to get me, I can come out Saturday after work. We can have a chat."

Iona's chuckle trickles down the phone line and sounds like water tumbling over pebbles in a brook. "Your dad will be at the hospital at three. See you then."

"Bye, Mom."

****

By the time Ivan Baranski delivers Audrey to the family kitchen, Iona has piled sauerkraut to cool on a dinner plate, and the potatoes are already mashed and fluffy in a bowl. She is up to her wrists in dough she is blending with sour cream. Her long hair, beginning to sparkle with silver at the temples, is tied back in a chignon reminiscent of the 1930s. Her nod to modern trends is acknowledged by the blue jeans she wears with her pink cotton blouse, partially obscured under a bibbed floral apron.

The back door creaks, and she is obviously delighted to see her child. Pure love rises in her eyes. "You are in time to grate the cheeses and mix them into the potatoes. I decided to make two kinds for tomorrow. He might not like sauerkraut. Not everybody does."

Audrey covers the space between the door and the kitchen table used as a work island in the centre, with two strides. She hugs her mother sideways around her shoulders, and then reaches for the other apron draped across a ladder back chair at the end of the table. "You can roll out the dough, Mom, and I'll put the filling in—like an assembly line!" Audrey loves to work with her mother. She has spent the day in a kitchen, but it wasn't like this. Iona has always made the work seem easy and fun, even when Audrey was a little girl.

"You think you can give your mother instructions, do you? Come now, let's see how we do. I want us to get them boiled and in the fridge. Then, tomorrow, all I have to do is fry them in lots of butter. Yes?"

"Most definitely yes. There'll be enough for an army. May I take a few home tonight to fry for my supper—like a taste test?" She giggles as she places filling by the spoonful on each round. Her mother comes along behind her and moistens the edges of the dough, folds it over on the filling to make a little packet, and then squeezes the edges firmly together by pressing them with a fork. The water has come to a gentle boil and they drop their creations into the pot for about four minutes. Audrey handles the timer while Iona turns the perogies and, when satisfied with how they look, lifts them out with a small sieve designed for the purpose. By the time she removes the last perogi from the pot, they have about six dozen cooling on paper towel-lined cookie sheets, ready to be fried tomorrow.

With big sighs, they both sit down at the table. Audrey doesn't want to stay for supper tonight. She wants to go home and prepare for her day tomorrow. "What did you want to chat about, Audrey? Does Amy still cause you worry?"

"Funny you should ask, Mom. I think Amy is seeing someone. I don't know who. She went out to meet him one night this week. He wouldn't come to The Station, but picked her up near the tavern. She didn't tell her mother."

"This is not your business, Audrey. Amy is over eighteen. She can do as she pleases and tell her mother whatever she wants. Do not let yourself be concerned."

"I know, but I think I saw her with Chester Wolski, the husband of the woman who owns the diner and used to manage The Station. You remember them? They have two little kids."

"Yes, of course. He is very handsome. Correct? What did you see?"

"I saw a truck like his, parked at the front of The Station. Amy climbed out and I am almost certain she leaned over and kissed the driver. It was on the same night she went to meet someone at the tavern. She came home late. Cheryl was mad she didn't go over when she got home, but it was after eleven and a work night."

"Do you know for sure the driver was Mr. Wolski, Audrey?"

Audrey focuses on her tea and avoids her mother's eyes. "I couldn't swear on the Bible, but I think so."

"What kind of truck was it?"

"The truck was a white one—a Ford and kinda' old."

"There are lots of old white Ford pickups around, Audrey. This is northern Alberta." Iona's expression is indulgent. She leans across the flour-covered table and pats her daughter's hand. "You pay no attention to Amy. She has her own life. As long as she pays her rent and half the bills, don't you worry. Now, I need to get this mess cleaned up and make a cheese-cake before your father and I eat. How many perogies do you want for your supper?" Before Audrey replies, she continues. "I will send home six of each. You can freeze what you don't want. Ivan! Can you take Audrey back to town while I clean up and start dessert?"

Ivan Baranski lumbers into the kitchen. He removes his reading glasses, and places his copy of the latest edition of *The Western Producer* on the counter near the coffee pot, which appears to be the one clean piece of kitchen real estate in the vicinity. "Not gonna stay for supper, my girl? Looks like good eatin' to me."

"You hold your horses, sir. This is for tomorrow and you might get a fried egg sandwich tonight."

Ivan chortles. His barrel frontage sways with the effort. "The girl has a sample of tomorrow's fare. What about me?" He fakes a pout, which certainly does not suit a man of his imposing stature.

Iona's expression is filled with love. Tendrils of silver detach from her chignon. "Take Audrey home and I will see what I can do. Now git, the pair of you. I have more work to do yet, if we want to entertain Audrey's friend tomorrow."

On the way back to town, Ivan makes a valiant attempt to grill his daughter, but Audrey can see what he's up to. "He's a friend and neighbour, Dad. He's been very nice to me. Mom was the one who suggested dinner. You have to promise you won't give him a hard time."

Chapter 14

Gaby

The Wolski project is moving right along. It's mid-July and crews are laying out the foundation, installing the septic, and finishing the power connection. The actual dig won't start on the wooden basement for another couple of weeks, but Gaby considers them to be ahead of schedule by a few days. She expects the sub-trades will be able to handle the load while she and Joe take a couple of days off to get married the end of next month.

She sets pretty flowered napkins on the dining room table and places a sandwich plate, laden with butter tarts, down in the centre. Joe is on a job site tonight to double-check elevations, while she has a meeting with Ronny Étang and Fiona Werbowski. A firm decision about the fundraiser ball for this year has become imperative. Will they revert to the normal October date, or stick with February? The ball was postponed from October, 1984 to February, 1985 because of Ronny's abduction last summer. Everybody needed time to decompress, so they rescheduled for early in the New Year. This gave them lots of time to talk to donors, print tickets, and think of various ways to raise money for the shelter, a welcome diversion from a focus on Ronny's near-death experience.

Gaby hopes they can keep the February date. The schedule is slower for her at work. Besides, there are many more events in the weeks and months prior to Christmas. February is quiet in a small town like Hayworth.

The doorbell rings and Gaby rushes to answer. The beveled glass reveals the stunning creature on the front step. Gaby still does a double-take each time she sees Ronny. Almost a year has passed since her ex-husband abducted her and kept her locked in an old cabin on John Fitzpatrick's property way out in the back of beyond, past the Petro-Canada Gas Station on the way to Carter River. When she came to Hayworth, Ronny tried to conceal her identity. She wore her hair as short as possible and dyed platinum blond. Not anymore.

The dark, long, and unmanaged curls of the woman who stands on the porch, tumble in all directions. She makes a feeble attempt to push strands behind her ears, but they jump out again. She giggles as Gaby approaches the door. Fiona, the police constable and community policing expert, stands behind her. Fiona is in street clothes and has her long, straight and dark hair pulled into a loose pony tail at the nape of her neck. Both women are in slacks and sweaters. The evening can develop a chill, even in July.

They push in, hugging, laughing, and both talking at once.

"Did you make these?" Fiona reaches for a sweet and a napkin as Gaby sets mugs of freshly brewed lemon tea in front of each woman.

"Yes. One of Joe's favourites. Help yourself."

"No need to offer twice. She's digging in!" Ronny nudges Fiona's shoulder.

Gaby doesn't miss the sensual comfort between the two. She gathers her thoughts. "The biggest issue is whether or not we plan for October or February. What do you think? Has anybody heard from donors or attendees?"

Fiona munches as she talks. "Regularly. The members like winter better than fall—not as busy. We agree. I think Ronny's abduction was fortuitous because we postponed. We would have never rescheduled otherwise."

"My abduction was convenient? This is your opinion? Eat up my girl. You may never get another meal at 15 Poplar Street!"

"Well, you know what I mean. Don't worry. Somebody will feed me if you won't."

The teases have an intimate quality. The conversation shared by the two women excludes Gaby, in that special way a couple has of communicating exclusively despite being in the company of others. Gaby understands. She and Joe are the same way.

"You two seem pretty cozy." Both women react with round eyes but don't respond. "Let's make our decision official and keep the ball in February. Are we in favour?"

Fiona and Ronny, in unison, share nods of confirmation with Gaby.

Ronny is all business. "Hayworth Printers will do the tickets again. Same arrangement as last year. If you remember, they add their logo to the bottom of each ticket along with the words 'courtesy of'. Seems fair to me. Once we have an exact date, I'll contact them. Then they'll have lots of time to do a print run when they have a spare slot."

Fiona rummages through a briefcase-like bag and produces a tattered list. "Here are the donors from last year. I've added a couple more businesses who contributed without being approached. I have three members in Carter River who will visit the businesses there to get their donations."

"How about I assign Amy to type us up a fresh list? We can make a few copies, assign who goes to which donor, and I'll manage the master sheet. I suppose we can start anytime, but I have a few commitments on my plate between now and late fall. We shouldn't have to do too much prior to mid-November, except for maybe Hayworth Printing, right?"

"I'll book the ballroom at the hotel. I don't imagine there will be much competition for a Friday in February, though. If we decide on February 15, we can have a Valentine's Day theme. What do you think?" Ronny, as manager at Segue House now, extends out to the community much more than she did prior to the episode with her ex-husband. She no longer hides herself, afraid someone from down east will recognize her.

The three women make up a schedule along with a list of priorities and responsibilities. They've done each task before. The chores have become routine. Gaby pours second cups of tea for each in turn and the conversation switches to what it always does—the disappearance of Roz Dover four years ago.

"I can't tell you too much. The investigators have interviewed the potential witness we talked about."

Gaby notices how Ronny seems to be aware of the identity of the witness, like Gaby herself is aware. Fiona must confide in Ronny.

"We have talked to other possible witnesses, but all we find are dead ends. Time is fast approaching for another community meeting. Maybe a new detail will turn up." Fiona sounds discouraged.

"I can't believe your potential witness had no information or observations. Was she asleep in her truck or what?" Gaby avoids the use of Charlene's name, in an attempt to respect Fiona's position. They talk around a lot of issues without a focus on names or places.

"We think she might have been mistaken, Gaby. When you work during the day and then sit up at night, weird thoughts happen. People go to sleep, yes, but they also imagine stuff. Memories become blurry over time." She nudges Ronny's shoulder. "Time we left for home. Work tomorrow for the three of us, right Gaby?"

****

The phone rings at ten o'clock the next morning. Amy answers, listens and tells Gaby there is a long distance call. Will she accept the charges from someone named Charlene Quinn in Nova Scotia?

Her first instinct is to refuse. Why would Charlene Quinn, in jail for murder, want or need to talk to her? Charlene stalked her for months. She was convinced Charlene killed Roz Dover. The horrible experience of sleepless nights, an investigation by the Canadian Counselling Alliance, the twist of fate which managed to get her out of her trouble—all this flashes before her eyes in the seconds she takes to decide to accept the call. Fiona hasn't detailed what Charlene said to the RCMP investigators who visited her and asked about what she saw the night Roz disappeared. Maybe Charlene will tell her. She nods up at Amy and pushes the flashing light on her phone.

"Amy, close the office door. Tell me if someone comes in." She knows she sounds abrupt. She knows she's tense. "Gaby Ridgway here, operator. I'll accept the charges."

"Hi, Gaby. Long time no talk. How're you doin'?"

"What do you want, Charlene?" She tries to keep her voice level; noncommittal. Her experience with Charlene Quinn was pivotal in her life. Her stomach churns. Her face and neck are flushed. She senses the symptoms of anxiety and stress, her constant companions from late June of 1981 until almost Christmas of that same year, as they return with a vengeance. Charlene was the reason she gave up family counselling and went into business with Joe. This decision was her silver lining at a time in her life when she began to question her own behaviour; when even her ethics were challenged.

"I have ten minutes. There are more rules in this place than you ever dreamed up for me in your therapy sessions." She titters. Is there a nervousness Gaby hasn't heard before? Charlene was always extremely confident. Even when she pouted and didn't get her own way, she never sounded hesitant.

"Get to the point, Charlene."

"Did the Werbowski cop tell you a detective came to see me a while back?"

"What for?" Gaby will not reveal any information, and sidesteps the question. There is an advantage in her awareness of how much Charlene prefers to talk about herself.

"Instead of me as the suspect in the disappearance of poor old Roz, they now think I might be a witness." She snickers. "In exchange for information, they said they would get me privileges. Boy, did I give them information."

"What do you want, Charlene?" Gaby forces her voice to remain calm. She might have been right. Charlene may well be a witness.

"I want you to know what I told the detective, because I don't think your friend the cop, and the rest of those idiot RCMP, will pay attention."

"I can't repeat what you tell me, Charlene. We've been through this."

"You're not my counsellor anymore. We can be friends and I can tell you whatever I want."

"We are not and will never be friends, Charlene. You reported me to the Canadian Counselling Alliance. You said I shared your personal information."

"Oh, I know you never went to the cops."

Her comment is so off-hand, Gaby finds it difficult to maintain control. Her complaint to the CCA and the resulting investigation were traumatic experiences in Gaby's life, second only to the deaths of her first husband and her parents years before.

"Pat, 'don't call me Pat, that's a girl's name', was the one who spilled the beans. I figured out it wasn't you. And Hayworth's hot psychiatrist, Rachel Wilkerson, started the ball rolling against me. I know every detail about what happened." Her voice is sticky and smooth, like honey mixed with motor oil.

Gaby, with a great deal more self-control than she thinks she has, repeats her question. "What do you want, Charlene?"

"Listen. I don't have much time. You know me better than anyone ever has. You can tell when I lie and you will know when I tell the truth. I saw two different trucks leave The Station the night Roz disappeared. I sat out front all evening after I left your place. I waited for Pat to get home. I told the detective how the Ford service truck went out and a few minutes later, Chester left in his truck. Maybe I was wrong. Maybe Chester was in the service truck and somebody else drove his pickup."

"What do you expect me to do with this, Charlene? If you told the police what you saw, then they can act on the information." She sounds very sure.

Fiona said she thought Charlene must have gone to sleep and imagined she saw the pickup truck leave the parking lot.

"I want you to tell your friend, Werbowski, I am positive I saw both trucks leave. Maybe someone else drove his pickup. Maybe Chester knows what happened to Roz but he wants to protect a buddy or somethin'. I have to go. Talk to the cops. Thanks for takin' the call, Gaby. I know you believe me." The phone line goes dead and in the sudden silence, the dial tone returns.

"I saw the light on the phone go out. Are you okay?" Amy peeks into the office, and keeps her voice to a whisper. "There's a couple out here who want to renovate their bathroom. I've shown them around while we waited for you."

Gaby, still confused about why Charlene chose to call, and whether or not the information she shared is critical, slowly and with an unusual effort, lifts herself out of the chair. *This is what it must be like when you're a hundred years old.* "I'll be along in a sec. Offer them a cup of coffee or tea, Amy."

****

Joe will be a little late—a piece of machinery broke down and needs to get welded before he comes home. No matter. She putters away in her kitchen, where she usually enjoys the quiet. Martha stirs on her pillow bed in the corner, eyes expectant and alert. "Don't worry, old girl. I'm a bit rattled. It's okay. Let's get you supper, and we'll go outside on the porch to wait for your papa."

As Gaby picks up the stainless steel bowls tucked into a corner of the kitchen, Martha gets up, stands, and waits with typical patience. Once her food and water are down, Gaby pours herself a glass of white wine, surveys what could well be described by any professional decorator as a magnificent great room, and sighs.

The kitchen is immense, with two islands and a walk-in pantry. The cabinets are custom designed by a friend and go right to the ceiling. The countertops are solid surface and in a rich taupe. They resemble crushed stone. The two couches positioned to flank the fireplace are slipcovered in white canvas. They are over-sized and plush. The dining room furniture is the suite she dragged from Ontario way back in 1977. There was never enough room for all of the pieces at 15 Poplar Street, but the heavy oak five-legged table, six chairs, and the ornate sideboard fit in fine here. The high ceilings could have served to swallow up every scrap of furniture, but they decided to cover them in western red cedar. The ceilings now serve to accentuate the space. The house gives her peace. Building this place and moving in with Joe were two of the best decisions she has ever made. The events where Charlene was involved played a significant role. Maybe she should thank her lucky stars, but unease wraps around her like a bulky sweater on a muggy day. She stifles an unexpected shiver.

Gaby and Martha wander out on to the front porch, or veranda as Gaby prefers to call the space. The view fills her eyes. The house is situated on a knoll. From a distance, the land appears flat and unassuming, but as you start to walk up the near kilometer-long driveway, the elevation not discernible to the naked eye, soon becomes clear. Joe bought this land years ago, when he decided to invest in Hayworth regardless of the economic forecasts which were most often doom and gloom. He brought her to view the property when it was a vast field of frozen stubble. As she sits in her rattan rocker, she can see all the way down the drive, past the subdivision growing steadily below them, and into the town itself. They own a considerable amount of land—five acres to be precise. No one will ever be able to smudge this picture.

Martha stands and lets out a tiny whimper. Joe's big blue monster of a truck has turned into the drive. He'll be here in a couple of minutes. She leaves Martha on the step and returns to the kitchen to pour him a glass of wine. She wants to tell Joe about her talk with Charlene Quinn. She thinks he might be cross with her because she accepted the call. She needs his advice about whether or not she should tell Fiona her impressions.

****

"You won't break a confidence if you tell Fiona what happened. Fiona might appreciate your observations."

"I thought the same, but I let on to Charlene that what she said didn't matter because I couldn't speak on her behalf or influence anybody."

Joe observes her over the rim of his wine glass. His frown is lopsided but his eyes twinkle. "You know, if you had asked me at the time, I would have said 'don't take the call'. If you took my advice, you wouldn't be in the glue now. Tell Fiona. Charlene's call won't matter in the grand scheme. Based on

Fiona's interview with the Wolskis, I think the RCMP figure Charlene Quinn is full of crap and I'm pretty sure I agree."

"Okay. I'll call Fiona." Gaby takes one last swallow from her glass and stands. "Barbecue? I have steaks in marinade and a salad already thrown together."

Chapter 15

Patrick

"How can you have a going away party for people who have already gone away?" Patrick wants ideas to make sense. Maggie and Rose have accosted him on his way upstairs to his apartment after work. Their plan doesn't add up.

"We wanted to have a July 1st party here at The Station but they were already moved and everyone was busy. Greta has settled in and she said we could have a barbecue out back for Chester, Amanda, and the kids this Sunday. We have presents for Mason and Melanie already." Maggie bounces up and down, unable to contain her excitement. Her long hair flies around her shoulders and she flips handfuls out of the way. Patrick absently thinks of Audrey and how she likes her hair tied back as tight as possible. Hair can tell you a lot about a person.

"I don't have to work Sunday, so I guess I can come." Patrick is hesitant, like always, but he knows he wants to go to the party with Audrey, if she is interested. Chester will be there, so he isn't sure if she will go. "What does Amanda say?"

"She will ask Nancy and Danny to take over in the diner and then they can come. We're excited because Greta has two kids around seven and four. They will be good company for Amanda's two." Rose is dressed in a nightie and housecoat. She sports a yellow plastic hair band. The northern summer sun still blazes through the front windows of both Number Two and Number Three as the sisters stand in the foyer with Patrick, at a little after eight o'clock in the evening.

"Do you want me to check with Audrey?"

Maggie cannot hide the little grin that flutters at the corners of her mouth. "Are you two an item?" She giggles.

"Now Maggie, leave Patrick alone. He can bring anyone he wants." She turns her attention back to Patrick. "Shall we invite her, first, and then the two of you can make your plans? Then she'll know she's included as part of The Station family. She's been here since before Christmas, but hasn't taken part in much with us. Does she spend a lot of time with her parents?"

"She works different shifts at the hospital and goes out to her parents' farm on the weekend for dinner. She's quiet." Patrick finds he's protective of Audrey's privacy for reasons he doesn't fully understand. "You invite her and then we'll see."

Maggie runs upstairs to Audrey's apartment. She sticks close to Patrick's heels. He can hear her knock on the door of Number Four as he hurries up the next flight to his own place. Audrey answers. He pauses for a second and listens to Maggie's muffled but enthusiastic introduction to the topic. Then he lets himself into the attic, as everyone refers to his apartment on the third floor.

The company of Audrey for the Wolski barbecue would be nice, but Patrick has serious concerns about whether or not Audrey will want to go. She is convinced Chester is involved with other women, and she seems most often threatened when he's around. He will promise not to leave her stranded. Chester won't stand a chance because he will remain close. They will be able to visit with other guests and avoid Chester Wolski if necessary.

They enjoyed such a good time when they ate supper out at her folks' place. Iona Baranski went overboard. Audrey couldn't wait to tell him how she helped with the perogies. She even said they could get together and make them one afternoon.

They arrived at the farm about four-thirty. Iona and Ivan met them at the door. Patrick liked them both right away. They are humble, hard-working, and kind immigrant farmers who have done whatever they could in their attempt to support their daughter. Both of her parents are tall and ample. Ivan's voice rolls and booms. Iona's is soft. They are both very direct—perhaps a cultural characteristic. "Tell us about your work." "Have you been in Hayworth long?" "Where did you come from?" "Who are your parents?" "Are you like Audrey and have to take pills every day?"

The last question was the hardest but Patrick replied to their directness in kind. "I was very sick for a long time. My mother was, too. She died when I was young." He avoided the story of her suicide and how he found her body. They wanted to know his story, but not the details. He could tell. "Her death changed me in many ways. Dr. Wilkerson says you have to treat schizophrenia like diabetes—not curable, but manageable if you're lucky enough to be able to stick to your medications and play by the rules. I think Audrey and I both stay on the straight and narrow, right Audrey?"

He could not miss the pure admiration in her eyes. He thinks the evening turned out better than she hoped. Now, if Chester doesn't get in the way, they might have another chance to go out together. Even if she has to work next Sunday, she'll be home by three in the afternoon.

Patrick stretches out on the navy blue leather sofa left to him by his friend Ben when she died. The television mutters away, but he finds it difficult to concentrate. He has left his door ajar enough to be able to hear when Maggie heads back downstairs after her talk with Audrey. He is patient. Patrick has learned patience over the last few years. A few minutes later, he detects two pairs of feet on the stairs. Maggie is on the way down to her apartment and Audrey is on the way up to his. He jumps to turn off the TV and makes his way to the door as her form appears in the opening.

"Can I go with you? I can't go by myself if *he* is there."

"Come on in, Audrey. I'll make us tea and yes, we can go together. I wanted to ask you."

She enters his spare, but clean and neat kitchen space. Years ago, Patrick kept no food in his apartment except cereal and ketchup packets. He has expanded over time and now could even fix a meal if pressed—at least breakfast with eggs and toast. He eats at the diner but grocery shops now, for more than sugary cereal and a quart of milk. He's proud of how far he's come.

She stands close to him. He can feel her bare arm brush the sleeve of his plaid shirt. He turns away from the pot, cups, and box of tea bags in order to reach for her hand. "We will go together. I won't let him do his 'Chester flirt routine' around you."

"I wouldn't call his behaviour a 'flirt routine', Patrick. He leers and makes me feel squirmy and dirty. I don't want to feel like that. He reminds me of when I was sick."

"I know. I know." He tries to keep her calm. "If you decide not to go, we can go somewhere else." He tries to be supportive. "Tell you what. If he gets creepy and you don't want to stay, we can tell everyone we dropped by for a few minutes but we promised your parents we'd come out to the farm. Good plan? Then we can jump in my car and take off." He gives her a conspiratorial wink as the saucepan reaches a rolling boil. Her warm hand is still tucked inside of his.

She leans over a tiny bit and places her forehead on his shoulder. "Thank you, Patrick. I knew you would understand." Her whispers blend with the bubbling of the water.

****

A couple of days later, Amy MacDonald wanders into the diner. Although she shares expenses at Audrey's for the summer, they don't see much of one another, according to reports from Audrey. Amy works regular hours and spends a lot of time with her mother. Audrey has different shifts, some are even split, so they don't eat together often. Amy is aware of his friendship with Audrey, but he thinks no other details have been shared.

"Not going home after work to run with Cheryl? What can I get you, Amy?"

"Oh, an iced tea, I guess. I'm waiting for a friend to pick me up. Amanda's not in today, is she?"

"No, not now. She worked breakfast and lunch. They are getting ready to dig for the foundation, and she went home to check on progress. Busy times at the Wolski farm."

"I guess." Amy is bored. She turns and peers out the window, looking up and down the road every few seconds, like she expects her friend to drive right past and she'll have to be ready to run out and wave whomever it is down.

Patrick delivers her iced tea to the table. He has a napkin for her as well and places both down in front of her. Business is quiet this time of day. Supper patrons don't start to arrive until a little later. He decides to try and make some small talk. "Do you like living at Audrey's instead of staying at Cheryl's? It must be different."

"Audrey's okay. I don't see much of her. It's great to have my own room and not have to sleep on a cot at Cheryl's like last year. She pays half of

Audrey's rent for the summer, and gives me money for food. I don't have to use the money Gaby and Joe pay me, which is good." She takes a sip of the tea and glances out the window again.

Patrick knows she wants to appear nonchalant but she can't camouflage her anxiety. *Is she involved with someone Cheryl disapproves of? Could the person actually be Chester?* He figures this could be the case, but their relationship would be difficult to hide in a small town like this. "Well, your friend should be by soon. Are you both here for supper?"

"Nope. I'll have to watch for the vehicle. Then I'll be up and out. How much for the iced tea? I'll pay now. Don't want to forget."

They settle up the bill. Patrick decides to busy himself at the counter. He knows the situation is none of his business, but he has questions. Maybe, if he can get a peek at the vehicle, he might uncover some answers.

Amy is up in a flash, grabs her shoulder bag, and flies out the door. Patrick meanders over to her table to collect the dirty glass and watches a white Ford pickup speed past the diner and down the road toward the outskirts of town. *Could the driver have been Chester? No! He wouldn't cruise past the diner to pick up Amy. He would know anybody could be seated right here by the window. Even Chester couldn't be so stupid. What if Amanda was at work?*

Patrick ponders. Audrey was sure she saw Amy get out of Chester's truck in front of The Station. She even thought Amy leaned over and kissed him. If this is true, a lot of people could get hurt.

****

He looks forward to meeting up with old friends he will no doubt see today. Gaby and Joe will be here. Ronny Étang will turn up. She and Fiona Werbowski stop in at the diner on a regular basis. As a result, he sees a lot of both of them. Maybe Fiona will come along, too. He expects Maggie will have invited Sean Knox. They spend a lot of time together. Perhaps there will be a wedding in the not too distant future. He wouldn't be surprised.

Patrick pulls on a clean white T-shirt. There was a time he didn't care whether his clothes were clean or not. If he happened to fall into the garbage bin or spill bacon fat on himself, what did it matter? Now, clean clothes matter. He prefers to smell like he just showered rather than like the deep-fryer.

Excitement and nervousness make him a little jumpy. The day has been hot. He has his windows open and he can hear Greta's children as they run around in the back. He has promised Audrey that Chester will not be an issue for her. He will run interference if he has to. If Chester causes any problems, he's confident they will relate to Amy MacDonald and not Audrey. He sticks bare feet into sneakers without laces, grabs his standard pecan pie off the counter, and stops long enough to lock his door before he rumbles down the stairs to knock on Number Four.

His hand barely leaves the wood when the door opens and he finds himself staring into the oval and tanned face of Amy. "I thought you'd be over at Cheryl's. She will be there, right?"

Amy feigns a cool and casual facade, but Patrick reads her like a cheap paperback. He figures she wants to see Chester and if she hangs around with Audrey and himself, they will make the opportunity easier than if she's with her mother. "Oh, I thought I'd go downstairs with you two. Cheryl is out for her run in this heat. She'll show up with one of her stupid pasta salads about a half hour after everybody else." She rolls her eyes and brushes thick dark hair off her forehead. The very low cut of her V-neck T-Shirt is not lost on Patrick any more than the length of her very short mini-skirt. "Audrey, your boyfriend is here!" Amy manages to shout across the apartment, even though Audrey is at the door to her bedroom, not twenty feet away.

"Hi, Patrick. Come on, Amy. We talked about this. Patrick is not my boyfriend. We are friends. We have lots in common, as you know." She meets Patrick's eyes with a pleading in her own. He tries to understand, but would like to argue and say he would very much like to be her boyfriend; how he wants to be her boyfriend.

He decides to let the comment pass. "Let's go, you two. I think almost everyone is down there already. I see Joe's truck and Amanda's car. I think Ronny has walked over. Let's go."

By the time the three of them round the corner to the patio located off the back entrance to the manager's apartment, Patrick is, indeed, correct and everyone is already there. The children play together on the climbing and swing set Chester and Joe made for the Wolski kids last summer. Gaby and Joe open beers. Chester works the barbecue, and Maggie and Rose help Greta organize the buffet table.

Patrick leans over to Maggie. "Where's Sean today? Didn't think he'd want to miss a barbecue."

Maggie pouts a little, but forces a smile. "He and Fiona both have to work today." Then she brightens. "But he said he'd come over after his shift and we could visit then. Better than no time together at all, right?"

"You are absolutely right, Miss Woodward." Patrick gives a little mock bow and turns toward Gaby to accept a glass of club soda. He could have a beer if he wanted. His meds are under control, but the soda and lime suit him just fine. Gaby exchanges glances with Patrick and tilts her head toward Audrey. He nods. She pours another drink, a duplicate of his, and he takes it to her.

"When we start to eat, will you go over to Chester and get me a burger? I don't want to go over there."

"No problem, but I don't think you have to worry, Audrey." He leans down far enough to whisper in her ear. "Keep an eye on Amy. I think the action will be there."

Audrey slides her hand into Patrick's.

"Do you have information about us you would like to share with me? Did you not mean what you said to Amy when we were upstairs?" His voice has a hint of teasing.

She turns her face upward, stands on her toes, and gives him a tiny kiss on the cheek. Patrick is suddenly warmer than any day in July.

****

The afternoon and evening were a roaring success, especially to anyone without a keen eye for the subtle. Patrick was sure Amanda was aware of the sly glances which passed between her husband and Amy.

Once Cheryl arrived, she seemed oblivious. This surprised Patrick. She is such a professional, he thought she would notice. He guessed the skills of an astute social worker are not the same as a mother who lacks the previous eighteen years of experience.

He wished Fiona was around. Ronny stayed long enough for supper and to congratulate Amanda and Chester on their move. Then she was off. He still finds it a challenge to relate to her with that crazy and curly dark hair. She could be in disguise, but he understands the short, platinum hairdo was the disguise all along. This is the real Ronny.

Soon, the group started to break up. Rose and Gaby gathered all the paper plates and plastic cutlery into a garbage bag. People picked up serving dishes. Chester cleaned the grill while Amanda rounded up the children. Although only eight-thirty, and the sun would be up until after ten, the children still needed their sleep. Greta had already hustled hers into the apartment to clean up before bed.

Audrey stuck to Patrick's side like glue. He liked it. There were good points and bad points about how Chester focused his handsome face squarely on eighteen-year-old Amy MacDonald. He was positive Audrey did not have to worry. Cheryl, on the other hand, may have her hands full with Amy. She will be here for another month or more before university starts. A lot can happen within a couple of months.

"I think the party's about done. Do you want to go for a walk?" He leans over from his perch on an upended log used as a stool in the backyard, as he pulls himself back from his reflections on the afternoon.

"Let's. The evening is beautiful."

Chapter 16

Audrey

She knows the day is sunny. She absorbs the warmth on her eyelids and sees the light filter through, red and pulsating. The thin blue cotton curtains, made and hung by her mother, do little to prevent the bright light of morning from bursting into her bedroom. She hears the rattle of dishes in the kitchen. *Is Amy up already? Why would Amy wander around at this hour on a Sunday?*

The forces of reality insert themselves behind her closed eyes and into her brain. She did not imagine last night. He was here. Patrick was with her through the night, but he's not here now. She reaches out one arm to survey the empty space beside her on the three-quarter bed her father unceremoniously lugged into this room ten months ago. Patrick was here. She's sure he was here. She can remember the scent of him—sort of fresh and soapy mixed with a hint of Mazola. She can remember his touch and how he held her face in his hands when he kissed her. The experience wasn't like she had always imagined—not like in the movies. They were clumsy. They giggled and fumbled. She remembers she said she thought they needed more practice. *Did I say that? I can't believe I said that!*

She hears the familiar creak of the bedroom door as the knob is turned and it inches forward. "Are you still asleep?" Patrick's voice washes over her, and blends with the warm summer breeze as it drifts in through the window.

"No," she whispers back. She opens her eyes and sees him as he's poised there with two mugs of tea. He graces her with a beam of pleasure.

"I have to work at eleven, but I thought we might have time for tea before

I go back upstairs to get ready. Okay?"

Audrey wiggles into an upright position and stuffs the other pillow behind her back. She pats the mattress beside her. "Come sit down here with me. Thanks for the tea."

"Are you okay? We didn't talk much last night, like we'd already decided. You're not mad, are you?"

Her eyes start to fill with tears, so she tries to make a joke. "No, I'm just happy I didn't imagine, this time."

His lips are turned up and his expression is one of pure pleasure. "You most definitely did not imagine us, Audrey." He sets his mug on the night stand and runs one finger down the side of her face. "You are beautiful this morning."

In this moment, Audrey realizes her hair is loose and not pulled back with a rubber band. She can't remember the last time her hair was down. She's oddly unfazed. His finger has guided a few stray strands away from her cheek and back toward her ear. She puts her hand on his. "Thank you. So are you." Then she blushes. She refuses to feel embarrassed as the light streams in and her roommate is still asleep next door.

Will I always feel like this? As much as she hates to admit it, right now she would like to see him go so she can decompress and think about their night together. She needs space.

"I have to go upstairs, shower, and go to work. Amy is up. I heard her a few minutes ago but she hasn't come out to the kitchen yet." He leans down and kisses her forehead. "I will see you later." His hand brushes hers and he's gone. What remains is a half-filled tea mug and the scent of Red Rose blended with rumpled sheets.

Audrey sits for a few more minutes, long fingers wrapped around the clay mug. She listens as Amy's door opens and then the bathroom door closes. She pushes back the covers, places her mug on the night stand beside its mate abandoned by Patrick, and wraps her naked self in a yellow floral dressing gown which hangs to the floor. She shoves her feet into soft sheepskin slippers. She considers her hair but lets it fall around her shoulders. She opens the door, retrieves both mugs, and pads into the kitchen.

She waits. Amy will appear in a minute. The toilet has flushed and she can hear the water in the basin run. Audrey is like a statue in a housecoat. She knows Amy will have to make a comment. She braces for what she is sure will come.

"Hi. You must have enjoyed a nice evening. I heard Patrick sneak out and run upstairs. He could have stayed. I don't bite." She stands in her blue baby-dolls and smirks, or maybe leers, at Audrey. "What would Cheryl think?" She wrinkles her eyes and giggles. "Besides, what would Mr. and Mrs. Baranski think?" She places the back of her hand against her forehead and pretends to swoon. "Mercy, me. What has the world come to?"

"Are you finished?" Audrey refills the kettle. "Do you want a cup of tea?" Her heart pounds. What *would* her parents think? What might Amy say? The night spent with Patrick wasn't her smartest move. The contented, mushy sensation she was carrying around like a warm puppy starts to ebb away.

In an instant, Amy's all business. "Listen, Audrey. I think it's great about you and Patrick. It took the two of you long enough. You're both over twenty-one and your relationship is nobody's damned business. Yes, I'll have tea. No work for me today. And...I wanted to rattle your chain a little, but don't worry." She leans into Audrey and their shoulders touch.

Relief spreads through Audrey in a wave. "Thanks, Amy. Nobody knows but you."

"Listen. Nobody *knows* but me, but everybody *thinks* you two are an item. Don't fool yourself. The folks of Hayworth pay attention!" She feigns an expression of surprise as she reaches across Audrey's shoulder for the teabags. "Besides, I have news of my own; information the busybodies of Hayworth *don't* have a clue about."

The two young women curl up at either end of Audrey's fifteen-year-old autumn-leaf-patterned colonial sofa, legs crossed, with toast smothered in strawberry jam served up on Audrey's new dishes. As she sips her tea and munches on her toast, Amy provides the details about her plans.

"I have a date with Chester Wolski tonight." She peeks out over the top of her mug, eyes wide and challenging.

Audrey is afraid to criticize her but knows no good can come of this. She keeps her voice even; nonjudgmental, like Dr. Wilkerson. "He's married, Amy. You need to think of Amanda, and Mason, and Melanie."

"Oh, for heaven's sake! I have to leave in another few weeks. Can't a girl have a little fun?" She giggles as she leans over and gives Audrey's slippered foot a nudge. "You like to have a little fun."

Audrey can't overcome the urge to defend herself. "Patrick isn't married, Amy. I don't think our circumstances are the same. You know they aren't."

"Listen. I'm to meet him tonight down by the Creek Tavern. He has the service truck because he's on call. The plan is to tell Amanda he has to go fix a flat or deliver a part, and come into town. Brilliant, right?"

Audrey has heard this someplace before. She can't put her finger on what makes Amy's plan sound so familiar. "How will he fake a call, Amy? If you telephone and pretend to be someone in distress, whoever answers the phone, if not Chester, will know."

"Oh, it's easy. He told me the service will ring the house whenever he wants to get out. He says they will do him a favour anytime."

"You'll see him tonight? What about Cheryl? Don't you have Sunday dinner with Cheryl?"

"I'll tell her I have to go help Gaby measure for a kitchen at somebody's place. She'll never check up on me. She trusts Gaby. She'll believe me."

Audrey puzzles at how cool, calm, and collected Amy seems to be as she creates a complicated web of lies and deceit. Her plan involves others, even her now, in order to pull off the deception. "I can't lie to Cheryl, Amy. She's your mother. I won't lie to her if she asks me."

Amy's face clouds over. She puts her plate and empty mug on the floor beside the sofa and unfolds her legs to stand up. She moves closer to Audrey, stares down, and meets Audrey's reluctant eyes. "Now listen, Missy. I've confided in you and I expect you to keep my confidence like I promise to keep yours. Chester is a little bit of fun, period. We're not in love, for God's sake! Nobody will get hurt. He's harmless. Now, tell me you won't say a word to Cheryl..If she asks, which she won't, say I said I was with Gaby, or tell her you don't know where I am. It's the truth because you won't know where I am. Can you do this?"

Audrey nods. Amy as a roommate until September might not be the best idea. Maybe the money isn't worth the trouble. She's conflicted. She wants to talk to Patrick.

****

Audrey hears Patrick when he walks past her door on his way to his apartment on the third floor. He said he would see her later. Amy has already left. She told Cheryl she was meeting a friend for supper at the hotel and left about seven o'clock. She created a more logical lie than a site job with Gaby on a

Sunday night.

Audrey did not approve of her clothes. She wore a short sun dress with a very low front, which cheapened her. Audrey worries Cheryl might ask her a question. She does not lie. She would get anxious and confused. If you can't speak the truth, keep quiet. Audrey is happy Amy did not ask her about her attire.

About ten minutes after Patrick went upstairs, she hears him return. She has hold of the door knob when he knocks.

"Hi! Were you right by the door? I ran upstairs and changed my shirt. Are you okay?" Audrey knows Patrick is analyzing her face. She cannot hide how she feels—another problem related to truth. "Where's Amy? Over at her mother's?"

"No. Come in. Tea?" She hasn't moved from the door and Patrick has to sidle his way into the apartment.

He turns and puts a hand on each of her shoulders before he plants a kiss on her forehead. "What's the trouble? Are you mad at me?"

"You? No! Why would I be mad at you? I'm worried about Amy but I don't think I should talk about the reason."

They both stand in the kitchen and share the tasks of tea preparation. Patrick fills the kettle while Audrey assembles cups and tea bags. "You can tell me what's on your mind, Audrey. I don't have a lot of experience with this couple-situation, but I think if we are to be a couple, we can share thoughts and trust each other, don't you?"

"Oh, I trust you, Patrick. Amy told me she wouldn't tell anybody how you stayed over. I assume she expects me not to tell anybody what she's up to, but I think her behaviour is wrong."

The kettle has boiled. The two snuggle up on the sofa, each with a mug of tea. Audrey is comforted by the touch of his thigh against hers, and the smell of him near her face. She could sit like this forever; like the world can't intervene unless they allow the intrusion. This must be the couple-situation he talked about.

"Okay. You don't have to share information you don't want to, Audrey. On the other hand, we have to hope she won't get into any sort of trouble."

"Chester makes me nervous. You know. I've talked about him enough."

"What's happened between Chester and you? Did he make a move? God, Audrey! He thinks he can flirt and fool around and nobody will react because he's so cool. What's happened?"

Audrey can sense Patrick tense up beside her. She's anxious for him to know Chester didn't bother her in any way. "No. Amy went to meet him tonight. She told her mother she would be out to supper with someone at the hotel and then she went to meet Chester over at the Creek Tavern."

"What? Audrey, are you sure the person she met was Chester? Amanda worked all day with me. It's the reason why I was late. We were today's staff, and we didn't finish clean-up until after eight. We were busy. What the hell?"

Audrey doesn't know what to do. If she tells Patrick the whole story, how will he react? Will he tell Amanda? Her palms are sweaty. She puts her mug on the floor beside the couch. "Maybe I'm the problem, Patrick. He makes my skin crawl, but everybody else seems to think he's a handsome, flirty guy who loves his kids and works on cars. It must be me."

Patrick reaches out and pats her on the hand. "No, Audrey. I think the same way you do and I don't know why. It's always bothered me how he was out on a service call, in the company truck, the night Roz Dover disappeared. He's said over and over he didn't see a soul. Charlene Quinn was parked right in front of The Station most of the time. I told the cops they should talk to her. Maybe she's a witness and not a suspect, but I've never heard if they did or not."

Audrey's voice is soft. She can't control the tremor that accompanies her words. "Amy said Chester would have the answering service telephone the farm and say there was an emergency and then he could meet her at the tavern. Anybody who sees the truck would think he has a call when he's out with Amy. I know I should not have told you, though. I expect Amy will be mad at me."

"Did she say, in so many words, the answering service for the Ford dealership makes fake requests so Chester can get out of the house?"

"Well, I don't know if they use the service on a regular basis, but Amy said they would call tonight; and she left at seven and now it's almost nine and she's not back. I guess the plan worked."

"Well, let's have more tea, watch TV, and see when Amy gets home. You and I can ask her how her evening went and see what happens. Maybe she'll spill the beans about Chester in front of me and then you won't have to worry about what you've said. I want her to tell me about the whole scheme with the answering service, because I want to be the one to tell Fiona Werbowski."

"Patrick, we can't get involved. Amy may have stepped out with a guy who's married, but her behaviour isn't worth involving the police."

"No, but maybe the answering service covered for him the night Roz Dover disappeared. They said there was no paperwork for the call and no one at the hotel remembers someone who needed a boost. The whole situation seems too weird."

"I guess this means we're to sit up half the night instead of going to bed?" She snuggles into the crook of his arm and rests her head on his shoulder.

"We will have a lifetime of nights to go to bed," he whispers as he kisses her hair. "I think there's an old episode of *Gunsmoke* on Channel 5."

****

It's well after three in the morning when Amy trips through the door. Patrick and Audrey have long since fallen asleep together on the living room couch. They both jump when they hear the key in the lock.

"What? Have you two waited up for little old me?" Amy feigns surprise, and speaks in a stage whisper, presumably in an attempt not to alert Cheryl, across the hall, of the time of her return to the building.

Audrey giggles and glances at Patrick. "I guess we didn't wait up, Amy. We were both asleep."

"Oh, did you two tire yourselves out earlier in the evening after I left?" Amy leers at them and staggers as she removes her sweater and tosses both it and her purse on the counter.

"Where did the two of you go?" Audrey glances at Patrick. She wants to encourage Amy to mention Chester's name so Patrick will hear for himself whom she was with. Then she cannot be accused.

"Oh, we drove out to a quiet little spot he knows about—way out in the country." She winks at Audrey.

"You don't think anyone was curious about the service truck?"

"Audrey! Little Patricks have big ears. No. No one would be curious about the truck." There's an irritating whine in her voice.

Patrick nods to Audrey and takes over the conversation. "The person I know who might drive a service truck at night is Chester. Were you out and about with Chester Wolski tonight, Amy?"

"Come on, you two! You haven't gone all judgmental on me, have you? We had a little fun. No harm done."

"How did he manage to wangle a service call at the same time as to have a date with you, Amy?" Patrick's voice is soft, but Audrey thinks there's enough authority in his tone to compel Amy to answer him.

"Oh, the answering service people call him and pretend. They fake calls all the time. No big deal." She leans forward and peers at both of them from across the space between the kitchen and the couch. "I want to go to bed. You two should do the same. Night, night." She grabs her purse and swishes into the spare room, slamming the door behind her.

Patrick and Audrey sit and stare at one another for a few seconds before Patrick breaks the silence when he whispers, "We have to tell Fiona Werbowski about this, Audrey. I think our questions found a few answers tonight."

Chapter 17

Patrick

Patrick is unable to put into words how much he respects Dr. Wilkerson. She gave him his life back. She helped him to learn about his schizophrenia; how to live with his condition; how to manage his medication; how to make a life for himself despite his illness. He came to understand how he need not end up like his mother, at the end of an orange electrical cord with a blotchy and contorted face and mercifully closed eyes. He knows he must work every day to manage his disease—like a recovering alcoholic or drug addict. There are no breaks. A few days after Patrick learns from Amy about her involvement with Chester, he looks forward to his session with Dr. Wilkerson.

"I don't want you to think I'm crazy, Doc."

"Now, Patrick. You know if I think you're crazy, I'll tell you." This is their private joke.

The absolute last accusation she would make would be to tell him he's crazy. He knows this, but he also realizes certain ideas can be too "out there" to be normal.

"Tell me what's troubling you."

"Chester Wolski made a date to see Amy MacDonald—you know, Cheryl Nadler's daughter? She's here for the summer and works for Gaby Ridgway." Rachel's nod gives him the confidence he needs to continue. "She told Audrey and me about her date to meet him at the Creek Tavern. He was on call and made arrangements with the answering service to telephone him at home and fake an emergency so he could get out of the house."

"I understand the moral issue, Patrick, but what, in particular, troubles you today?" Rachel's soft auburn hair hangs down to her shoulders, and rests in waves on the pale pink silk of a blouse with about a hundred buttons up the front. Her heavy watch rolls around on her wrist. It has always appeared to be more like a bracelet than a watch.

"The same thing happened the night Roz Dover disappeared. Don't you remember? The police questioned him as a witness because he was out on a service call. He claims he gave somebody a boost over at the hotel, but there's no record with Ford."

"You think Chester fakes service calls to meet girls, Patrick?"

The idea sounds foolish when said in those words, but he sputters on. "I asked the RCMP—Fiona Werbowski—to check to see what Charlene Quinn saw. She was out in front of The Station for hours. I don't know if they learned any new info from her or not. Fiona wouldn't be allowed to tell me if they did. If Charlene didn't hurt Roz, then maybe she saw what happened. If the answering service pretends he has calls, maybe the cops need to talk to them, too."

Dr. Wilkerson's expression remains blank as she jots down a couple of notes. "My suggestion would be for you to speak to Constable Werbowski again, Patrick. She is not the main investigator, but she is the police officer who works within the community. She's the one who organizes the meetings. She won't be able to tell you what's happened, but I am positive she will listen."

"What if Chester did meet Roz? What if he faked a call and left Amanda to go see her? What if he killed her?"

"Slow down, Patrick. Too many ifs. You know assumptive reasoning gets you into trouble. First things first. Talk to the RCMP. Don't decide for yourself that Chester Wolski's bad behaviour with Amy means he killed somebody more than three years ago."

"Okay. I see Fiona at the diner often. I'll talk to her. Can we change the subject now? I want to tell you about Audrey. I need to know if I'm on the right track. I've never done more than buy a girl a coffee at the diner or walk home beside someone. This is serious and I don't want to make any mistakes. I don't want to mess up our friendship, either."

"Tell me what's happened, Patrick. You know I can't talk about Audrey, but I can listen to you tell me about your involvement."

"She's a sweet girl, Doc. We spent the night together and we did okay for a couple of amateurs." He blushes beet red. He feels his old acne scars pop out on his cheeks.

Rachel's expression never changes. "Do you two consider yourself to be a couple now?"

Patrick is unsettled by the question. "I guess. I think so. I went to her folks' place for supper. It was before we made love, but yes, I think we're a couple."

"Does she feel the same?"

"I don't know for sure. I want her to."

"Maybe your next step is to talk together. Then you will both know where you stand."

****

The most important advice Patrick gains from his session with Dr. Wilkerson is he needs to have two conversations—one with Audrey, and one with the RCMP, specifically Fiona. Audrey should be with him, too, and they shouldn't talk to Fiona at the diner since Amanda might be there or turn up.

His obsessive thoughts drag him in another direction. Patrick wants to talk to Gaby because she knew Charlene, but he can't go to Dodd's Contracting when Amy is there. He can't talk to her at the diner, if she happens to show up, because Amanda would be there. He wants to talk to Fiona but he does not want to go to the police station, which makes him so anxious he can't think straight. His mind is muddled.

"How's life out at the farm?" Patrick cleans off the remaining dirty tables after the lunch crowd. Amy's revelation regarding her rendezvous with Chester happened a couple of days ago. "You guys must enjoy the rural life."

Amanda, behind the counter, places clean glasses and mugs on shelves. Her red hair is tied up with a navy blue ribbon. She's cute. Patrick has always liked Amanda. He knows a bit about her difficult childhood and he admires her for her accomplishments. He relates.

"Oh, there's ups and downs, Patrick. I like to be near the job site. There isn't a whole lot of progress yet—you know, site preparation—and Chester's folks are a big help with the kids, but Chester seems to be gone on service calls a lot more. Maybe they aren't more often, but each one takes longer cause we're outside town." She gives her curls a little shake as she turns to face him. "Life will settle down once we get into the new house. I can hardly wait." She grabs the empty tray, nudges the swinging door to the kitchen with her hip, and disappears.

Patrick stands and watches the blue ribbon and red curls bob along behind the saloon doors. He continues to spray the urethane tops of the tables. He should ask her if Chester only goes out to help stranded motorists, or if he uses the Ford service truck for other errands when he's on call. The question might break the ice.

When she returns to the front and starts to double-check the cash in the till, he makes his move.

"Amanda. Does Chester always have someone who needs his help when he takes off in the tow truck? Does he ever use the company vehicle to come into town, you know, to pick up a part or come to the diner to get you?"

Amanda turns to face Patrick full on. "What are you getting at, Patrick? Are you insinuating Chester takes advantage of his employer? You think he uses a company vehicle for personal use? Why do you care?"

Patrick's face feels hot when it turns red. He gets sweaty in an instant. *Why is she acting so formal? She sounds like she's rehearsed what she said in front of the mirror a hundred times.* "No. No." He hurries to smooth the situation over. "You're right about the afterhours work, though. I guess I've seen him in town a lot."

"Where Chester is and what truck he drives is none of your business, Patrick. None of your business," she repeats.

Patrick thinks she seems nervous. "You stick to your job and your pretty little girl friend. Don't be worried about what my husband might or might not do. Now, can you get the dishwasher started again? Danny's about to leave for home and I have the dinner prep to take care of."

Patrick continues on with his work but makes up his mind then and there to talk to Fiona Werbowski again. He's troubled; details don't add up—like a riddle he can't solve. He doesn't know why, but he senses a clue hidden in this information somewhere.

****

Later on in the afternoon, Sean Knox shows up at the diner to pick up coffees for the two constables. Fiona remains in the car. Patrick pours the coffees, adds milk to Fiona's just the way she prefers, and leans over toward Sean. "Can you ask Fiona to call me tonight, Sean? I need to speak to her and I don't want to talk here."

"What about?" Sean Knox is all business. He's a different guy when he's out of uniform and with Maggie Woodward. Patrick thinks he likes Maggie's Sean a lot better.

"I can't talk here, Sean." Patrick's whisper is almost a hiss. "I get home around eight- thirty. Can you guys call or pop by then?"

"Unless there's an emergency, we'll be there. What apartment are you? Six, right?"

"Yes. I'm in Number Six. I might have Audrey Baranski with me, too. Tell Fiona." He hands the cop his two coffees and raises his hand as Sean digs for his wallet. "These are on me today. I appreciate the meeting later."

Time drags all afternoon, like the wall clock has glue on its hands. Patrick is in a constant state of hot and sweaty anxiety. He wants to talk to Audrey before Sean and Fiona show up. She might want to be included. She might not. He worries she'll see the patrol car in the yard and wonder what's happened.

Supper service is busy, which is standard during the summer. Folks don't like to cook when the weather is hot. Amanda made salad plates for the special tonight, complete with potato salad, baked ham, and deviled eggs. She does the best deviled eggs of anybody. A nice cool supper and ice-cream or lemon meringue pie for dessert.

By the time he gets cleaned up and ready to lock the diner doors and go home, the clock already reads past eight. Amanda offers him a ride but he declines. He doesn't want her to see a cop car in the yard, so he jogs almost the whole length of Hayworth to get to The Station. Since there is still no sign of Fiona, he raps on Audrey's door.

"I ran home," he pants. "Where's Amy?"

Audrey nods toward the bathroom.

"I asked Sean and Fiona to come and talk to me. I have to tell them." He whispers with his mouth close to her ear. "Sorry if I smell like French fries. Do you want to come upstairs with me to talk to them?"

She nods and glances back into the apartment. "Amy, I'll be upstairs with Patrick. I have a key. See you later." She reaches out to grab her key and follows Patrick.

Once inside his apartment, Patrick starts to have second thoughts. "What will Amy think when she sees a cop car in the front lot?"

Audrey is nonchalant. "Oh, she'll think Sean's come to see Maggie. She won't be the least bit bothered. Even so, Patrick, are we getting into other people's business? If Chester Wolski wants to run around with Amy, what does their behaviour have to do with us?"

He pats her arm and runs water into the sauce pan. "They should be here any minute. Let's see what they have to say, okay?" He sighs with relief. He's home and has Audrey there with him.

The big old Caprice crunches on the gravel when it rolls into the front lot. He hands Audrey her tea and motions her to the sofa. "I'll get the door."

Patrick is surprised Sean doesn't stop at Maggie's for a minute on the way past, but he supposes she would be used to not being acknowledged when he's at work. "Hi, guys. Thanks for coming."

"This better be good, Patrick."

"Hear me out. Fiona, I only want someone to hear my theory. Okay?"

"Okay, Patrick." Fiona glances across the open living space toward Audrey, curled up on the very end of the navy blue leather sofa. "Hi, Audrey. Haven't seen you in a while."

Audrey nods at Fiona, but remains silent.

"Come sit down." He's placed kitchen chairs across from the sofa.

Fiona starts. "What's on your mind, Patrick?"

"Fiona, did you ever follow up with my idea about how Charlene Quinn could be a witness and not a suspect?"

"Patrick, is this the reason you asked us to come up here tonight? You know I can't talk to you about interviews, but we did follow up on your theory. Suffice to say, there are many pieces to the puzzle."

"Charlene Quinn is not the reason why I asked you here, Fiona." He stops and takes a gulp of hot tea. He almost burns his mouth and is a bit breathless when he begins. "Chester Wolski seems to be stepping out with Amy MacDonald—you know—Cheryl Nadler's daughter. Anyway, Amy is staying at Audrey's for the summer while she works for Gaby and Joe." He is encouraged by Fiona's nods. Sean stares straight ahead like he does not have a clue.

"Go on." Fiona's tone is cautious.

"Amy told us how Chester was on call the other night and he planned to meet her at the Creek Tavern in the tow truck. When I asked her how he would manage, she told me he gets the answering service to telephone him with a fake breakdown or boost needed, or another made up activity. Then he gets to go and, in this case, take Amy for a little drive."

Fiona leans back on her kitchen chair and glances over at Sean. Neither says a word to one another.

"Anything else? Audrey, do you agree with Patrick's information?"

Her voice is tiny, almost childlike, when she replies, "Yes"

"Patrick, what's your theory?"

"Well, I don't know what Charlene Quinn might have said but we know Chester claims he received a service call the night Roz Dover disappeared. We also know there was no record of the call and it's pretty hard for you guys to follow a lead when it goes nowhere. Maybe the call was a fake, like the one he put together a couple of nights ago in order for him to go out with Amy. Maybe he went out in his service truck to meet Roz Dover and the situation deteriorated somehow."

"There's lots of maybes, Patrick." Sean stands. He's heard enough.

Fiona is still writing in her notebook. "We'll check up on this, Patrick. I will talk to the answering service employees again. The only information we asked them about before was a record of the service call, and it appeared the paperwork couldn't be located."

"Because there never was any paperwork." Patrick can't keep the sarcasm out of his voice.

"Now, you two, this is nothing but speculation and amounts to very little, and certainly not evidence. I do not want to hear how either of you have spread rumours around town about Chester Wolski."

"You need to talk to Amanda, Fiona. I asked her about whether or not Chester ever uses the company truck for personal business and she took a big hissy fit, like she had information but wouldn't say. She sure told me to focus on my work and mind my own business."

"Don't ask Amanda any more questions, Patrick. I appreciate you two speaking up about this, and I will discuss your observations with the investigators in charge of Roz's case. If they need you to come in and make a formal statement, will you?"

"Of course, Fiona. Audrey, you, too?"

Audrey hesitates. "Cheryl and Amy will be upset if they think we have meddled in their affairs, Patrick."

"They will never know from us, Audrey." Fiona addresses her concerns "We're interested in the behaviour of the answering service the night Roz disappeared. The information you've shared with us will give us reason to dig a little deeper."

"Okay. If the investigator wants to see me, I'll come down to the police station. Can Patrick come with me?"

"By all means. You leave the details to us. Maybe what you've told us isn't important; maybe it is. We'll have to wait and see."

Patrick is disheartened. He parrots Sean. "Lots of maybes, Fiona."

After the cops thump back down the two flights of stairs and Patrick hears the patrol car leave the lot, he holds up his sauce pan toward Audrey. "Gonna stay for another cup? We can watch a little TV if you like. I thought I'd have a shower. What time do you have to be at work in the morning?"

Audrey beams as she nods toward the stove before she replies. "Why, Mr. Hollinger! Whatever are you suggesting? My work day starts at eleven tomorrow. I believe I can sleep in a little, if I need to."

His heart completes a little flip as he crosses the apartment and places a gentle kiss on her forehead. "You make tea while I get out of these smelly clothes and give myself a hose-down."

Chapter 18

Amanda

In her tiny office situated behind the kitchen in the diner, Amanda grabs her big hobo brown leather purse, her blueprints of the house, and her notebook before she flies through the saloon doors. "You two hold down the fort. I hope I won't be long." She sees the unasked questions as they pass between Nancy and Patrick, but she doesn't care. They should have started to frame her house by now. Here they are, past the first week in August and all she has to show for her trouble is power and a septic field. The house is laid out with sticks in the ground and orange tape to outline the footprint—the full extent of the work. *Why isn't the basement finished? What do Joe and Gaby think they're doing?* They said four months and by God, she expects to hold them to their commitment. She intends to be in her new house by early December.

By the time she pulls her car into an angle spot in front of Dodd's Contracting and Interiors, her anger has escalated to hurricane force. Her hands shake as she gathers up her papers off the passenger seat and then tries to wiggle her plump behind out of the compact Tercel.

She throws open the front door. The gentle tinkle of the bells overhead assault her sensibilities. These people have to do their jobs. She owns a business. She can't get it in her head not to make meals on any given day. If she tells people turkey dinner will be the special, she better goddamned well have turkey dinner. She wants to stomp her feet. *Have I stomped my feet? Am I being childish? Well, I don't give a rat's ass.*

Gaby appears from the office at the back, all cute and skinny. Her hair flies around her face like usual. She has on a long pink sun dress and looks like a middle-aged flower child. Amanda tries, with little success, to straighten her blue stripped blouse that hangs down over wrinkled blue slacks. The blouse doesn't manage to disguise her rounded belly.

"Good morning, Amanda. I didn't expect to see you today. You must be excited about your new house. Can I get you coffee?"

"I've had my fill of coffee, Gaby, since I've already done a day's work in a hot kitchen. Is Joe around? Do either one of you know when my house will get started?" Amanda can tell Gaby is a little put off by her tone, but she can't seem to control herself. She is so mad, the trembling in her hands continues to worsen.

"Amanda. What's the matter? Joe has the schedule under control. The contractor hired to dig the foundation should be there next week. We have lots of time. The weather is expected to be good, now. We want to have the basement complete before we dig the well, and there's an old well down back Joe wants to get filled in. He says the hole is a hazard for the children. It will be done next week."

"Gaby, there will be no work on the property beyond a hundred foot radius of the foundation. Didn't I already give those instructions when we started? Chester and his brothers have plans for the rest of the acreage." She begins to get sweaty. *Don't they have air conditioning in this stupid shop?*

"There's no extra cost, Amanda. The well is a safety hazard. The fellas' will already be there with the backhoe. Don't give it a thought."

"Did you not understand me, Gaby? This is my property and my decision. No one is to dig or fill in, or whatever, beyond a hundred feet. Have I made myself clear?" Amanda wonders if she has gone too far; if her anger has jeopardized the whole job.

Gaby's face has become devoid of expression. "I will make your wishes clear to Joe. Now, are there other details I can address for you today?" She turns toward a noise in the back of the shop when Amy MacDonald appears with two tile boards. They display the floor tile Amanda was considering for the bathrooms.

"Hi, Amanda. I thought I'd show you these again in case you wanted to decide on the floor tiles today. I can pull out other samples, if you're interested."

You can get the hell out of my sight. That's what I'm interested in today.

"Thanks, no. I prefer to work with Gaby. We've known one another a long time; we put up with each other's moods. Right, Gaby?" She tries to smooth over her previous behaviour, but isn't convinced Gaby is pacified.

"What else would you like to deal with this morning, Amanda? Amy, I'm expecting a phone call. Come and get me if the call comes through. You may continue to price the new tile boards in the back unless another customer needs help." Gaby redirects her attention back to Amanda. "Okay, if I recall, you asked for bigger samples of the bathroom tiles you like and they arrived with a stack of other boards yesterday." She points to the tile boards leaning against the wall. "Are they what you expected?"

Amanda knows Gaby is being professional. She focuses on the products and not on her. "May I compare them over here at the table under the brighter light? I find the dimness in here difficult, Gaby. With a lighting store next door, you'd think you could manage better fixtures in this place. She flounces across the showroom. She knows how she must look. She does not give a damn. She perches on a stool as Gaby places the tile samples down in front of her. *Gaby works for me, not the other way around. Gaby can't always be in control, even though she seems to think she is.*

Gaby points to the first of the two floor tiles. "You liked both samples when we discussed this before, Amanda. One is about double the price of the other. With bigger samples, are you better able to choose which one you prefer?"

Gaby's formality starts to aggravate Amanda and her anger, reduced to a simmer at this point, returns to a boil. "I suppose you think I should pick the most expensive one, right? You don't have to play fast and loose with my money, Gaby. You know I inherited the cash for this house. It doesn't mean you have to spend every cent."

"You have excellent taste, Amanda. You tend to choose higher end products because of your preference for quality over price. I am happy to provide whichever tile you want, regardless. To be clear, I wrote a contract with the basics covered. You wanted to upgrade, which is your option. Those costs tend to add up over time. We can still cut corners. There's lots of time to return to basics, if you want or need to."

Gaby stares straight into her eyes. The sensation is disquieting. She feels like a fish on a hook and this makes her even more annoyed than she already is. "We don't have to change a single detail. I want everyone to know I make the decisions and nobody else, okay?"

"Of course, Amanda. I've never thought otherwise. After you pick your bathroom floor tile, we still have to determine hardwood. Did you want to decide today, and be finished with the flooring upgrades?"

Butter would not melt in her mouth. Amanda wonders if Gaby learned how to deal with people and maintain her poker face because she worked as a counsellor for all those years. As she's about to agree to explore her hardwood options, Amy appears around the corner.

"Gaby, the call from Thermadore is holding on Line One. Do you want me to tell him to call back?"

"No. Excuse me, Amanda. This is the guy who will tell me if we can get your self-venting cooktop here in time for your kitchen installation. If he can't, then we will have to make adjustments in the design to accommodate an overhead vent. I'll be a moment." She dashes to her office, and leaves Amy and Amanda to stare across the showroom at one another.

"Would you like to see more samples while Gaby's on the phone, Amanda? There's another bathroom tile board. It came in with the shipment yesterday. I determined the price already, in case you might be interested. The size is perfect."

Amanda would rather eat dirt than deal with this young woman who seems to have captured the eye of her handsome and flirtatious husband, but her house is more important to her than any flighty teenager. "Bring the sample out here so I can see it. I imagine it's more expensive than the pricey one Gaby already showed me."

Amy is very professional. "I'll double-check Amanda, but I think the charge would be about a dollar a square foot less. Let me go get it."

She returns a moment later. It becomes clear to Amanda that Amy took the trouble to set the sample aside earlier. She lifts the somewhat heavy board on to the work table. "What do you think?"

The minute Amanda lays eyes on the eight by eight pale grey mottled tile sample, she knows she has made her choice. Perfection. "I love this one, Amy. I think this might be my final decision."

"There is a nice selection of coordinated countertops, too. Let me get your cabinet door sample and we can review countertops, okay?"

Gaby returns at that moment. "Well, Gaby, I guess your helper, here, paid attention. I think I like this tile the best. If I am given a chance to compare vanity top samples, we might be able to get the bathroom decisions made today." An expression of relief passes between Gaby and her assistant. It does not escape Amanda's attention.

****

The diner is busy throughout the afternoon. Amanda hoped to leave early, but Nancy needed to go somewhere, and she had to stay. Now she won't be home until around eight-thirty. She and Chester need to have it out about Amy and what he might be up to. Maybe, after watching Amy this morning, she's been wrong and he's more attracted to Audrey Baranski. She's pretty sure her husband has his eye on one of them, and she wants to have a chat in order to straighten him out.

By the time she leaves the diner, the August air has started to cool down. She can smell the musky scent of canola in the fields. The farmers will start to combine anytime now, if the weather stays warm during the days. Chester's brothers are run off their feet with the huge number of acres planted in canola and wheat. Tesia Wolski seems to do little else besides make meals and take care of her grandchildren.

The drive home gives her time to get herself worked up again. She wants to get out of her in-laws' house. She wants Chester to smarten up. She wants to be in control. She's overwhelmed with fear for how the good in her life, since she moved to Hayworth, might all slip away, and the result will be Chester's fault. If he didn't see the need to chase every skirt in town, their lives would be much different.

She tries to recall when their problems began. She thought he wanted another baby and when she became pregnant with Melanie, he seemed to be fine with the situation. She remembers she was moody, unlike her pregnancy with Mason where she wasn't sick and she floated on a cloud through the whole nine months. Her second pregnancy was a bitch...and she was a bitch; but her mood swings shouldn't have mattered. Chester should have cared for her regardless. But this was when their relationship changed—when she was pregnant with Melanie.

As she pulls her car into the driveway, she is struck by the peaceful domesticity of the view. Tesia Wolski sits on the front porch while Mason and Melanie, out on the lawn, roll around and play together. The scene would soothe her, if Amanda were in the mood to be soothed.

She wiggles out of her vehicle.

"Long day, Amanda?"

"Yup. The evening's almost over. I wanted to get home early enough to have time with the kids, but so much for those plans." Her disappointment and annoyance bounce across the door yard. Both children observe her with troubled faces. "Hi, you two. At least I'm home for baths and bedtime."

Melanie runs into her arms. "No bath. No bed. Stories, Mommy, stories."

"We'll see. You and Mason go inside now. The air has started to cool off. I'm right behind you." She takes a moment to pat Tesia on the shoulder as she makes her way past, but she's tired of saying thanks every time she turns around. Amanda knows she has trouble being grateful. She spent most of her formative years forced to be grateful to someone—a foster family, a social worker, an employer. She does not want to be forced to be grateful anymore.

On her way through the kitchen, she leans down and whispers in Chester's ear as he sits and reads a newspaper discarded by his father. "We have to talk. After I get the kids to bed, we will take a walk over to the property and we will have a conversation. Understand?" She hisses in his ear. His eyes never leave the paper, but he nods. Her father-in-law is in the living room snoozing in front of some stupid sitcom on the TV. The kids don't even disturb him when they tumble past.

By the time the children are settled, dusk has begun to creep across the prairie landscape. Amanda and Chester trudge down the veranda steps and toward the path leading from the family home to their building site. The walk takes about ten minutes. He tries to hold her hand but she pulls away. She will not be swayed by his charm tonight.

"First, you know as well as I do how we need to keep Joe and his workmen away from the old well. Gaby told me today that when they come to do the foundation, Joe wants to have the guy dig out and then fill in the hole."

"Well, it would save me doin' it if Joe thinks he can get the job done."

Amanda is shocked at her husband's attitude. She almost screams her response. "I told her in no uncertain terms that there will be absolutely no work done outside of our hundred foot radius, but it scares the shit out of me. He insists the well is a safety hazard and you know Joe Dodd as well as I do."

"Maybe I should get the tractor and fill the hole in myself. If I do, then he can't complain and we kill two birds with one stone."

Relief washes over her. "Can you do it right away, Chester? We need to do this now. We should have finished the job after your father bought the land. We could have said we were worried about the kids."

"I can try. The machinery's pretty busy this time of year. Leave the job to me. Did you talk to them about when they expect to do the foundation?"

"Yes, I went over there today and read the riot act to Gaby. She wasn't very happy, but she said they were scheduled to do the work for the foundation and basement walls next week, which is how I found out they wanted to fill the well in at the same time. She said the new well wouldn't be drilled until after the basement was completed—some crap about crew schedules, weather. Whatever." She waves her hands in a signal of dismissal. "You have to get the tractor out here this weekend, Chester."

"Jeez, Amanda. I don't know. I'm on call all weekend."

Amanda stares up at him, unable to disguise her look of absolute disbelief. "What the hell are you doing on call again, Chester? You want the service truck so you can run around town and meet your little girl friends. Is this the story?"

"What? What are you talking about?"

"After all we've been through, does the answering service still make up jobs to give you an excuse to get out of the house?"

"What?" He stops and peers down at her. He's standing beside the orange tape used to mark out the placement of the walls for the house.

Amanda is reminded of cop dramas on TV. Crime scenes are always marked with tape. "Patrick asked me, all casual-like, if you use the Ford tow truck for personal business. Has he seen you catting around Hayworth when I think you've been asked to go help some poor bugger with a dead battery? Who is she? Cute little Amy MacDonald? God! Is she over eighteen? Or maybe Audrey Baranski? She's a little loony tunes and more Patrick's speed."

Realization surges past her anger which begins to boil over. "Hey, now I understand. Patrick's knickers are in a knot because he has the hots for Audrey and you want to chase her, too. Which, Chester, the crazy one or the little girl?" There are tears in her eyes. Her face is knotted as she tries not to cry.

He presents his blank facial expression—the one he uses when he doesn't want anyone to know his thoughts. Every time the cops come to talk to him about what he saw the night Roz Dover vanished, he pulls his look. He's a master. She knows he won't incriminate himself tonight.

"Amanda, we should start back. Did you bring the flashlight? Listen, you don't have to be worried. You know I flirt. I like to flirt, but you're my girl."

He attempts to put his arm around her shoulders, but she shrugs him off. She's not ready to accept his explanations. She wants to stay mad a little while longer. "We could be in a lot of trouble, Chester. You need to stick close to home. Get the well taken care of. Stay away from other women, even if you are just flirting. We have to work together."

She examines his face through the enveloping gloom of late evening. He tries again and she permits the plaid-shirted arm to wrap around her. She leans into his side. No matter what, she always feels safer when they are together. She hates his flirting, but she owes him for so much.

"Let's call it a night, my love. Don't give the well another thought. I'll get the tractor this weekend."

Chapter 19

Gaby

"Do you mind if I take a quick run out to the Wolski site? I feel I have to get another visual, Gaby. Since Amanda told you, in no uncertain terms, how she only wants one hundred feet cleared, I need to walk the area again."

They have finished supper on Friday evening. Gaby told Joe about Amanda's state of mind when she was in the shop earlier in the day. "Do you have to go out there tonight?"

"I'll have light until at least ten. I know I shouldn't care, Gaby, but I can't seem to let this old well issue go. The hole needs to be filled in. I know the location is pretty far from the house, but if one of the kids, or one of their little friends, fell in the damned shaft, what would I ever do?"

Gaby heaves a sigh as she studies this mountain of a man she has adored for all these many years now. They are like a single finely tuned unit. She could not have imagined, when he came to assess the little house on Poplar Street before she decided whether or not to purchase her rental property, how this aging and balding, middle-aged contractor with white cat hair covering his ass would become the love of her life. She understands his concerns without any explanation.

When Joe was small, his younger brother drowned in a creek near their family home. For years, he thought he was at fault because he lost track of the little tyke when they were out for a walk. He eventually traveled back east and talked the event through with his ailing mother. In truth, Adam returned home on his own and Alice Dodd told him to run out again to find his older brother, Joe. Alice was the one who sent Adam to his unfortunate death.

This realization has not relaxed Joe's attitude when the topic relates to the safety of children. After they accepted the Wolski contract, they went out to the land purchased by Chester's father, Borys, and tramped through every last foot of the place, through thickets and brambles as well as overgrown fields and pastures. The one acre building lot, set in the middle of the expanse of farmland purchased by the Wolski family, felt huge as they walked the ground step for step.

Joe came upon the well, despite its location low to the ground with a small mound of jagged stones piled over the access opening. Years ago, the owner would have constructed walls about three feet high and a crudely rigged mechanism to lower a bucket down into the water. Any remains are scattered with the rocks and hidden in the high grass. There are bits of collapsed timber strewn about as well. At the time they decided, since a new well would be drilled for the house, they would budget enough money to dig out the structure and fill the area in to remove any hazard.

Since Amanda's visit to the store today, Gaby is quite sure there will be a resulting problem. Joe and Amanda can't both get their way and, as much as she would like to err on the side of the customer, she knows her Joe only too well.

"Do you want to come? You and Martha can ride along." The blue heeler and husky cross lifts her eyebrows at the mention of her name, but remains firmly planted on her mat at the end of the kitchen cabinets.

"No. You take Martha. I want to start to make a few calls to invite people to our little summer dress-up party." She widens her eyes at Joe's questioning expression. "If we want to go through with this surprise wedding, I need to give people notice they're invited."

"We're to refer to this affair as 'summer dress-up' to prevent people from turning up in blue jeans?" He chuckles as he reaches for his truck keys and Martha's leash.

"We're in Hayworth, Joe. There will be people here in blue jeans." She roars with a guffaw that bursts from her face and echoes throughout the great room. "On a more serious note, I'll still invite Chester and Amanda. I've made up my mind not to take her behaviour today personally. Maybe the stress with the house and the diner, and temporary residence with her in-laws, has started to get to her. You go out and have a walk around. Maybe you'll decide the well is far enough away not to matter."

****

"Hi, Cheryl. This is Gaby. I didn't disturb your supper, did I?"

"No, not at all, Gaby. Wonderful to hear from you. I was about to call you. Great minds think alike."

"What did you want to talk to me about, Cheryl? Have you decided to get into a house of your own?"

"No. Certainly not! I remain content here at The Station. Greta Seeley has worked out surprisingly well. I was worried at first, since we already knew one another, but the situation is no different than Patrick. We all live in the same building, no problem."

"What did you want to talk to me about?"

"Oh, Gaby, you go first. You called. What can I do for you?"

"Come to a party. Joe and I have decided to have a little summer dress-up party on Sunday afternoon, August 25, and we would very much like you and Amy to attend. We will start at two in the afternoon and have a buffet lunch." Gaby is well aware of Cheryl's dietary idiosyncrasies. Cheryl will be Cheryl.

"An afternoon tea party. What a wonderful idea. May I contribute a dish?"

"Well, I thought I would take the easy route and have the party catered by the hotel, but if you find time to make your pasta salad, I will tell them there's no need to include pasta with the other salads, sandwiches, and sweet trays. You'll come?"

"Of course!" Cheryl's response floats through the receiver. "I would not miss one of your parties unless I happened to be at death's door. Will you ask Amy yourself, or shall I tell her?"

"I'll mention the date to her tomorrow at work, and tell her I've spoken to you. Then she will know you're both invited. Now, since the party details are settled, what did you want to talk to me about, Cheryl?"

Cheryl seems to hesitate for a mere fraction of a second. "Do you know who Amy has been seeing, Gaby? I thought maybe she would have talked to you. She is terribly fond of you and she trusts your opinion."

Gaby slips into counsellor mode although she's in conversation with one of the best social workers in the area. "Are you worried about her, Cheryl?"

"She's met someone on a number of occasions over the past weeks. She tells me she goes out with friends, but Audrey never accompanies her. I guess Audrey knows, but I don't want to put too much pressure on the girl. She is very fragile."

"Amy's never hinted about a relationship to me, Cheryl, but if she talks to me in confidence, you know I won't tell you what she said. I would suggest you talk to her yourself."

"I think I must be a hopeless mother, Gaby. I pray she isn't involved in the wrong sort of situation. I'm excited you invited me to your party, though. Sounds like a fun afternoon."

Gaby worries Cheryl might feel she's out of the loop somehow. "Cheryl, Amy has helped me a lot this summer. She's a pretty good kid. You know she is, right?"

"Yes. Yes. But I guess the worry comes with the territory. I'll take your advice and have another chat with her. Thanks, Gaby."

****

"Ronny, how are you? Did I catch you in the middle of supper? Joe ran out to a job site and I thought I would give you a ring to invite you to our party." All this comes out in one mouthful of words.

"No, we're done. Fiona and I are ready to dig into ice-cream. A party? When?"

"Good, Fiona's there, too. Saves me another call. Joe and I want to host a summer dress-up party on Sunday afternoon, August 25, and we would like the two of you to come. This isn't the usual potluck, more like an afternoon tea and we will have caterers. What do you think? Will you come?"

Gaby holds while Ronny repeats the invitation to Fiona. She can hear the muffled giggles as Ronny returns to the phone. She isn't sure she has ever heard Fiona giggle. "We'll be there, Gaby. I think Fiona has that Sunday off. If you invite Maggie Woodward, then Sean Knox will be able to go, too. Good timing."

"Perfect. I wanted the date to work. You guys can bring someone, too, you know."

Ronny's voice takes on a softer tone. "Oh, I imagine we'll come together. Can Fi talk to you for a minute? She has a question."

"Sure, put her on. The party is at two o'clock, by the way."

"Looking forward to it, Gaby. Here she is."

"Hi, Gaby. Thanks for the invite. Sounds like fun. Can I ask you a question about Amy MacDonald?"

"Of course. Twice in one night. What's up?"

"What do you mean, twice in one night?"

"When I called Cheryl about the party, she asked me if I knew whether or not Amy is dating someone. I have no information. She will talk to Amy again, which is the best option in my opinion. What would you like to know?"

"Kind of the same topic. You don't know whether she's involved with anybody, eh?"

"No, Fiona. What's going on? Why don't you two finish your ice-cream and come out to the house for tea. Joe took a run to Wolski's house lot to walk the property again. He's concerned about an old well. Come over here for a while and we can visit."

She waits again, this time while Fiona talks to Ronny. "We'll be there in twenty minutes, Gaby. Put the kettle on."

****

The two women arrive at the Dodd/Ridgway home as Gaby puts black currant tea bags into her green Fiesta pottery teapot. The matching mugs are lined up on the Corian counter. She runs over and swings open the beveled glass entry door to welcome two of her favourite people. The three women have been through a lot. They trust one another. Fiona shares more than she should regarding her work, in reference to the ongoing Roz Dover disappearance investigation, but neither Gaby nor Ronny would ever repeat a word outside their circle of three.

Gaby watches Ronny kick off her sandals and pad in bare feet across to the kitchen. Fiona is always a little more reserved. Her straight dark hair isn't pulled back in the usual necessary chignon at the nape of her neck. Instead, it's permitted to fall loose around her shoulders. She appears much tinier without her uniform and all of the necessary attachments. Gaby can never seem to get used to Fiona as a civilian. They pile on to stools at the island. "Where's Martha?"

Ronny always appreciates Gaby's affectionate old dog. "Oh, she went in the truck with Joe. My company cannot compare to a drive down a gravel road in the big blue monster." She laughs as she pours their tea.

"Gaby, I have a few concerns about Amy and I might need your help— in confidence, of course." Fiona becomes very serious. A chill runs down

Gaby's spine, despite the warm August evening air.

"Okay, my dear. Let's hear what's on your mind?"

"Patrick talked to me the other day. He told me how Amy MacDonald is seeing a lot of Chester Wolski. According to what he and Audrey Baranski understand, Chester fakes service calls to get out of the house to meet her. Patrick's all in a twist. He thinks maybe this is what happened the night Roz disappeared. We have said publicly there was no record of the call for assistance from the answering service. When we interviewed them, they determined the record was misplaced or thrown out."

"Charlene called me more than a month ago." Gaby's voice is soft. The words thud like bricks dropped on the stone topped island. "I know I should have told you, but I thought you guys had already interviewed her and I would muddy the waters."

"What did she say, Gaby?" Fiona is alert and now becomes the cop she is; no longer a girlfriend sitting in her kitchen drinking black currant tea out of a Fiesta mug.

"She said she thought the investigator who interviewed her figured she lied in order to get special privileges. She said she is sure she saw both the tow truck and Chester's old Ford pickup leave The Station. She insists she was wide awake, there to spy on Patrick at the time. She even has a theory, if you can believe her."

"Gaby! Why in God's name didn't you tell me about her call?"

"You talked to me about the interview. You said the police assumed she fell asleep and confused the trucks. You didn't need me to tell you a sociopath and murderer presented another theory."

Fiona's expression is somewhere between annoyed and curious, as she sips her tea. "Okay, tell me her theory, Gaby. What did she say? And, by the way, you will have to come down to the police station tomorrow and tell this to the investigators."

Gaby heaves a sigh as she reaches for the teapot to top up their mugs. "She thinks maybe someone hurt Roz and they came to get Chester to help clean up the mess. Maybe there was no emergency service call when two trucks left The Station. She was adamant. She thinks Chester Wolski might be covering for someone."

Fiona is quiet. Ronny observes her friend with a concerned expression Gaby compares to the way Joe studies her when she attempts to work through an issue. In a sudden burst of clarity, Gaby has come to understand the relationship which appears to have formed between her two friends. *Good for them, but back to the point. What does this have to do with Amy?*

"Let's examine this logically, okay?" Ronny pipes up for the first time. "I'm no investigator, but what could be happening? If Ford employees are taking advantage of the use of the tow truck as a way to get out of the house, then the answering service is compromised somehow. I would be very interested to hear what they have to say when confronted. Maybe somebody was involved with Roz, their meeting went sideways, and they called Chester to help. Now Chester has to cover somehow. Did the dealership say Chester was on call August 6th, or could somebody else have had the truck?"

"I don't know. I will have to review the case notes tomorrow and tell the detectives you'll be in, eh Gaby? Maybe we will have to revisit the information provided by both the dealership and the answering service."

"Are you mad I didn't tell you about my call from Charlene?"

"No. The additional information wouldn't have mattered before Patrick told me about Chester and Amy with the tow truck. We need to find out what the Ford tow truck drivers are up to. Let's go home, Ronny. I have a mountain of work to do tomorrow. I imagine Joe should be back anytime, too. We'll get out of your hair."

****

Fiona was correct and Joe pulls into the driveway about five minutes after the two women depart in Ronny's big old black Buick.

"Better?"

"As a matter of fact, a lot better, Gaby. I arrived out at the lot and when I climbed down from the truck with Martha, who should be walking across the field from the house but Borys Wolski himself."

"How's Borys? I haven't seen them in ages. I suppose he's busy right now—harvest time, house building, grandchildren under foot."

"My impression is he's busy. He dotes on those two kids of Chester and Amanda's, almost as if his other two sons don't even have families. In any event, we walked out to the well and he listened to my concerns and told me to clear the area out and then fill the hole in. He said he still owns the property."

"Did he ask about the cost?"

"Oh, I told him right up front that there would be no extra charges. He said Amanda can do whatever she wants with her house, but he still has rights when issues relate to the piece of land itself. I don't imagine she will be very happy, but I plan to take care of the area right at the beginning of next week when the equipment shows up to start the foundation. You must have had some company by the looks of the mugs in the sink."

Gaby reviews her telephone conversation with Cheryl, as well as her visit from Fiona and Ronny. In order to respect the confidences of all parties involved, she decides to do no more than talk around the edges of the issues. "I called Cheryl to invite her to the party. She thought Amy told me her life's details so I would know if she's dating someone. The fact is, I don't know a scrap of information. I also talked to Fiona and Ronny. They had just finished supper and decided to come over for tea. Fiona still obsesses about the Dover case like the rest of us. She thinks there might be a detail they've missed relating to the answering service Ford employs for afterhours calls. I'll be interested to see if this trail leads anywhere."

Joe's expression is quizzical. "Is there a remote chance Ronny and Fiona are a couple?"

Gaby slaps her thigh and howls. "Ya think? Man, are we dense? Should have noticed ages ago—ever since Ronny was kidnapped. Couldn't be happier for them, if we're right. They make a great couple. Wanna see what's on TV?"

****

The next morning, Amy arrives at the shop bright and early. She seems to have dressed with care. The day promises to be warm and sultry once the early morning coolness dissipates. She has chosen to wear a red and pink cotton sun dress and has a white fine knit sweater draped over her shoulders.

"Gaby, are you in the office?" She pats Martha as Gaby puts down the quote she has been rewriting, and comes around the corner.

"I'm right here. You're ahead of schedule. I expect today to be quiet, since most farmers are out in the fields."

"I'm really excited about your party, Gaby. Cheryl told me you called her last night." She leans closer. Gaby can sense the young woman's shoulder touch hers—an act of intimacy and, in the end, conspiracy. "Tell me, will Chester Wolski be invited?"

Chapter 20

Amanda

Although almost impossible to see the building site from her in-laws' property, Amanda hears the heavy equipment as it rumbles down the makeshift driveway toward her future home. She can sense the vibration as the Construction King backhoe, driven by Curtis Weaver, approaches what will soon be the hole to mark the official start of the build. Curtis lives down the road and drives the 1970 Case 580 like he has a Ferrari beneath him. He does Joe Dodd's digging work.

She butters Melanie's toast as fast as she can, and almost tosses the plate down in front of her little girl, in order to race to the kitchen window and try to catch a glimpse.

"Mama!" Melanie protests the loss of her mother's attention. Amanda knows she wants peanut butter. "Mama! Come!"

"Chester left a half hour ago, Amanda. I'll go on over and keep track of the work if you want. When do you have to get to the diner?" She knows Borys is trying to be supportive.

Amanda scrapes a tendril of curls away from her face and wipes her hands on the yellow flowered cotton apron belonging to her mother-in-law. She had hastily wrapped it around her waist when she started to help her children with their breakfast. "I told Danny and Patrick I might be as late as ten-thirty, so I can stay for a while. You go on over, Papa. I'll get the kids organized so Mama can watch them, and then I'll catch up. Mason, you stay put. You need to help your grandma with Melanie today. You can't go with Grandpa."

Mason pouts. She manages to place a hand on his little denim-covered shoulder as he's about to jump down from the table and make a beeline for his grandfather. "Stay put now, boy. After lunch, you and I can take a walk back over and see how the men are doin'. Whatcha think?"

The six-year-old directs a broad grin toward his grandfather's face. Amanda knows Mason thinks he has one-upped his mama. "Thanks, Papa. I need all the help I can get these days."

As the screen door slams behind Borys, Tesia returns to the kitchen after she made a quick trip upstairs to get dressed. Her long hair is pulled into a ponytail. She's dressed in short blue-jean-like capris and a sleeveless yellow polka-dotted blouse. Amanda thinks they could pass for the same age. Either she has aged faster than normal, or her mother-in-law has found the fountain of youth.

"You go ahead after Borys, Amanda. I think I can keep operations under control at this end."

Amanda nods her thanks, rips off the apron, throws it over the nearest pressed-back chair, and virtually leaps through the screen door and off the veranda. Borys is about a hundred feet ahead of her, but she'll catch up. His characteristic lumbering gait won't win him any races.

Damn Chester! He promised to get a tractor from one of his brothers and take care of the old well. Like so many other commitments, he makes a promise and then he doesn't follow through. Well, as long as Joe understood her very clear demand to leave the spot the hell alone, Chester can borrow a tractor after harvest and do the deed himself. As she gets closer to the site, she can see they have already started to peel back the topsoil before they begin to dig the eight foot deep hole where the footings for her new house will be poured. She gave them strict orders to save the soft loam. She wants to have the yard landscaped after the build. This area used to be pasture land and the earth doesn't get much richer than right here. *At least they're doing as they're told, so maybe that's a good sign.*

She stands beside her father-in-law and watches Curtis manoeuvre the old backhoe. The machine roars. She taps Borys on his sleeve and nods before she picks her way across the gravel and mud to where Joe stands and supervises.

He leans down to listen to her but then shakes his head and motions for them to move over to the other side of the parked vehicles.

"Nice to see you managed to get here, Joe."

"Don't worry, Amanda. We'll get the basement dug this morning and the forms will be built for the footings before the end of the day. I have the cement truck booked for seven-thirty tomorrow. We're right on schedule."

She sighs. She thinks he can't hear the expulsion of air as she attempts to show her impatience, but she's pretty sure he can read the expression on her face. "You said this week, Joe. I thought you meant Monday."

"The site was too wet. We were forced to wait until the area dried out. There will be good digging now. Enough moisture in the ground, we don't have dust flying all over the place. Are you gonna be around all morning?"

"Nope. I have to go to the diner, but Borys will keep an eye on the work for me."

"Think I need to be supervised, do you?" He seems amused and not the least bit concerned his client worries she has to be on top of his work. "Gaby told me if I saw you to tell you she'd be out this afternoon."

"Does she think you need supervision, too?"

Joe laughs loud enough to almost drown out the backhoe. "Gaby always visits a site at the start of a build, even if she has to show up after hours—a little tradition we have, Amanda. I'm sure she'll be disappointed you won't be around. Anyway, I have to speak to Curtis about the footing for the chimney support. We'll talk lots later, I'm sure." He gives her a little salute and then picks his way past the piles of fresh earth while he waves to his equipment operator.

Amanda wanders back over to her father-in-law and stands on her tiptoes to shout in his ear. "I have to go back to the house and get ready for work. You call me if you have any concerns about the job, or if there are questions you can't answer. I'm trusting you to be my site foreman now, Papa." She pats his arm as she looks up into his handsome face.

He moves a couple of steps closer to the marked off site as she starts back toward the farm.

****

The day spins by at the diner. Service is brisk. Amanda felt like lunch started an hour early and ended an hour late. Danny and Patrick managed breakfast on their own. Danny will be off at three this afternoon. She and Patrick will work supper. Nancy was supposed to be in but has a summer cold. Patrick agreed to work a double. He said his friend, Audrey, might come in for supper. Amanda said she could sit in the staff booth and Patrick could visit with her if there aren't too many customers. She thinks they made plans but Patrick rarely says no to extra work. He hates to let her down.

At about two-thirty, the phone rings. "Hayworth Diner. Amanda speaking."

"Hi, Papa. What's wrong? Come home? Are the kids okay?"

"The kids are fine. Joe found something down the well. We've already called the RCMP. You'd better come home."

"What do you mean—Joe found something down the well? I gave him strict instructions last week to leave the old well alone." Amanda can't seem to get her breath, like she's forgotten how to breathe, or her lungs aren't able to move air anymore.

"Amanda, are you okay? You're white as a sheet." Patrick pushes through the saloon doors from the kitchen where he's unloaded the last of the cutlery from the dishwasher.

"Ask Danny if he can stay, Patrick. I have to go out to the farm."

"Are you there, Amanda? Ask what?"

"No, Papa, not you. I asked Patrick to catch Danny before he leaves. I'll be home in half an hour and I'll kill Joe. He explicitly went against my orders."

"Not his fault, Amanda. I told him to go ahead when he came out last Friday night to walk the site one last time before the work started. I said I was worried about the children, too. He told me about his younger brother who drowned in a creek behind their house when he was a kid."

"I don't give a shit about Joe's childhood. I told him to leave the area alone. Chester could cover over the well later. What did they find?"

"Blue canvas fabric and bones." His voice is soft and Amanda can barely hear him. Under normal circumstances, his voice booms and rumbles. This particular tone is weak and sad. "Maybe not important. Maybe someone wrapped a dog in an old cloth and threw the carcass down there years ago. We don't know. Will you come home now? Gaby Ridgway is here and I think I see police cars on the road."

"I'm on my way. Did you call Chester?"

"Yeah. He said he'd be home after work. He was the one who said the bones are a dog."

Amanda couldn't be bothered to say good bye. She simply hung up on her father-in-law and rushed into the kitchen for her purse and keys.

"Emergency, Amanda? I called my wife on the other line, and I can manage to hang in until eight. I hope the diner will be quiet tonight." Danny is a great cook. He has made a tremendous effort to help her throughout this whole process, both when she bought the diner and then when she had to learn how to run the kitchen. If not for Danny, Patrick, and Nancy, she doesn't know what she would do.

"Seems like there's a glitch out at the job site and, of course, nobody but me can deal with the problem." She makes a half-hearted attempt at a joke but her excuse falls flat. Her face is as white as her hair is red.

Amanda dashes to her car and peels out of the gravel lot, lucky there are no other vehicles nearby. They'd be sprayed with rocks for sure. She tries to stick to the speed limit but knows she's driving way too fast. After what seems like an hour and not fifteen minutes, she drives her car straight into the job site—down the ruts and pot holes of the track cut through the field to make access easier for workers, so they don't have to go to the farm and drive across from there. Eventually, there will be a fine gravel driveway, with grey crushed rocks and mowed grass on the sides.

There are vehicles everywhere, including an RCMP patrol car and a black van with the RCMP emblem on the side. Amanda's heart races. Her palms are wet. Her forehead drips with sweat. She hopes people think her condition is because of the August heat. She can't let anybody see her fear. Everybody knows Roz Dover's car was located almost exactly where they have dug the hole for the basement of the house. Back then, the place was covered in bush and the outbuildings of the abandoned farm were obscured from view. You couldn't even see the green Pinto from the Wolski property next door. She is aware that there is not a person on this job site right now who doesn't wonder if what they found in the well might be—could be—Roz Dover's remains.

****

She sits in her Tercel. The afternoon sun blazes down. She clutches the steering wheel with sweaty palms as she tries to control the shaking. The view through the windshield is chaotic. Borys stands off to the side of the basement—the beautiful hole that marks the start of the creation of her dream house—and talks to Joe Dodd. They don't exactly talk. They watch the break in the brush created by the backhoe, which mowed down the vegetation to get to the damned overgrown well. Another cop car rolls into the site, followed by a normal sedan, but Amanda guesses the car belongs to one of the detectives. Fiona Werbowski and Sean Knox, both in uniform, stand with Gaby Ridgway. *Why the hell is she still here? Who knows? Maybe Fiona asked her to stay. They're thick as thieves.*

Amanda becomes increasingly agitated as her father-in-law turns toward her car. He's noticed she's there. She cranks down her window and is assaulted with the smell of freshly turned soil and pressure-treated lumber. She's parked right beside the materials pile designated for building the wooden basement walls.

"I gather we have a situation?" *Stay calm.* She decides to get out of the car and Borys opens the door the minute she touches the handle.

"Once I called the RCMP, the whole scene was out of my control. Everybody turned up in fifteen minutes. What took you so long?"

"I needed to make sure I was covered at the diner, Borys." She finds she can't bring herself to use the more familiar "papa", like this man no longer cares for her. "I wish Chester would come home." She also wishes her philandering husband had done what he said he would do and filled the well in. How could she have ever guessed Joe had some childhood trauma?

"Chester says he'll be here soon. He thinks they found dog bones and the well will be filled back in before dusk." Borys does not sound confident.

"I hope he's right." *What a stupid comment for him to make. The investigators won't need ten minutes to figure out they've found a person. And Chester wrapped her in his goddamned mechanic's coat!* She starts to shake again and leans against her car for support, as she ignores the dust and dirt caked on the side panels.

Out of the corner of her eye, Amanda sees Fiona begin to approach across the bare earth rutted by vehicles and equipment. The yard is a mess. She picks her way along in her street boots. "I brought rubber boots but not work boots. Didn't know the place would be so torn up." Her remarks are made to both Borys and Amanda once she gets within ear shot.

"Hi, Fiona. I guess I have a mess on my hands, and we're not talking about the yard." She tries to direct a grimace-like smile toward the RCMP constable.

"Borys, you've lived here a long time. How old do you suppose the well is? I can't even remember if it was discovered when we found Roz Dover's car."

"Older than me, for sure." His voice booms above the sound of the digger in the distance. "I would think a hundred years. There's been nobody on this property for a long time. The houses fell down and grasses grew up around the woodshed and rubble. We never even saw that girl's car from the house. Unless you were searchin' for a well, you'd never know the hole was there."

"Well, Joe found the hole. How did he do it?"

"By accident. He walked the property before work ever started and came upon it then. When he drove out last Friday and we talked, he told me he thought the well was a safety hazard for Mason and Melanie. I gave him permission to dig out the rocks and then fill dirt in."

"Yes, he told me about your conversation." She turns to Amanda. "He told me you didn't want the area touched, Amanda. Why not?"

Amanda is suddenly queasy in the mid-afternoon heat. "Chester said he would take care of the problem. I didn't want to pay extra for Joe to hire someone to do what my own husband could do." She squirms and thinks perhaps her mind has been read.

"Funny. Must have been a misunderstanding because Joe said there would be no added charges for the additional well work. He wanted the job done while he was on site. It was important to him."

"Yeah. Yeah." Amanda waves her hand dismissively, in a faint endeavour to suggest the unimportance of Joe's issues. "Joe's brother drowned, I think. I know about his childhood trauma. Like I said, we intended to do the work ourselves. We would have filled it in by the fall. The equipment is busy this time of year."

Borys stares down at her and his shocked expression creeps under her sweaty skin. She has spent most of her life attempting to hide her cynicism and lack of trust in almost everybody. She learned to protect herself a long time ago. She makes a mental note to try and keep her feelings in check when she's around anybody but Chester. She knows he will have to wear this. *His stupid mechanic's coat, but he felt compelled to wrap the slut up.*

Sean trudges over to join the group. "Forensics will pitch a tent, Fiona. They expect to be here most of the night. We need to clear the area now. I'll go talk to Joe and Gaby. Then they can move their crew out. Curtis will stay with his machine. Saves them getting someone else." He nods toward Borys, glances down at Amanda, and then scans the yard for Joe and Gaby.

"Okay, Amanda." Fiona gives directions. "You two might as well take your vehicle back to the farm. Use the dirt track and avoid the field. The detectives will want the area kept as clear as possible."

"Will you keep us informed about progress?" She makes every attempt to sound civil, but feels her control slipping away.

"I imagine the request to stop work has already been made, Amanda. It's pretty much how these situations go. As for information, I would guess there will be lots of questions, but let's provide forensics the opportunity to do their job for right now, okay?" Fiona repeats her request. "You and Borys go on home. Call Chester and tell him to go to the farm after work and not come over here."

Amanda catches her father-in-law's eye. "We'll leave in a minute, Borys. I want to go over and tell Joe and Gaby they're fired. I'll find somebody else to build my house. Somebody who can follow goddamned instructions!"

Chapter 21

Gaby

"I can't get over how calm you are."

"What's to be anxious about, Nina?" Gaby has her elbows on the table and sips white wine from a long-stemmed goblet designed for water. She surveys the clutter of dirty dishes on her dining room table. It's the night before her so-called Sunday afternoon tea. She and Joe have assembled those members of their families able to make the trip to Hayworth—no small feat, in and of itself.

Nina, Gaby's younger sister, and her husband Craig, flew in this morning from Kingston, Ontario. They are bunked at the Hayworth Hotel. Craig has never visited before, although Nina has been here a few times in the last eight years. They rented a car and Nina spent the day giving her husband the big tour. Their four children are at home with Craig's sister and brother-in-law. The trip was last minute. Inclusion of the kids would have been a stretch.

Gaby leans into Joe. "Are you nervous, big guy?"

"Me? No way. My only fear is that you'll change your mind at the last minute."

"Not a chance." She raises her glass to him and takes another sip. "I'm in this for the long haul."

"You may be sorry." Both of Joe's older sisters are at the dinner table as well. Anita is the one who makes the remark. Although she comes across as pleasant enough, Gaby is always leery of her temperament. Anita runs hot and cold, but she's here and Gaby feels this is the most important part.

Christine's response is defensive, although she punctuates her thoughts with an expression of patience. "Gaby won't be sorry, Anita. She's landed herself a great guy." She reaches over and pats Joe's arm. "I am so glad we could come."

Gaby knows they both wish their husbands and Chrissie's two girls could have made the trip, but circumstances prevented the whole family from attending. They arrived yesterday, as well, and booked into the hotel.

"Now, you know the Hayworth people invited tomorrow have no idea this is a wedding. A lot of them think we're already married. Right, Joe?"

Joe nods. "The surprise is sure to be fun. Go through the list, Gaby. I don't think the family has met many of these folks. When you guys come to visit, we run around and do stuff together. We might talk about these Hayworthites one way or the other, but you haven't met many of them."

Gaby refills wine glasses before she begins. "Okay, let's start with Rose Woodward. She lives over at The Station in Number Two."

"Yes, right below where Joe used to be." Christine is anxious to let them know she has met a few of the guests.

"Correct. She works for Dr. Gunton, a local family doctor.

"Didn't her sister, what was her name, Maggie, live with her?"

"Not any more. She lives across the hall in Number Three, now. That's the apartment Ronny Étang moved into after Ben died and Joe settled the estate. Anyway, Maggie works at Segue House, the women's shelter, and she's been dating Sean Knox from the RCMP for almost a year now. They make a cute couple."

Joe's eyes scan around the table. "People make the same remark about us."

"Have you had too much wine? Settle down, now." Gaby taps Joe on the hand and giggles. "Speaking of Ronny, she will be here. I imagine she and Fiona Werbowski, another RCMP and good friend of Ronny's, will come together. I work with them to plan the Segue House Annual Ball and Fundraiser. They are wonderful women."

"Is Ronny the one who was kidnapped?" Nina pipes up, in an attempt to clarify.

"Yes. Ronny came here four years ago, almost in a self-imposed witness protection situation. Her abusive husband, a guy named Duncan Taylor, found out where she was because of a newspaper clipping with a story about how great our RCMP/Segue House Ball and Fundraiser is every year. I never knew who she was until after he grabbed her. She rented 15 Poplar then, but I sold the house to her a short while later."

Joe pipes up at this stage. "Then there's my buddy, Patrick. God, there was a time when I didn't even want to stand near the guy. He's lived up in Number Six at The Station since 1977. Thanks to Ben Tullis and a good shrink, he's a different person. He'll come with Audrey Baranski. She's a local girl who moved into Number Four after I finally gave up the lease." He follows this remark with an explanation. "I didn't want to put too much pressure on Gaby, here, in case our good intentions didn't work out. We knew we could roll back the clock if circumstances went sideways."

Gaby's voice is soft as she teases him. "I played a long game." She glances around the table. "And you'll get to meet that 'good shrink', too. Rachel Wilkerson will be here."

"Anyway," Joe continues. "Audrey suffered from mental health issues, too. She's okay now. She and Patrick seem to get along. Like Maggie and Sean, I think they make a cute couple."

"You have turned into a bit of a romantic, Joe. Man, after your love-life history, I'm surprised."

Anita can always find a way to toss out a curve ball insult. Gaby knows Joe's history, which isn't particularly sordid. He was married once and when the relationship didn't work out, he lived with someone else for a while. When the second relationship disintegrated, he moved west. It was ages ago—1966, if her memory serves her. Joe needed to sort out the issues related to the death of his brother, Adam, and how the loss impacted everyone in his family.

Gaby takes the spotlight off Joe and continues. "Then there's Cheryl Nadler and her daughter Amy MacDonald. Anita and Chrissie, you've met Cheryl. She and I worked together at the Hexagon, although we were in different divisions. She works with adoptions and I was in family counselling. Cheryl still lives where she has for years—in Number Five at The Station. Cheryl was fifteen when she gave up Amy for adoption, from what I gather. She's very private but proud of her daughter."

"Amy's the young woman who works at the store."

"Yes, Nina. She's inexperienced, but she's helped me have a normal life this summer. Joe might go out to a site after supper, but I have tried to manage my work days to end at five o'clock."

"Any other old Station friends? What about Chester and Amanda?" Chrissie isn't up to speed on the latest developments out on the Wolski property. Gaby remains uncomfortable with current circumstances and doesn't want to reveal too much.

"I don't expect them. Their house build has been shut down for ten days, ever since they found human remains down an abandoned well on the property August 14. Amanda isn't very happy with Joe and me. I invited them, but will be surprised if they turn up."

"Why would they blame you because a body was found out there? What happened?" Craig, of course, wants the gory details.

"Amanda told me not to dig out and fill in the well, back a few hundred feet from the house. She said she and Chester would take care of the job, but you guys know me. I didn't want there to be any opportunity for one of their two children to have an accident. When I expressed my concerns to old Borys Wolski, Chester's father, a few days before we dug the hole for the foundation, he told me to fill the damned hazard in. He said he owned the property and he could give me permission. We dug out the old rocks from the collapsed wall and, as they say, the rest is history. Amanda was pretty mad. She fired our asses." He raises his eyebrows as he grimaces at Gaby. "I think it marks the first time I have ever been booted off a job site. Now the whole place is shut down until they make an identification." He looks at Gaby to continue.

"Everybody is pretty sure the remains are those of Roz Dover, but you know the RCMP. They won't speculate about a situation like this. I haven't talked to Fiona since the day we were out at Wolski's. I still think information from the night Roz disappeared doesn't add up."

"Well, none of the problem is your affair, right? No one can blame Joe because the body was found on the property." Anita seems defensive.

"We have a stake in this, Anita. The Wolski house barely has a foundation dug, but we have materials and products ordered. We have commitments and bills we can't honour with just a deposit cheque. There are a lot of loose ends. On top of this, my old nemesis, Charlene Quinn, may or may not be a witness for the RCMP. They've been to interview her and she's already made contact with me once." Gaby brushes a stray curl behind her ear and sighs. "I've been through enough with Charlene Quinn to last a lifetime."

"What about people you used to work with?" Nina, as is her habit, tries to change the subject when the atmosphere feels the least bit tense.

"Well, the whole gang will be here, judging by the responses. They're suspicious because we have gatherings of Station residents often, but previous work colleagues have never been included before. A few of them will figure a special occasion is afoot."

"List them off. I need a refresher."

"Let's see. My old boss, Pearl Markowski, will be here. Clark Alden, Pearl's boss, will also attend. He was excited, all in a flutter, when I called him. Edith Findley is still with the Family Counselling Division, so I needed to ask her. She would have been apoplectic if I left her out and she heard." Gaby knows full well she would not have considered leaving Edith out.

"Don't forget the big guy," Joe inserts.

"Frank and Margaret Spencer—the Pastor never changes—and Elliot and Celina Banks will also be here. Celina is a hoot. You will love her. Too bad the weather is warm and she won't have to wear her poodle coat, eh Martha?" Gaby leans over to pat her dog, stretched out beside her chair as usual. "Martha loves Celina's poodle coat."

"This is becoming quite the affair." Chrissie, elbows on the tables, smiles with contented pleasure as she sips her wine.

Gaby presses on. "Two of my favourite people accepted invitations— Rachel Wilkerson, whom I already mentioned, as well as Mimi Long and her husband Tim. Rachel has decided to stay in Hayworth full-time starting this fall. Mimi was our secretary when I worked at the Hexagon. She and Rachel were extremely good to me when I was under investigation. You learn who your true friends are when you're ass-deep in a crisis."

"Members of our two building crews will be here, plus Murdock Blackney, the Justice of the Peace."

"I think you paid attention, Joe!" Gaby giggles and turns to their family. "Here's the plan. Murdock will arrive well ahead of time and hide in our home office until everyone else gets here. I want to stay upstairs and out of sight. Joe will be official meeter and greeter. Once everyone is settled in and has a drink, he will call upstairs to find out what's taking me so long and I will come down the stairs in all my glory. Then Murdock will appear, Chrissie will slap on the 'Here Comes the Bride' record, and we'll be ready for a party."

"What about Martha?" The dog lifts her beautiful face toward Nina as the question is asked.

Gaby bends down to pat her dog once more. "I think Martha will walk me down the stairs. Right, old girl? You and I will marry your papa. It was Joe who brought Martha to me in the first place."

****

The day holds great promise. By one-thirty, Gaby is dressed and sitting at the upstairs foyer window in her rattan rocker. She has a perfect view of their guests as they arrive, confident they cannot see her. She is still happy with her dress, purchased many months ago. This particular garment appealed to her, with its simple empire waist-line and ivory lace fabric that floats to the floor. The sleeves have small caps. She slides her hands into the pockets. They were a surprise and she loves them.

Gaby admires Martha, gussied up with a big pink bow attached to her collar. She shook a couple of times, but has now admitted defeat. The bow will stay. She took longer to get the dog's bow to remain in place, than she did to get her wedding dress on.

Nina came up and tried to fix her hair. Her sister decided to call the effort a messy chignon—whatever. She has her curls captured in a tiny bun at the nape of her neck. Nina gave her a thin hair band, covered in little crystals, to hold back stray tendrils—not an accessory she would wear every day, but it works with the dress. Rose Woodward should love it, since she wears a plastic hair band most of the time.

Almost everyone is here. The noise downstairs has become a bit of a din. People get their drinks and wander out on to the patio in the back. Gaby sees what she expects is the last car to pull up. Elliot and Celina pile out. The couple present themselves to the world in the exact same way they did the first time Gaby met them. He spends most of the time with his gaze fixed on his shoes. Celina, on the other hand, has no trouble compensating for his general reluctance with life in general. Their relationship has never ceased to amaze Gaby. Celina is dressed as only Celina can, in a form-fitted, low-cut, and very short electric blue dress. Her heels must be six inches high. Her blond hair bounces around her beautiful face. Gaby can make out her baby voice as she tells Elliot they are late. She hears Elliot point out the event is an afternoon tea, for God's sake, and a couple of minutes won't matter. *Joe and I might actually pull off this surprise.*

"Will you be down soon, Gaby?" Joe's deep voice rattles up the curved staircase to the foyer above.

Gaby stands, pats Martha as she tells her to heel, picks up her little bouquet of pink roses chosen to match Martha's bow, and makes her way down the stairs. At the precise moment her gown would be visible to the guests below, Nina turns on the record player and she hears the office door open. Murdock Blackney, round and resplendent in a navy blue suit, takes his place in front of the fireplace.

Of course, there are gasps. Gaby expected there would be gasps. What she is unprepared for is the spontaneous round of applause as she takes one step at a time, with her dog by her side. Martha surveys the crowd, seems to satisfy herself they are friendly, and continues her trundle to the bottom beside her mistress. Joe is there. He takes Gaby's hand. The three of them approach Murdock. Gaby and Joe have eyes for no one but each other. Martha sits with one big paw placed strategically on the toe of Gaby's shoe.

The ceremony is quick—a formality of sorts. Murdock Blackney, with his head in a perpetual tilt to the left like he questions everyone and everything, reads from his little red book. They exchange their rings; rings stored in a drawer upstairs for as long as Gaby has owned the dress. He then, in his capacity as the JP, introduces them to their friends, and the ceremony is over.

Now the party starts in earnest. Of course, there are lots of introductions of their family members to their friends and former colleagues. Gaby and Joe circle among their guests. He pours wine. She passes wedding cake while Nina, Anita, and Chrissie manage the rest of the food. Nina's Craig has been in charge of parking, and now takes his post as bartender for those who don't drink wine.

As they hug, Celina's huge breasts squish into Gaby's paltry ones. "We are too excited you invited us to this, Gaby. Elliot and I adore you both. We are delighted. What a surprise!"

Gaby leans back a bit to better face her beautiful young friend. "All the times you've been in and out of the shop while we design your new bathroom, you didn't suspect?"

"Never even imagined, Gaby. You two can keep a secret. Even Miss Martha, here, never let on, did you old girl? I brought you a present."

Martha likes Celina. Gaby is suspicious the coat might be the attraction, as Martha gazes up at Celina with her one brown eye and one blue eye, sad and expectant. Celina reaches in her over-sized designer handbag and produces a stuffed poodle almost the exact colour and texture of her beloved coat. She giggles and bends over. Such behaviour threatens to result in a serious wardrobe issue if Martha doesn't reach up toward the gift before Celina's boobs drop out of her dress.

"Here you go, my friend."

Martha takes the stuffed toy in her mouth and immediately gives the poodle a good shake.

"It has to be dead, Celina."

"My mistake. Next time, I'll kill her present first. Come on, Martha. Let's go show Uncle Elliot what you have."

Maggie Woodward and Sean Knox sidle up to Gaby the minute Celina drifts off in search of her husband. "We are thrilled for you, Gaby! I think your idea to host a surprise for us is the best." Maggie stands on tiptoe and kisses Gaby on the cheek.

Sean has made a huge impression on Maggie. There was a time when the girl flinched if you patted her shoulder. She notices the couple never seems to relinquish the hand of the other.

"Fiona wants to talk to you, Gaby. There's news about the case. She wants to tell you herself." Sean gives her a half-hug with his spare arm. "Thanks for the invitation. This gives me lots of ideas," he whispers in her ear.

She takes her plate of cake and starts to manoeuvre through little groups of guests. The trip to get to the patio where Ronny and Fiona sip wine and admire the distant prairie views, takes longer than she expects. Of course, everyone has to congratulate, admire her dress, comment on the surprise, and express their appreciation to be included. Gaby realizes, after eight years in this community, Hayworth has become her home. The people around her today are the proof of her epiphany.

Of course, Amanda and Chester Wolski did not come. Gaby and Joe talked about this last night. They decided they would start the ceremony once everyone else arrived. Amanda never called and said they wouldn't come, but Gaby knew in her heart the young woman was too angry and upset to join in an afternoon tea party.

"Cake, you two? I need a break. Can I hide out here?" Gaby sets the silver tray of wedding cake down on the patio table and drops into one of the matching chairs.

"You don't have a drink, yet, Gaby. Let me run and get you what? White wine?" Ronny is up and on the move before Gaby has a chance to settle.

"Wine would be wonderful. Joe said we would do a toast in a few minutes. I guess I will need to get a drink." She embraces the pure comfort of getting off her feet.

"Chester was arrested this morning." The words sound hollow and distant, like thunder on a prairie evening."

"The body is Roz Dover?"

"Yes, they're the remains of Roz. We were forced to wait for the dental record comparisons. I won't go into details, but there was still a lot for forensics to work with. A body down a cold well lasts a little longer, I gather. She was wrapped in a blue mechanics coat, too. I wanted you to know how our whole discussion around the answering service proved to be the pivot point. The detectives let me talk to them and we found out the details of what happened; what has been happening right up until the body was found."

"What did the service have to say?"

"I have to shut up about the details since an arrest has been made and charges will likely be laid, Gaby, but suffice to say the answering service employees did not want to be accountable if their behaviour relates to a homicide."

Gaby spies Cheryl Nadler as she hovers at the patio door. She thanks Fiona for keeping her in the loop and Ronny, who has fetched her a glass of wine, before she makes her way back inside.

"Amy and I are flattered to have been invited to your wedding, Gaby. We were surprised, weren't we, Amy?" She acknowledges her daughter, the mirror image of herself, but with a modern twist.

"How come Chester isn't here, Gaby? I thought you said you invited him and Amanda."

"I did, Amy, but perhaps they didn't come because of the whole business with the well. She wasn't very happy with Joe. Maybe they made other plans. She fired us, you know." Gaby knows Amy is disappointed not to see Chester.

"Well, Amy has one more week before she finishes her job and heads back home to Halifax and university. We appreciate all you've done, Gaby. Don't we, Amy?"

"Yes. The summer's been a blast. I hope we can work together again next year, Gaby. The money's great."

"You've been a big help. We have to see how contracts go this year before I can commit to next, Amy." Gaby is in no position to make promises, considering they are currently in the middle of a house contract which has fallen apart at the seams.

"Can I have everybody's attention?" Joe's voice resonates throughout the house. Everyone moves toward the sound. He has taken a spot in front of the rock fireplace. "Where has my beautiful bride drifted off to?"

Gaby, wine in hand, gives him a wave as she circles around from the patio doors.

"There she is." He holds out his hand to help her as she stands up on the elevated slate hearth beside him. "I want to make a toast—first to the beautiful, smart, and kind Gaby Ridgway. You are my best friend and I love you. Second, to our wonderful family who traveled up here to the back of beyond in order to help us celebrate on this day. Third, to each of you, our friends and colleagues for all these many years. You have been there through some very rough patches. You have supported our business. You are our community. Thanks for sharing this day with us. Enjoy the food and the drinks." At this point, he clinks his glass with Gaby. Their guests do the same and everyone claps.

The afternoon is light years beyond a huge success. After the locals depart, Gaby is anxious to return to comfy clothes. Her sister and sisters-in-law start to clean up and get food put away. Craig and Joe move furniture back to rightful places, empty garbage, and reorganize cars in the driveway.

By seven o'clock, everyone is ready for a cup of tea and a final visit. Tomorrow, they leave to go back east. Both of Joe's sisters, as well as Nina and Craig, will catch the one flight out of Hayworth in the morning. They will fly to Edmonton together and then on to Toronto. Once in Toronto, Anita and Christine will continue on to Halifax while Nina and Craig will catch a commuter train to Kingston. Compounded by the time changes involved, it will be very late when they get home tomorrow night.

This is good bye. Since Joe and Gaby won't take vacation until Christmas, tonight and tomorrow is their time. Gaby finds it hard to wind up the day. As much as she wants to take a long walk across the field with Joe and Martha, she hates to see the sisters go.

****

Gaby and Joe return to the shop on Tuesday, like every other week. They have always closed on Sunday and Monday. Joe has been very worried about the status of the Wolski project. Yesterday, they took a drive out past the job site. There was no sign of life there or next door at the Wolski farm. One would think the brothers would be out on the land, but there seemed to be no activity.

"Chester was charged yesterday. Maybe everyone was at the police station or holed up with a lawyer. Fiona told me the site was released back to the family, but Joe, I don't think we can proceed until we hear from somebody. I know Amanda was mad, but maybe she needed to blow off steam. She's in a terrible mess. Then again, maybe we are fired for good. We can't let on we know about the arrest. I'm not sure what to do."

As they enter Dodd's Contracting and Interiors together through the back, they don't realize a big farm truck is parked on the street in front of their business. A few minutes later, after coffee has been made, Gaby and Martha approach the front door to turn the sign and open up, only to be greeted by the imposing form of Borys Wolski.

"Come in. Come in. I hope we didn't keep you waiting, Mr. Wolski. Did you come to see Joe? He's here in the shop with me for a while this morning. We're about to start to regroup after the weekend." She babbles to fill the space between them. She is sure he knows she knows.

"Coffee smells good."

"It does indeed. Come on over to the table and have a seat. I'll get you a cup. Joe! Borys Wolski is here. Maybe you can come up front while I get coffee for us."

Joe meanders out, coffee in hand. "Hey, Borys. What brings you into town today? I thought you and your boys would be busy on the fields this week. The forecast says cool nights and warm days. Perfect weather for all you farmers." He extends his hand.

Gaby sees Borys shake Joe's hand but he doesn't respond to the remarks. He takes a seat at the design table and keeps an eye on Gaby. She hurries to return with his coffee.

"How do you take your coffee, Mr. Wolski?" Gaby shouts, aiming her voice down the short hallway.

"Black. Thank you."

She returns with two cups, hands one to their guest, and places hers on the table. She doesn't sit. "What can we do for you, sir?"

"Please, call me Borys. You are a friend, correct?"

"We most certainly are friends, Borys." Joe leans across the table, ever so slightly.

"You will not tell anyone what I say?"

"Of course not!" Gaby's heart pounds. "How can we help?"

"There is not help. My son was arrested. They have charged him with murder. Amanda wants to continue with the house but I want her to stop until after this mess is cleaned up. It is important I pay you for all work to now and any materials you have already ordered and bought. No debts. I want no debts."

"You are very thoughtful, Borys, but Amanda has the contract with us. She was upset when she fired us on Wednesday."

"Amanda won't pay. She says this is your fault. She says she will hire someone else to finish. I want her to stop. She is like a crazy woman. The children miss their papa." His voice trembles. "Very, very hard." He reaches for his cheque book.

Gaby and Joe exchange glances. Gaby knows they might as well accept his cheque and deliver the products they have in the back shop out to the farm. Then, if Amanda decides to hire another builder, they will not have lost more than time.

"Okay, Borys. I'm saddened Amanda couldn't come and talk to us herself. This puts you in a terrible position."

"She says I gave permission about the well, so I have to pay." He surveys each of them in turn. "I can pay. It is okay. I can pay."

"Give me a few minutes to compile an invoice. Joe, when Amy shows up, send her to the office, okay?"

"Does this girl still work here?"

"Amy Macdonald? Yes. It's her last week, why?"

"Amanda hates her. Talks about her. Calls her bad names. She says the girl was involved with Chester. I can't believe. If I believe, I will lose faith in my son."

"I'm afraid I don't have information, Borys."

"When Amy gets here, I'll send her to the office."

Gaby takes about ten minutes to go through the contract and tease out how much is owed over and above the initial deposit. She draws up the invoice and returns to the showroom as the bells above the door tinkle and Amy bursts in.

Joe stands. "Hi, Amy. I need your help in the office. Come with me."

Amy, who appears bewildered since Joe is rarely in the office and never gives her instructions, nods at Gaby and follows him.

"This is her?"

"Yes, Borys."

"She is a young girl, a child." His big frame bends and his shoulders shutter.

Gaby places the invoice in front of him. "We have materials on hold at the lumberyard and I have other products stored in the back. You can take whatever I have here with you, and I will call the lumberyard and have them deliver the materials they have set aside. Will those arrangements work for you?"

He writes her a cheque. "It is why I brought the big truck today. I will keep the materials in the barn until we know what will happen." His ruddy face is reddened by emotion. His blue eyes have puddles and appear about to overflow. "You and Joseph have been very kind. I am sorry about the contract, but I don't think the house will ever be built and I don't think Amanda will ever pay. She is a hard person."

He unfolds his tall frame, stands, and reaches out to shake Gaby's hand. "Pray for us, Gaby. We are a family with many troubles." The sun is blocked from streaming through the front door as his broad back fills the space. He engages the truck and pulls round to the back, where Joe waits to load materials.

"Was the man at the front Chester's father, Gaby?"

"Yes, Borys Wolski."

"Man, you can tell where Chester gets his looks."

Chapter 22

Amanda

"Are you visiting Chester, Amanda? The morning is half over." Tesia pours juice for the children.

"I have to go down to the diner and tell the staff Chester's been charged. I imagine the story is all over town by now. When I wasn't at work yesterday, people no doubt figured it out."

"Daddy gone." Melanie picks Cheerios out of her bowl with her fingers. No one corrects her.

"When will Daddy be back, Mommy?" Mason, as usual, gets right to the point. Tesia tries to hush the children.

Amanda is overcome with waves of anger; waves she hasn't felt since she was a child in foster care. Sometimes, no matter what you do, the world goes against you. "Eat your breakfast, you two. Grandma will make you toast." She takes a breath. She has to get out of here. "Where's Borys?"

"He went to town to see Dodd's."

Spurts of her anger continue to fly around inside her brain, like swirling snowflakes with nowhere to land. "He's gone to pay them off, hasn't he?"

Tesia keeps her eyes focused on the place settings in front of the children. "You said this was his fault. He will pay."

"Joe went against my express orders, Mama. Then Borys told him to go ahead. None of this would have happened if people did as they were told. They would have my house almost framed by now." Her voice begins to sound shrill, even to her own ears.

"But they found a body, Amanda. More important—they found Roz Dover and her family will have closure." Tesia's voice seems soft, like she doesn't want to spook a frightened animal.

"Do I care about Roz Dover's parents? I care because work on my house has stopped and my stupid husband is in jail. Now I have to use my money to hire him a lawyer and I have to handle every detail myself, as usual." She grabs her purse and turns toward the door.

"Kiss, Mommy?"

Amanda runs back and gives each child a peck on the cheek before she tears off to her car.

****

Last Sunday was horrible. The RCMP arrived at their door as Borys and Tesia were leaving for church. Four cop cars rolled into the yard. Amanda remembers how she scanned the occupants in search of Fiona or Sean, since she knows them better than the others. Of course, they would have taken the day off in order to go to the Dodd party. As a result, a few of the members who arrived on the scene were from Carter River.

"We have a warrant for the arrest of Chester Wolski." A young female member, with M. Wiley on her name tag, was the officer who approached the screen door. Two other burly police stood behind her.

Amanda remembers she was at a loss as to what to say or do. She never thought, in a million years, this would happen. She didn't believe their situation would come to this. Chester sauntered over to the door. She could see him as he turned on the charm like someone might turn up the gas under a pot on the stove. He thought he could wiggle out of this because he's good looking. M. Wiley did not seem impressed, and a part of Amanda was pleased.

They didn't put handcuffs on him, which was thoughtful if you consider the children sat wide-eyed at the kitchen table. Mason jumped up to go see the police cars. Amanda grabbed him by the shoulder and told him to sit back down. She thinks, now, he will have a bruise.

Once Chester was outside, out of ear shot of the children but in front of both his parents and her, as they stood on the other side of the screen, M. Wiley told him he was to come with them to the police station. His arrest was in relation to the murder of Roz Dover. They must have identified her.

Amanda had harboured a faint hope the RCMP wouldn't be able to, but her parents arrived in Hayworth the minute there was news of a body, and must have provided dental records.

M. Wiley instructed the family to please stay at home. They would be contacted if required. It could be a couple of days.

Amanda asked if Chester needed a lawyer and was told he was entitled to representation. Chester turned and told her to get him a lawyer. She called Murdock Blackney after the cops left the property. Murdock wasn't home. She had to wait.

Her mind churned all day Sunday. When she finally contacted the lawyer, Murdock said he would go down to the police station and get the lay of the land. Then he would call a friend of his who is a criminal attorney.

She laid awake most of the night and worried all day Monday. Chester will take the fall for this. He wrapped her in his damned mechanic's coat. Everybody and their brother knows he always wears one of those to cover his clothes at work, and even at home when he's in the barn. He always has spares in his truck.

She isn't worried he'll talk. Someone has to run the diner, finish the house, and manage their children. If he admits to the whole episode and says her death was an accident, he might be out in ten years—appropriate punishment for a man who cheats on his pregnant wife.

On Monday, he was formally charged. She stayed at the farm. His parents went and stood in court while the charges were read.

****

When she arrives at the diner, breakfast has started to wind down. Danny, Nancy, and Patrick watch her as she goes into the kitchen and puts her purse in her office. She goes back through the swinging doors and behind the counter to retrieve the framed photograph of Mason and Melanie she has always kept there. She'll take it to Chester as a reminder of why he is about to make this sacrifice; a reminder of the importance of their decision and how she will take care of their children and try to rebuild a life for them.

After she puts the photo in her bag, she checks the restaurant for stragglers. Once the place has emptied out, she calls her staff together. Nancy and Patrick sit down in the booth at the back. Danny leans against the divider which separates this booth from the next, and Amanda takes her place. She stands at the end of the table like she's poised to write up an order.

"I don't know how much you people know, but Chester was arrested Sunday morning and charged with Roz Dover's murder yesterday."

"I heard the body they found was Roz." Patrick is the first to speak up.

"Yeah, everybody in town knows Roz was in the well." Danny keeps his eyes focused firmly on the table in the booth. "How's Chester holding up?"

"I don't know. They told me not to come near. Murdock Blackney doesn't do criminal stuff but he took care of getting a lawyer. Chester's parents went to court yesterday. I'm on my way over this morning. First, I wanted to talk to all of you. I'll be here when I can, but will the three of you be able to manage all the shifts?"

"I suppose you'll want me to work splits. It means a lot of prep work if we have to go back to the lunch menu we use when there's only one cook." Danny can summarize the most complicated of circumstances. In this case, lunches have to be made in advance so the cook can be around for breakfasts and suppers.

"Right. Expect seven days a week for a while, until we figure out what will happen. I appreciate your help."

"The wait for a trial might seem like forever, Amanda. Will he be able to get bail?" Patrick points out the obvious.

Amanda sighs. If Chester pleads guilty, this whole mess could be buttoned up in a couple of weeks. Her goal is to reinforce this idea once she gets in to visit. "I hope bail's an option, Patrick, but difficult to predict in a murder charge. Keep your fingers crossed. I'll be back after I talk with him. I'm off now." *Did I sound enough like the supportive wife to satisfy the bunch? I hope I did.*

****

Small town cop shops are boring. You walk in the door and see a cluster of desks. There are a few offices and then a corridor that leads to an interrogation room and a couple of cells. She approaches the first desk, identifies herself, and says she's there to see Chester. She explains how she was told she could come in today.

The young woman, not a police officer and someone unfamiliar to Amanda, nods and says she'll be back in a minute. Amanda gazes around as she waits.

There isn't any security to speak of. Her purse has not been inspected. The thought crosses her mind she could very well have a pistol hidden in her bag and no one would be the wiser.

Sean Knox appears from the back corridor. "Hi, Amanda."

His face is devoid of expression. Amanda thinks he seems blank most of the time, even when he picks up coffee at the diner.

"I put Chester over in the first interrogation room."

"I thought we could have a private talk, Sean. This is pretty serious. You guys have mics and stuff hidden in there?"

"No. I'm sure there are plans for the future, but for now you get a plain old room. You're entitled to have a private talk, the same as with a lawyer. None of our business." He follows his little speech with a brisk nod, and turns.

She trails behind him down the hospital green corridor. He uses a key to open the door. "Ring the buzzer when you want to leave, okay?"

"No problem, Sean. Thanks. Oh, by the way. Can I give him this?" She reaches in her purse to pull out the picture of the children. She notices how Sean takes a step back and his hand drifts toward his weapon. She decides, as much as she would love to poke fun at his nervousness, not to acknowledge the behaviour.

Chester remains seated at the metal table when she walks in. His hair needs a comb. He could be ten years older, suddenly. *Good. Let him sweat. He deserves this.*

"Hi."

"Hi."

"How are the kids? What about Mom and Dad?"

She ignores his questions for the moment. "What have Murdock and his fancy lawyer friend said?"

"They say they can get me off, but they don't think I'll be able to get bail."

"What do you mean, get you off? You need to plead guilty, Chester. You need to tell them you gave the little slut a push, she fell, and you panicked. That's our story!"

"I could get twenty-five years in jail, Amanda. I didn't kill her and I don't want to go to jail. The lawyer said he could get me off."

"Maybe if you hadn't wrapped her in your goddamned mechanic's coat. What an idiot. Like you needed to be nice to a dead body before you toss it down a well. Jesus! Tell them you shoved her and she fell on a rock. Tell them it was an accident and she died."

"I don't know if I can do it. Maybe if you tell them the truth...."

"Are you out of your mind? We have two children. We have a business and a new home—albeit a hole in the ground right now. I do not intend to tell the RCMP one damned scrap of information different from what I've said all along! You will tell them you screwed around behind the back of your pregnant wife. You convinced the answering service to call you and fake an emergency. You went to meet her. You fought and she fell and hit her head. You wrapped her in your dirty mechanic's coat from the service truck and threw her in the well. You will tell them this, Chester. You will tell them this for our kids; for our future."

"What future? I have to give up my future because of what you did?"

"No, not because I hit the little tramp on the head with a rock. You have to give up your future because of what you did to me."

"Why did you have to go out there?"

Amanda leans over and whispers in Chester's ear. "Funny in the end, when you think about it. You would have beaten me to your rendezvous," she wiggles her shoulders as she draws out the word, "if you hadn't stopped at the bar to pick up off-sales beer. She saw your truck as we bumped down the old dirt track. Here I am, pregnant and fat with a toddler asleep on the front seat, and she skips over to the door expecting you. Too stupid to remember you were supposed to be in the tow truck. She squeaked like a little mouse when I started to get out."

She leans back and turns to grab the other chair in the room. She's started to enjoy this—a cathartic chat of sorts. "She tried to run away from me, back to her car. She thought she could run away. I picked up a rock the size of a small turnip and was up behind her, even pregnant and sick, long before she got back to her ugly green Pinto."

Chester stares across the table. His eyes are full of abject terror. Amanda hasn't seen this exact expression since the night Roz died. She thought he could hide his fears behind his mask of blank vagueness, but maybe he isn't as skilled as she thought. She learned how to hide her truth a long time ago, in foster care, when she knew for certain no one loved her. She can take care of herself.

"Here's the deal, Chester. You tell your new, expensive lawyer—the one I hired and the one I can fire—how you want to plead to some lesser charge than murder and get a deal. Tell them her death was an accident. You might get lucky and get to serve five, six, maybe seven years." She examines her fingernails before she points to the picture of their children. "You think of them, Chester. They need to have a future and we can't have their lives ruined because you couldn't keep it in your pants."

****

Amanda avoids the diner and points the car straight for the farm. The idea that he might roll on her and tell the truth never crossed her mind in the four years since she killed Roz Dover. Chester cheated on her. He was an asshole. She was pregnant. Her hormones were wacky. She was out of her mind with jealousy. From the very start, her intention was for him to pay for his infidelity by taking the blame, if the body was ever found. Now, there's a problem. She needs a plan.

The RCMP haven't come to talk to her because she's the wife. They talked to Tesia who, of course, does not know a thing. She never does. They spoke to Borys, who told them about the well and how he gave permission to Joe Dodd. Joe Dodd and his goddamned dead brother!

"Hi, Mama. I see Borys is back. He's unloading a bunch of stuff into the barn and I passed the lumberyard delivery truck coming this way."

Tesia lowers sheets into the washer located beside the kitchen sink. Amanda has a separate space designed for both a washer and a dryer. No one will ever catch her with clothes hung out when the temperature hits thirty below, or see her when she takes them in when they're stiff as a board. What a joke. She will have a dishwasher, too. "How is Chester? Did they say we could go to see him?"

Amanda doesn't know if he can have other visitors besides her and the lawyers, but she tells his mother he can't. There's no point in courting an opportunity he might use to talk to his parents. They could testify. She can't take the risk. "Where are the kids?"

"They went down to the barn with Borys. He said he could keep an eye on them until the big truck gets here and then they'll come back to the house before he goes over to your place." She sighs.

Amanda tries not to think the worst of Tesia, although she always thinks the worst of people. Her mother-in-law doesn't make eye contact. Maybe she knows something.

For whatever the reason, Ben Tullis jumps into Amanda's mind. Ben brought out the best in her. Ben loved her and love made her a better person. Chester's love performed the same function for a long time, and their relationship was wonderful before he started to cat around. She could handle the flirting. God! He's so attractive. He would walk into a room and every woman there would stare with her mouth open. She could handle marriage to a handsome and faithful man. He would always come home with her.

Their relationship changed when she was pregnant with Melanie. After she inherited the money from her first husband, her confidence returned. She no longer cared if he loved her. She would have left him if not for Roz Dover.

She makes an effort to be kind for a moment. "Chester seems pretty good, Mama. He's tired, you know. RCMP lock up can't be comfortable. He asked after you and the kids. I took him the picture of them I kept down at the diner, you know, on the shelf behind the counter? He was happy to see it."

"Will you work more at the diner today?"

"No, I think I'll stay away from Hayworth for a few days—let the gossip settle down. I don't want a whole bunch of people I don't know asking me questions. I have no answers. Murdock Blackney found him a good defence lawyer. The guy says he won't get bail. We could be in for a long haul, especially if they move him to county lock up in Carter River."

Tesia gasps and puts her hand over her mouth. "Carter River is two hours away, and fall is here, Amanda. We will have to take turns to go and visit him."

"I don't know, Tesia. Right now, I think I might take the kids away for a while." She tries to sound casual, like what she means is a little drive to the lake or into the city.

"Away? Where? School starts in a couple of weeks, Amanda. You can't take the children on a trip when your husband is in jail and charged with murder!"

Amanda's eyes narrow as she stares across the kitchen at her mother-in-law, snarled in the floral sheets she's attempting to load into the washer. "You need to know, Tesia, I think I am capable of doing whatever I want. Right now, I'm off down to the barn to get the kids." She ignores Tesia's shocked expression.

Chapter 23

Patrick

"Patrick, come in the kitchen when you have a minute. I have a question." Patrick is concerned about Danny, who clearly has the hardest job. He and Nancy can back each other up but Danny has to do his work alone. They both take care of as many tasks as they can to help, but Patrick still worries. Danny has been run off his feet all morning. For some twisted reason, the diner is a lot busier since Chester was arrested three days ago. He went to jail on Sunday, and here they are at Wednesday and business has almost doubled.

With Amanda not there to share shifts at the grill, Danny has become short-tempered. He reminds Patrick of what the cook used to be like when he first started to work and Danny had it out for him. Now they work together well, but this whole mess with Chester has put a strain on the team, as they try to cover.

"On my way. I have another order for you, too."

Patrick pushes through the saloon doors with an armload of dirty dishes. He hands Danny the order slip, which saves the older man a trip to the pass window for retrieval.

"Thanks. When do you think Amanda plans to come back in? I can't work from six in the morning until eight at night with a couple of hours off in the middle of the day. I can't do this forever. My wife is ready to kill me already. I could go to work at the hotel and make more money while I work less hours. You could, too. Even Nancy, if she wanted. Amanda doesn't know how lucky she is."

Danny has worked up a head of steam and Patrick knows he might as well let the guy run off at the mouth until he peters out. He's learned a lot since he came to work here eight years ago, back when Margo Johnson owned the place. "Maybe you could call her, Patrick. Find out what the hell's the score. Jeez, I know a person has other concerns on their mind when their husband's been arrested for murder, but come on! The rest of us have lives, too."

Patrick takes a deep breath before he speaks. "Let's wait until after the breakfast crowd gets out of here. Then the three of us can talk about what to do. Do you think if she's gonna be gone for a long time, like more than a month, we should ask her if we can hire another cook? Or maybe not open for breakfast for a while? Try to think about other options."

By a little after nine, the diner has emptied. Patrick gets the dishwasher he oftentimes thinks of as his personal friend, humming and blinking. He feels secure when she's working away; when there are no breakdowns. He and the vintage Hobart countertop dishwasher are a lot alike.

Nancy, Danny, and Patrick sit down in the staff booth at the back of the diner.

"I think you should call her, Patrick. And the idea of letting us hire another cook works for me. There's always a bit of training involved, but once we're up to speed, it'd be good. What about you two? Do we need extra staff to wait tables or bus for you? Does Audrey need any extra work, Patrick? Maybe she could come in and help either one of you when she's not at the hospital."

"I can ask her. She plans to come down for supper tonight—says she has to eat here in order to see me and she's pretty much right." He blushes. He wants his relationship with Audrey to work. She can hang out down here while he works whenever she wants.

"Will you call her? I can't go home today without information to pacify my wife. We've been without help since Sunday. Today's Wednesday and no end in sight. We need a plan." He leans over and pokes Patrick in the shoulder. "And you are just the guy to call the boss."

"I'll call her before lunch starts up. I knew all along Chester was involved, you know. I'm glad they arrested him. He had his eye on Amy MacDonald."

"What?" Nancy's eyes widen as they flit from Patrick to Danny and back again. "How do you know?"

"Well, she's lived with Audrey this summer. She told Audrey and me how he gets the answering service to fake an emergency when he wants to get out of the house in the tow truck and go pick her up. I figured the same thing happened the night Roz disappeared." His voice gets quiet and he focuses on the urethaned table top. "I told Fiona what Amy told us. I think Fiona went back and talked to the answering service. I don't know."

"Sounds like you might have helped with the investigation, Patrick."

"Yup. I also told her a while back that if Charlene Quinn didn't kill Roz, maybe she was a witness and someone should go to Nova Scotia and talk to her. I don't know if they did though."

"Well! You have been quite involved in this, Patrick. I'm proud of you. There was a time when you thought no one would believe you." Nancy turns to grace him with an expression of pure motherly indulgence.

"And the rest of us would have thought the story was one of your dream-things." Danny coughs, and unsuccessfully tries to hide the bit of emotion he permitted to seep into his voice. He starts to haul his ample self out of the booth. "Okay, back to lunch prep. I still want to get home for an hour or two. You call Amanda, Patrick, and then tell us what she says."

Patrick trudges through the kitchen into Amanda's office to make the call. He has a deep sensation of foreboding, like life will change forever once he hears his boss' voice.

****

"Hello, Mrs. Wolski?"

"Yes. Who is this, please?"

"Patrick, down at the diner. Can I speak to Amanda for a minute?"

"One moment, please."

There is a long silence with muffled mumbles. Amanda's mother-in-law has the phone mouthpiece covered with her hand.

"She says she will call you later, Patrick."

"No, ma'am. I have to talk to her now. It's very important."

More muffled mumbles.

"What's wrong, Patrick? This better be an emergency. I have a few more important topics on my mind than your work schedule."

Patrick thinks Amanda has become increasingly abrupt and thoughtless since she inherited her money. The stress of Chester's arrest has served to make her worse. He attempts to find solutions rather than look to her for answers—his way to calm her down.

"Amanda, Danny can't work twelve to fourteen hours a day every day. Maybe we need to open later, or close one day a week, or hire another cook to work the hours you used to do. The diner is busy. We're worn out. Will you be back soon?" The words tumble out. He didn't want to sound anxious; to cause her to worry, but he can't help how he sounds. If Danny quits and goes to work at the hotel, they will be out of jobs.

"Listen to me. Call Greta Seeley. She'll help you guys hire another cook. And find a part-time waitress, if you want. Tell Greta I said she should help and do interviews, too."

"Can't you come in and do interviews, Amanda? The diner belongs to you. We want to do our best to take care of your business for you."

"I do not intend to show my face around Hayworth anytime soon."

"Don't you visit Chester? You have to come into town when you go to the jail."

"I came in yesterday and it will be the last time for a while. Don't torment me, Patrick. I may leave the area for a break; take the kids on a holiday; get away from the farm and this mess."

"Mason starts school in a couple of weeks, Amanda. You can't take off. Your husband's in jail. You have to be here...for him, for your in-laws, for us." His voice has raised an octave, as he starts to get anxious and worked up. Dr. Wilkerson said to take deep breaths. He tries.

"Keep your panties on, Patrick. Don't be such a whiner. Call Greta. She'll take care of the details. Tell Danny, if he needs to hire another cook, hire one. Don't call me anymore."

The phone goes dead. Patrick stands with the receiver raised to his ear until the dial tone kicks in.

When he leaves the office, Danny is standing, hands on his hips, waiting to hear what transpired on the phone. "Well? Is she on her way?"

"Nope. Not for a while so far as I can tell. She said we should call Greta Seeley. She keeps the books and she will take care of any new hire like another cook and a part-time waitress. She said Greta could even sit in on the interviews, if we have any."

"Good. What do you mean, she won't be back for a while?" Nancy has blasted through the swinging doors with an empty and damp tray. She unloaded the dishwasher while Patrick called Amanda.

"She told me she has a plan to take the kids on a trip, but school starts soon and her idea doesn't seem right." Patrick knows he's always anxious when situations appear unreasonable to him. He becomes obsessed when he is not able to interpret information in a logical sequence. Amanda is illogical in Patrick's eyes.

"She can't leave town. Her husband's in jail, for God's sake! What's the matter with her?" Nancy's expression is one of stunned shock. "She has responsibilities."

"I even told her so; almost the exact same words." Patrick sighs. Danny has taken off his apron and is about to go home on a two hour break. He has lunch prep done. They have little more to do than heat and plate. "She told me she couldn't face people in town and she wasn't about to come back."

"I think I'll stop at the hotel on my way home. I'll see if Mike Vukovic wants to do more than prepare vegetables. He's a good guy. Call Greta, Patrick. Get her down here later this afternoon, before supper starts. Call Audrey, too. Maybe we can make this work, especially if we don't have to deal with crazy Amanda. I'm outta here." With a muffled yawn, Danny heads for the door. "See you in a couple hours."

"Nancy, I guess you get to keep an eye on the front while I call the bookkeeper. Of course, you can call and I'll take care of customers. Preference?"

Nancy snickers as she wraps one arm around Patrick's shoulder. There was a time when she would have turned up her nose if she found herself beside him—although she never, ever said one word to make him feel bad. He tries to share the moment with her. He likes Nancy a lot, but he still can't help but believe their situation will deteriorate very soon.

"Do you think we can get through the weekend before we commit to anybody, Nancy?"

"We can...but why the reluctance?"

"I don't know. I think Amanda might throw a monkey wrench into our whole situation. Dr. Wilkerson would say she isn't making good decisions. I'll talk to Greta, but maybe we can hold off until the weekend before we hire anybody."

"Fine with me. I hope Danny doesn't make any commitments. We don't want his friend Mike to quit the hotel today, do we?"

Patrick replies in the negative as Nancy returns through the saloon doors into the main diner when they are both alerted by the bells above the plate glass door.

****

"Hi, Greta. Patrick here, from up in Number Six?"

"Hi, Patrick. Is everything okay? Is there a problem in your apartment?"

"Oh, no, not at all. I'm calling from the diner."

"Poor Amanda! Poor Chester! Have you heard any news? I kind of thought she would call me, but not a word."

"She hasn't been in since Chester was arrested, except for a minute on her way to the jail yesterday. She says she won't come in and we should talk to you. We can hire another cook and a part-time waitress. The place is busy and we're working, like twelve hours a day every day. Danny has a friend at the hotel who might come in to cook, and Audrey might want to pick up a few waitress shifts when she's not at the hospital."

"Wow. Sounds like you guys have the details figured out, but there's lots of paperwork before people start to pull their weight. Maybe I could come down later on today to talk with you. When's a quiet time?"

"Around four, after coffee and before supper. Today's Wednesday. Supper isn't crazy. Not like the weekend."

"I'll have the kids with me after school, Patrick. Perhaps I should call Amanda and tell her."

"You can try, but she might not even answer. She refused to take my call but I told her mother-in-law we had an emergency—and there will be one if Danny gets fed up and goes over to the hotel to work. They've offered him a job once already and he turned them down. He doesn't want to run out on Amanda any more than I do."

"I'll be there after school. We'll talk about the situation, okay?"

"Okay, Greta. See you later."

****

Danny returns around two-thirty to start supper preparations. He talked to his friend, who will wait for a formal job offer, but is interested. Greta Seeley, with her two kids aged seven and four, show up about four o'clock. Nancy makes a pot of tea.

"I called Amanda and she asked her mother-in-law to tell me to handle employees as I see fit. I can't say I'm not worried." Greta sits in the booth across from the one the staff use. Patrick has provided her two children with crayons and placemats with pictures of circus clowns. They busy themselves. Greta's children are extremely well behaved. Patrick has noticed this at The Station. They never interfere, interrupt, or get in their mother's way. They never try to compete for her attention when she collects rents or checks on a repair in the building. They accompany her, but stay in the background.

Greta makes no secret of how she chose to give her kids up to foster care a few years back. She worked and got the training she needed to keep people's books. He imagines how much of a challenge and hardship it must have been. Now she can work from home and, at the same time, manage The Station.

Patrick decides not to mention the fact Amanda said she might take off on a trip. "We're worried, Greta."

"And tired out." Danny leans against the back of her booth, so he can keep one eye on the kitchen. He has three pork roasts in the oven.

"Well, I see no reason why we can't hire another cook. You have someone in mind, Danny?"

He nods. "Mike Vukovic. He works up at the hotel. He does preparations for the chef. He could handle the work load here with a bit of training. Of course, the hotel wants us to work up there. I expect they won't be happy when Mike comes down here to the diner. What about Audrey? Will she pick up a few shifts to give you and Nancy a break?"

"Likely. She plans to come in later for supper with Maggie and Rose. We can find out then."

"Great, Patrick. We can work around her schedule at the hospital. Maybe we need to hire a dishwasher, too. Somebody to bus tables." Nancy has said little to this point. She knows Amanda on a more personal level than Patrick does. Maybe she already knows their boss won't be back anytime soon.

"Let's start with Mike and Audrey for now and see what happens. Let's wait until Monday before we offer anybody a job, though. I will put the necessary paperwork together. I hope Amanda will see her way clear to return to the diner in a few weeks. I imagine a trial for Chester will take a long time." Greta frowns as she continues talking. "Margo has friends who are lawyers and she says she was told a trial could take a year from arrest to verdict. That's a lot of stress on a wife with two kids, a business, and a house to be built. The extra staff will be a big help. I don't envy her."

"Well, not to change the subject, but let's get my children fed. Me, too. I think I want the special tonight, when Danny gets it out of the oven." She focuses her attention on her kids for the first time. "Tell Nancy what you want and we'll have our supper."

****

Patrick peeks over the saloon doors to check, and sure enough, Audrey has cautiously opened the plate glass door. Her eyes scan the diner. He pushes through so she can see him and he can watch her face light up as he approaches. He loves to see her expression. He can't ever remember anybody who looked at him like that in his whole life. Right in front of Maggie and Rose, he leans over and kisses her on the cheek.

"You ladies are here for the pork roast special, I presume." He attempts a "formal waiter" approach, but Maggie and Audrey start to giggle.

Rose waves her hand in dismissal. "Lister, mister. I knew you back when you wouldn't even say hello. I knew you way before you became the handsome manager at the Hayworth Diner." There is respect in her eyes. Rose has been very good to him over the years, and he appreciates how she treats him. He also likes to be teased by her.

The three women choose a booth about half way down the dining area. Patrick provides menus and water. The place has quieted down a bit. It's close to six-thirty. Maggie and Rose prefer to eat late when the days are warm. He leans over and whispers in Audrey's ear. "Will you stay and walk me home at eight?"

His heart skips a beat when she responds. "I think I can manage."

"You hang around your boyfriend's place of work as long as you like, Audrey. I won't be offended if you don't want me to drive you home." Again, Rose acts like the mother, although she's not much older than Maggie, perhaps a couple of years.

"Speaking of boyfriends." Patrick decides to try and pump Maggie for pertinent information. "How's Sean these days? He must be busy since Chester was arrested."

"Patrick, you need to know—well, everybody needs to know—Sean and

I never, ever discuss work when we are together. We decided from the very beginning, since I work at the shelter and we cross paths often due to cases, not to talk about work ever. I have no idea about the Wolski case. Why don't you talk to Amanda, if you want to get the latest?"

Patrick's voice is soft. He doesn't want Danny to overhear and think he's gossiping. Nancy has already gone home. "She hasn't been in to work since he was arrested. We don't know when or if she'll be back. We may have to hire extra staff to pick up the slack."

"Well you can't blame her, Patrick. I imagine every Tom, Dick, and Harry is coming in here to get the scoop. I think I'd want to lock myself in the house and never come out. I feel sorry for her." Rose is almost abrupt in her assessment. "Let's order, girls. Does everyone want the special?"

****

After Rose and Maggie finish supper, which includes lemon meringue pie and tea, they pull out of the parking lot around seven-thirty. Patrick serves Audrey a second cup and sits down across from her for a minute. He reaches out to hold her hand. The dishwasher is loaded and the place is empty. Someone may turn up for a late supper, so they will stick around until eight. Patrick would be surprised if there are more customers tonight.

"Glad you stayed to walk home with me, Audrey. I have a proposition for you." He attempts a playful leer, but she is too interested in what he has to say to notice. "Greta Seeley was here today. We don't expect Amanda will be back to work for a while and she said we could hire extra help. Greta suggested I ask you if you're interested in picking up some shifts. Nancy said she would work around your schedule. I'm fine with extra hours, but she has nieces and nephews she wants to spend time with and we're here every day. I thought, at least this way we might get to spend more time together while this mess with Chester is on the front burner."

"Sounds like fun. I did a little bit of waitressing when I lived in Edmonton—not much, though. I thought everyone was out to hurt me and I quit."

Patrick pats her hand. "I don't think you have to worry now, do you?"

She giggles. He loves the sound; the one telling him she knows she's safe.

"Greta said to wait until the first of the week. I think she wants to make sure Amanda won't be back in the near future."

"You tell Greta I'm interested. Extra money would be great, since Amy leaves the end of next week."

They walk home together later in the evening. They take their time and hold hands. Patrick thinks expenses might be easier for Audrey if they shared one apartment instead of renting two. Maybe he should get out of the attic, but it's too early to tell. He'll wait for a while. He's managed to learn patience over the last few years. He thinks he'll talk to Dr. Wilkerson first. Always good to have a second opinion.

****

The next day is busy as usual. Too bad they have to wait until Monday to hire people. When the bell above the door jangles, Patrick is in the back with Danny who has returned from his afternoon break. Nancy prepares to take off.

Patrick places himself behind the counter as the big man approaches. "Hi, Mr. Wolski. What can we do for you today?"

"Are the other two staff here? The cook and the waitress?"

Patrick has always been curious why Chester's parents have never darkened the door of the diner. He doesn't think they were thrilled about Amanda's purchase of the place. "Yes, they're in the back. Nancy was about to finish for the day."

"Get them to come out here, please."

"Of course, sir. Is there a problem?"

"Go get them both."

Patrick does as he's told. Nancy has removed her apron and has her purse in hand. She's ready to take off. Danny is back in his chef's whites. "What's this about, Borys? I have half a dozen meat loaves to get ready for the oven." Danny knows Borys—a connection to his wife's family.

"I will not be long. You need to know we intend to close the diner indefinitely as of Saturday night, eight o'clock. Amanda cannot cope. She has many difficulties. The children are upset."

Patrick watches Danny and Nancy, who both stand like statues with their mouths open. "But Greta told us we could hire extra staff and run the place, Mr. Wolski. We thought we could manage the diner for her."

"I have talked to Greta and it is a bad idea. Amanda needs to focus on

Chester, not on business. Greta will deliver to you your cheques on Saturday afternoon. You will each get two week's extra pay and all the overtime you have worked."

"How long, Borys?"

Borys Wolski looks at Danny. "Closed? Long enough you should find other work. You have a young family to feed." Then he shakes hands with each of them in turn, and leaves without another word.

Danny lifts his shoulders and turns his hands palm outward. "I guess the shoe's on the other foot. We'd better go up and have a talk with the restaurant manager at the Hayworth Hotel."

Chapter 24

Gaby

"I'm off to the post office, Amy. I won't be too long."

"Alright, Gaby." She expels a dramatic sigh. "Once I get this pile of tile samples priced, I guess I'll start to dust displays if you're not back. You'll soon get to do this grunt work again yourself."

Gaby thinks she understands why there's a certain sadness in Amy's eyes, and why every task seems to aggravate her even more than the last. "Grunt work!" She giggles. "I think you have been well compensated for the 'grunt' work you've done for me this summer, my dear. See you in a bit." She calls for her dog and they take off out the front door and down the street.

The clear summer morning is not too hot yet, although there is the promise of a near perfect late summer afternoon developing, with slate blue skies, a tinge of change in the colour of the poplar leaves, and no bugs. Gaby pushes her curls behind her ears and sticks her nose in the air. She sniffs like Martha; inhales the aroma of downtown. She considers deep breaths to be her therapy. She bends a bit at the waist to ruffle the dog's soft ears. "Good girl. You heel."

Martha gazes up with an expression of, "Does this look like I'm not heeling?"

An RCMP patrol vehicle is angled parked in front of the federal government building, a small brick affair with granite steps and a big front window. There are lots of offices inside, but most people think of the structure as the post office. Gaby recalls the day she received her letter from the Canadian Counselling Alliance. It declared her vindicated. In the end, vindication didn't matter. It was December 10, 1981 and a fierce snow storm raged around her. It was on that very day she began to think about abandoning the field of family counselling forever—almost four years ago.

As she and Martha approach the steps, Fiona bounces out the double doors. "Hi! I was about to pop by the store to see you, but I've been a little busy."

"Why don't you come out to the house tonight, Fiona? Come for supper, or tea, if you don't want supper."

"I'm not off until seven. Too late for food? Can we ask Ronny? She expects me to stop by her place and bum a sandwich after work."

Gaby slaps her friend on the arm. "Bum a sandwich after work! You are a grown woman. Don't you cook?"

"Not much. Often pick up a special at the diner. Anyway, there's updates on the Dover case." She leans closer to Gaby and pretends she does this in order to pet Martha. "I can't tell you every detail, but I can reveal a bit. You and Ronny have been a part of this from the start. I figure you should know."

"Now you have me very curious, Fiona. I'll call Ronny when I get back to the office. I'll tell her you will pick her up after work and the two of you will come to my house for supper. Is it okay that Joe will be there, considering whatever you want to talk about?"

"Since the two of you haven't been married a week, I think I can approve the both of you at the supper table." She giggles. "Besides, Joe was the one who found Roz. He deserves to be privy to this information as well."

****

Amy hasn't been herself since Chester was arrested. Gaby understands the girl's anxiety, but she has become sullen and unresponsive in the shop. Gaby has decided to terminate their arrangement as of tomorrow, Saturday. There's still another week before she leaves for home.

After she gets the mail, Gaby calls Amy into the office. "What's up, today, Amy? Are you anxious to be back at university?"

"No. I'm worried about Chester. He's all I can think about. Do you believe he killed that girl?"

Gaby analyzes Amy's expression. There's more to her relationship with Chester than a few casual flirts. Maybe the rumours are true. "Amy, were you involved with Chester?"

She perches in Joe's chair at the desk on the other side of the office. Her face focuses on her lap and she picks at her fingers. In a trembling whisper she confides, "I think we were in love."

Gaby knows, from her days as a counsellor, how the most important aspect of sharing a confidence is to respect the person who reveals their secret. "You became close?"

"We used to meet when he was on call. We would go for drives in the tow truck. I was pretty sure we were serious, Gaby. You know, I was so important to him he would get the answering service to call the farm and fake an emergency, so he would have an excuse to get out of the house. Then we would meet down at the tavern and go off. He wouldn't risk his job if I wasn't important to him, would he?"

So...the information Audrey and Patrick revealed to Fiona was true. Roz must have felt the same way about her relationship with Chester. Gaby can imagine the bits and pieces of the puzzle as they start to nudge themselves into place.

"Amy, Chester is a charmer. He has always traded on his charm and attractiveness for as long as I have known him. He likes to flirt with young girls. He picked you. The truth of the matter is, he could well have picked Roz Dover, too. I don't know what happened to Roz, but you might be in the position to consider yourself lucky. Maybe there was an accident, or maybe he killed her on purpose. We don't know. The truth will come out in a trial. I know you're sad and worried." She gets out of her chair and moves closer so she can pat Amy on the shoulder. "But you are safe and sound, which is what's most important."

Amy does not appear convinced or pacified.

"How about you finish your work with us for the summer at the end of day tomorrow? I think it will be good for you to spend a little time with your mother before you return east."

Amy is a smart girl. She sees right through Gaby's ploy, but she isn't offended. "I haven't been much good to you the past few days, have I?"

"I understand. We've been upset, anxious, and concerned. The other point I want to make, though, Amy, is if you come back to Hayworth next summer, and if I can afford the help, I am happy to have you on staff. Let me know. If there is a job, it will be yours if you want to work here again."

The girl nods, as she tries to compose herself and rein in her emotions before she replies. "Okay, tomorrow I'm done. I'll start to reorganize the countertop samples and get rid of the discontinued ones—work I can accomplish before I'm through for the summer."

"Good. All good. I'll make coffee. I have to call a couple of people and I think Joe will be in any moment."

Gaby makes two phone calls. The first is to Ronny Étang, so their arrangements for supper can be finalized. Ronny is happy to accept and tells Gaby they will be there shortly after seven.

Then Gaby calls Cheryl.

"I know you're at work, but I wanted to alert you to a slight change in plans. Amy and I will go our separate ways as of tomorrow at closing time."

"Thank goodness, Gaby. I didn't want to interfere, but she has been such a mess since Chester Wolski was arrested. I've booked a few days off. I want to be around until the time comes for her to leave."

"Why didn't you talk to me? I would have done this for you if you thought her job should be finished up."

"Like I said, I didn't want to interfere. To be frank, Gaby, I was in the dark about her relationship, whatever it amounted to, with Chester. She lived at Audrey's. She often said she was meeting friends, but now I think every time she said this, she was with Chester Wolski. Do you think they were serious?"

Gaby avoids a direct answer. "I think Chester was being Chester. The scary part, Cheryl, is up until his arrest, I always knew he was a flirt. Maybe he's more, and we never knew."

"Well, I can't imagine Amy's mind is on your business. She isn't focused on me or home. Poor Audrey. I chatted with her a couple of days ago. She was in tears and said she was afraid to talk to me about Amy because she didn't want to break a confidence. She's a good kid. She's come a long way. I think she and Patrick are fond of each other."

"Oh, you are quite right. They're very cute. I also want you to know, Amy has been a big help to me this summer. I don't think we would have pulled off the wedding if I was tied to the shop all day, every day. She's good with customers and has serious organizational skills. If she's back next year, I'm happy to take her on again if we can afford to, and I have told her this. You should be proud of her. This is but a bump in the road."

"Thanks, Gaby, for your support. Amy and I will spend quality time together next week. Parenting is not as easy as one might assume."

"See you later, Cheryl."

****

After the shop closes at five, Gaby rushes to the grocery store to pick up supplies. Her plan is for Joe to barbecue chicken and vegetable kabobs. She grabs fresh raspberries and frozen yogurt. Supper will be simple, but she suspects Fiona won't know the difference.

By the time she arrives home, Joe and Martha have been for a nice long walk and the dining room table is set for four. He has managed to remember to shove a bottle of white wine into the fridge. They won't be here until after seven, giving her time to marinate the chicken, build the kabobs, and change her clothes. The day was warm, but evenings cool down in a hurry now. She chooses a blue sun dress with palm trees and sparkling water. She grabs a sweater.

"I see them on their way up the drive." Joe is out on the veranda, sipping wine and supervising the barbecue, although all he's done so far is turn the contraption on.

Fiona and Ronny are two of Gaby's favourite people. She feels comfortable in their presence.

"Come on in! Fiona, you are a different person when you're in your civvies. When you wear your hair down and don't carry a gun, it's like you could have graduated from high school this year." Gaby hugs her friend and they giggle at her description.

"How do you know I don't carry when I'm off duty?"

Ronny raises her eyebrows in response to Gaby's unasked question.

"Wine, everyone?" Joe has lumbered back in after he put the chicken on to cook. He plays his role as host, like always.

Dinner is fabulous in its simplicity, despite the last minute. They sit on the porch with their tea and watch the sky flood the fields with colour as the sun sets. Gaby is reflective. "Hayworth has changed a lot since Roz first disappeared four years ago. Do you think the atmosphere will change again now that her body has been found?" She asks the question to no one in particular, but knows she needs to direct the conversation toward the murder. She wants to know what Fiona has to tell her.

"One of my biggest regrets is, because we were so fixated on Charlene

Quinn, we never even considered Chester Wolski to be more than a potential witness. I don't know how many times I talked to him and he said he went out on a call and the streets were quiet. Our focus was on the documentation of witness statements."

"I still wonder about the possibility his old Ford left the lot, too." Gaby can't seem to get Charlene's telephone call to her off her mind. "She was adamant she saw both vehicles leave."

"I think Charlene is mistaken. She was half asleep. She sat in her old red Land Cruiser and paid more attention to Patrick's lights in his apartment than to what might have happened around her." Fiona peers over at Gaby through the increasing gloom. "She doesn't make the best witness."

"Gaby knows Charlene better than anyone, Fiona." Ronny hasn't contributed to the conversation until now.

"Charlene Quinn may have a lot of issues, but she's a stickler for detail. I learned that much during the time she tormented my lady, here." Joe pats Gaby on the arm. "I had the distinct impression she could stay up all night and be totally alert."

"You could be right, but there's no obvious explanation for two vehicles. Amanda was around four months pregnant and Mason was a toddler. She didn't take off to run for groceries. She told me she was sick as a dog most of the time. We even know, now, how Chester stopped at the Creek Tavern to get off-sales beer. We are clear he was in the tow truck. That part of Charlene's story—the time she says he left The Station—checks out.

"The other issue still bugging me about all of this," Fiona continues as Joe offers more tea, "is the valuable time we consumed when we felt whoever took Roz also took you, Ronny. I still wish you could have confided in me when you came here. We would have kept track of Duncan Taylor. We could have protected you." She leans over and gives Ronny a friendly tap on the knee.

"Water under the bridge, you two. Like I said, our whole community has been tainted, somehow, since Roz disappeared. We assess strangers with suspicion and abandoned buildings with a chill. I still remember when Joe and I wandered around in the basement of 15 Poplar after Roz vaporized...and then I asked the guy next door to go through his run down old garage. You never get over certain experiences. Let's go inside. The bugs have started to fly and my sweater seems somewhat insufficient since the sun's gone down."

They pile back into the house and make themselves comfortable on the over-sized, canvas-covered sofas on either side of the rock fireplace.

"I love this room, Gaby." Ronny gazes around at the kitchen island, the great room, and the high ceilings covered in cedar.

Gaby roars. "You said the same words to me before you offered to buy 15 Poplar, Ronny. I'm afraid this one's not for sale."

"Well, maybe in a year or two, you might be able to build a house for us." Ronny catches Fiona's eye. "My house isn't big enough for us to be roommates. We think we might go into partnership and build."

Joe and Gaby exchange glances. "I will be happy to build you your heart's desire. Just give me the word." Gaby is curious and she can't stand the wait any longer. "Okay, Fiona. You said you had news about Roz's murder."

"I don't know much, but Chester made a special request to see his parents today." Fiona stops to take a sip of her refreshed tea. "The circumstances are unusual because he knows he's only permitted visits from his lawyer or his wife. They made an exception because he said he was worried about his kids and needed to talk to his folks."

"Why would he be worried about his kids, Fiona? Amanda's a good mother. She must be at her wit's end about the situation, but they're out at the farm, safe and sound"

"I don't know. The constable who took the request reported how Chester said he was afraid his wife would take off with his kids. Seems like a bit of an over-reaction to me, but they gave in and let his parents in to see him, once he told the constable he would talk to the prosecutor to make a deal."

"Make a deal? What kind of position is he in where he can make a deal, Fiona?" Joe has leaned over. His elbows are on the knees of his chino slacks. He talks to her across the brim of his cup.

"Well, he says he didn't murder Roz but he knows who did."

"What? What does he mean?" Gaby almost lifts off the couch. Her insides vibrate. *What really happened out at the abandoned farm?*

Fiona continues. "There isn't a whole lot more to tell. When I saw you this morning, I thought maybe the situation might have progressed, but no such luck. He and his lawyer spent a long time with the prosecutor this afternoon. He was clear he wouldn't talk until he was sure his kids were cared for. Apparently, he held a picture of them throughout the meeting."

"We know what he has told them, right? We know Charlene Quinn was correct all along. Both vehicles left The Station late on the night of August 6, 1981."

"Speculation so far, Gaby. We still don't know, for sure, what Chester has said to the investigators."

About the Author

L. P. Suzanne Atkinson was born in New Brunswick, Canada and lived in both Alberta and Quebec before settling in Nova Scotia in 1991. She has degrees from Mount Allison, Acadia, and McGill universities. Suzanne spent her professional career in the fields of mental health and home care. She also owned and operated, with her husband, both an antique business and a construction business for more than twenty-five years.

Suzanne writes about the unavoidable consequences of relationships. She uses her life and work experiences to weave stories that cross many boundaries.

She and her husband, David Weintraub, make Bedford, Nova Scotia their home.

Email – lpsa.books@eastlink.ca
Website – http://lpsabooks.wix.com/lpsabooks#
Facebook – L. P. Suzanne Atkinson – Author

Watch for:

No Visible Means: A Stella Kirk Mystery

The first of a new series of mysteries, set in the Shale Cliffs RV Park
Coming in the spring / summer of 2019

www.ingramcontent.com/pod-product-compliance
Lightning Source LLC
Chambersburg PA
CBHW021013120726
47905CB00009B/2988